ANN ROYAL NICHOLAS

BOURNOS

ACKNOWLEDGMENTS

It is said you can find inspiration anywhere. It's also said to "write what you know." In my case, both statements are true. As it happens, *The Muffia* was inspired by true events—that is, a lot of what happens in the book actually happened. There really is a Muffia book club. We've been reading books and talking about them since 2002 when Muffia member Denise came up with the name—a vast improvement over "The Cliterati," a suggestion made by yours truly. We agreed that went a bit too far—even for us.

Though most everything that happens in the book, or some version of it, happened to me, other Muffs, or people we know, names have been changed. And since there are so many of us, some characters are composites of one or more members. All the members of the Muffia have read *The Muffia* and have given me, and it, their blessings. Thanks, therefore, must first go to my inspiration, the ladies of the Real Life Muffia: Michelle Joyner, Lisa Mohan, Carolyn Calvert, Sonya Walger, Lysa Hayland Heslov, Denise Gruska, Susan Hoffman Hyman, Betsy Salkind, Clare Foster, Janine Eser and Jann Turner. Without you women, life would be so much less than it is. All of you are funny, engaging, enterprising, brave, beautiful and flawed— as am I. I hope we're reading and arguing about books until we drop.

So many others inspired me in the writing of this book as well and helped me as I wrote: Agatha Dominik, Arbel Ben Peretz, Sirgiv Rossano, Cedering Fox, Claire Carmichael, Lynn Vannucci of Water Street Press and Hannah Dennison. Maybe some people can write in complete solitude and only for themselves but I can't, so thank you.

I also need to thank my fabulous agent, Liz Trupin-Pulli who just kept believing in me and the book despite numerous glowing rejections.

And because I could not have written, nor have launched this book into the world without the assistance of several wonderful women, I am donating ten percent of profits from the sale of this book and all subsequent *Muffia* books to charitable organizations that benefit women in the United States. We're willing to go beyond US borders too but until we've helped all the women who need help here, that's not likely to happen. I'm particularly interested in organizations that provide women of all ages with access to education and the means to start their own businesses.

Happy reading and thank you.

Ann

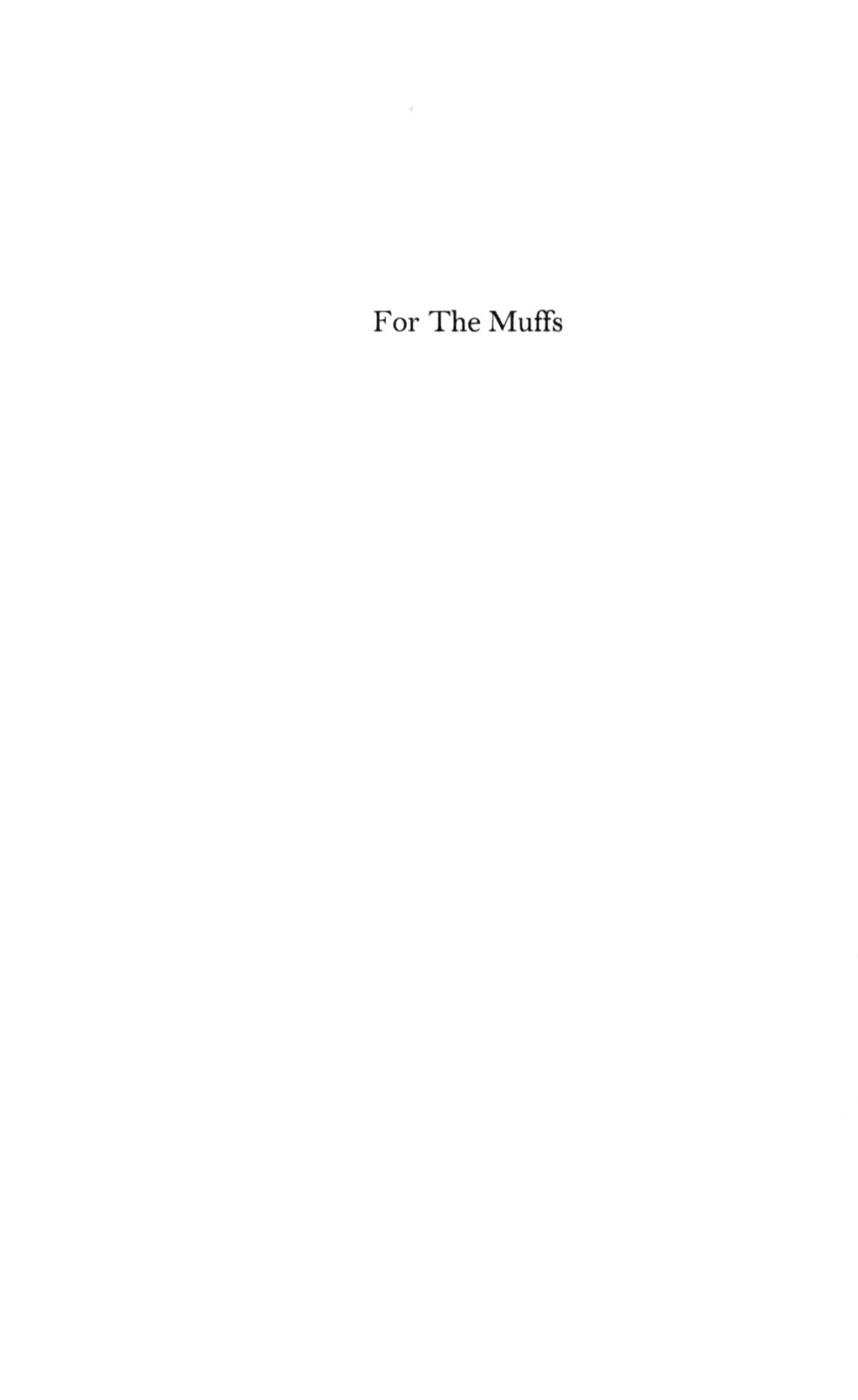

For The Muffs

PROLOGUE

Sunlight penetrated the hibiscus and carefully pruned live oaks growing alongside the architecturally ambiguous California house. It filtered through the arched windows and dispersed fuzzy shafts of light, which fell upon bodies writhing in ecstasy. Well, I mean, we were writhing and it *was* ecstatic—at least from my point of view beneath him.

Oh yeah, I remember chanting over and over. *Oh yeah, Baby, yeah.*

You're so sexy, he kept telling me which made me moan again and again, of course; to which I'd say, *God damn, you're good,* and *You're so fucking great.* You know, the usual things people say while in the throes of physical passion.

In between my moans he'd tell me, *You make me so horny, Baby,* and *Yeah, Baby, I love it when you scream.* As I recall, both of us were probably saying *Yeah, Baby* somewhat excessively.

You make me scream, I remember screaming. He really was incredibly hot—a fantasy man—handsome, penetrating green-gold eyes and a body like a Greek sculpture come to life.

Believe me, I was into it when it was happening, so forgive the seeming detachment from the event. It's a bad habit I've developed during my career assisting other people resolve their legal disputes—emotional distance. But I assure you I was right there and apoplectic while it was in progress.

He wasn't from California, or even an American. But so what? I found him a remarkably generous lover and maybe that's why.

I want to make you see the stars, he'd say. And the way he said it—*the stars?*

I . . .Oh, my God, the stars!

I remember glancing out the window at the oaks— the stars weren't out—in all their green-gray glory, swaying in the afternoon breeze, and I felt like some wild animal in nature engaged in a deliciously beasty act. And then I lost all sense of place and time. Could it have been love? Or just desire? I don't think it mattered at the time.

Oh God... I'm coming! I screamed.

Yeah, come on, Baby, come! he urged me unnecessarily; see, I'd already started down Orgasm Drive—I didn't need any help.

And so I came, over and over I came, and it was— words fail, really. But it was unbelievably great—the best I'd ever had, which I realize is what I always say after too long a time between orgasms. It's just that I don't want to take anything away from the event or the man. Men need to know, after all, that they've improved the quality of your life in some way.

The earth moved as it hadn't in far too long, and I did see stars—danced among them, to tell the truth. We came together in a release of consummated, long pent-up desire, which we'd finally acted upon with abandoned *joie de vivre* on that quiet Wednesday afternoon on the daybed in the solarium of my suburban Los Angeles home.

In one final explosive burst of sexual ecstasy, we moaned together with unparalleled pleasure and, with one last shudder, he collapsed upon me. There was nothing left in either of us, such was our mutual effort and joy. I was completely spent. But there was no getting around it: My new lover was dead.

"Udi?" I managed to squeeze out—the weight of him keeping me from speaking above a gasp. I knew he wouldn't answer—he breathed no more. But the silence of the afternoon was already starting to make me twitch with fear.

I tried again. "Udi?" Only quiet met my ears. Not even Stipple, my customarily ever-present, constantly meowing cat was in attendance. For some reason, the theme song from *Rent* popped into my head—*Five-hundred twenty-five thousand six hundred minutes…*

I had to get him off me. Or maybe the more accurate phrase was, I had to get out from under *him*. If I pushed, he'd roll off the narrow daybed and onto the tile floor, potentially causing further injury, which I'd have to explain—not that it mattered significantly if he was already dead. But I've watched C.S.I. a few times; why add to my trouble? Udi's death *in flagrante* would be unpleasant enough. But how to get him… *ugh*— I mean, he was heavy.

Oh my God, oh my God, oh my GAWD! What does a woman do in a situation like this? *Which* woman was the question? What would Hillary Clinton do, for example, if—OK, that's not a great image. How about Charlize Theron in the latest *Mad Max* movie? Or Beyoncé? They'd handle it, that's for sure. And Queen Latifah could just lift the guy, er… person and toss 'em on the floor.

The truth is, these women probably have built-in detection systems that would never allow them to have sex with anybody possessing a sub-par heart, but if they *had* made the same mistake, what would they do? I mean, it wasn't the first time a person's died having a rumble. And I don't mean just Nelson Rockefeller. Erotic expiration is actually quite common—it's the twelfth—well, perhaps thirteenth— highest cause of death in men over thirty. The only reason you don't hear more about it is for reasons of decorum. For example, what would people say at the funeral?

Trying to lift Udi's body again, I managed to shift my butt an inch or two closer

to the edge of the daybed before the dead deadweight of him collapsed back on top of me. This wasn't going to work, at least not in a timely fashion. I had to call someone for help—someone I could trust who wouldn't judge me. *Good luck with that, right? Who doesn't judge?* The point was, I had to call someone soon, before Lila came home from school and got completely freaked out and disgusted.

I had a flash, wondering if this would have happened if I hadn't gotten divorced, or if I hadn't moved back to Los Angeles, or if I hadn't been in the book club. And then finally I wondered if *that book* had anything to do with my seeking out and having sex with Udi in the first place. It was possible, I supposed. At this point, anything was. One thing I know was true: if I'd still been married, I wouldn't have been stupid enough to bring a man who wasn't my husband to my own house for a tryst. That would demonstrate a lack of self-restraint and I have almost too much of that.

Straining against him, I pushed on Udi's clavicle and *scroonched* my upper body up and over at the same time, probably no more than a millimeter. At this rate, I'd get out from under him in about four hours. Reaching above my head, I felt around for the phone. I couldn't see it but I hoped it would be resting in its stand on Grandma's cherry tilt-top table at one end of the daybed, instead of where I often found it—buried in the pink shag carpeting in Lila's room, battery dead after an extended phone session with one of her friends. But, no… There it was! Right where it was supposed to be. I managed to get two fingers around the stub of the antenna and snatch the phone out of the dock.

It would be only right to call one of the people who I believed might have—indeed probably *had*— gotten me into this mess in the first place. You see, I did blame what happened with Udi, and everything that occurred afterward, on *that book* and, by extension, book club; or, as we refer to ourselves, "The Muffia."

If I hadn't been a Muff, I would not have read that book, and if I hadn't read that book, I might not have gone down the path I did. But then, of course, there's really no way of knowing.

You may think you know where I'm going with this, but believe me you have no idea.

PART 1

CHAPTER 1

The Muffia—which we also reverentially refer to as "The Cliterati" is a twelve-year-old collective of nine book-loving women varying in age from thirty-three to forty-two, living in the greater Los Angeles area. We meet roughly every month at one of our homes to share a meal and talk about a book we are supposed to have read.

Of course, like the members of a lot of book clubs, we Muffs are friends in addition to being readers— many of us very old friends, the bonds of those friendships forged over, in some cases, twenty-five years, through struggles and successes. So even though the alleged reason for our meetings is to discuss the book one of us has assigned to the group that month, keeping the discussion "on topic" isn't always easy.

Speaking of making things easy, I've prepared brief character sketches of the members of the Muffia (including what I hope is an honest assessment of myself) to assist you, dear reader, in keeping the nine of us straight as you continue. We should, each of us, come into focus during the course of the story so skip this section if so inclined. But if you're the type who likes knowing who's who up front, let me introduce each of the Muffs, complete with marital status and email address:

Madelyn Scott-Crane (42)
MSC@MSCMediate.com

This would be me. I'm an attractive (one guy, later institutionalized, called me riveting) blonde, irreligious *divorced mom* with a daughter (Lila, 14). We live in Agoura Hills, outside LA, as does my ex, Lila's father, Brian. I'm the oldest Muff, but probably the most "toned" due to hours relieving angst (often self-imposed) by practicing yoga. I haven't been with a man on any outing that would qualify as a date in two years. I'm a lawyer turned mediator, though I don't get enough work to actually call myself either.

Quinn Cunningham (41)
cunningquinn@Talentpool.com

Single, never married, no children. Quinn is tall, with thick shoulder-length auburn hair that she often wears in an up-do. She has a job as a talent agent with a top agency placing celebrities in overseas commercials where they'll never be seen by their domestic fan base. She doesn't get the dates she wants most of the time, so she resorts to going out with actors who do a bad job of disguising the fact they want her only to get them onto a TV show.

Jelicka Gelman (41)
MissJelickaG@aol.com

Married, no children. Jelicka's too smart for her own good. An ex-screen-writer, she's also a horny, botoxed housewife with an incredible wardrobe who sort of looks like a double-blonded Angelina Jolie (those times when A.J. isn't traipsing around Vietnam or Africa)—same eyes and puffy lips. She's married to Roscoe (63) who's been taking Viagra but they're still only permitted sex once a week due to Roscoe's other medical issues. Jelicka's been faithful, but Roscoe probably wouldn't mind if she had an affair. She's a news hound, gossip and conspiracy theorist.

Lauren Busch (37)
LBSweet@aol.com

Married, two children (Amanda, 1, and Gavin, 3). Lauren's probably the richest, party-loving Muff—that would be keg party— but perhaps the least sexually adventurous, next to me. She's married to George, of the Anheuser-Busch beer dynasty, and they both partake of too much of the family brew. She's slightly overweight, in a healthy mid-western way, with green eyes and a great big toothy smile. She, like Jelicka, also enjoys dishy gossip.

Sarah Pizzo (39)
sapizz11@connect.net

Married, one child (Nate Jr., 5). Sarah's a brown-haired, brown-eyed, Catholic church-goer. She's cute and petite in an Audrey Hepburn/Tatou way. Her husband (Nate Sr.) is younger than she is and they're both terrible flirts. She rarely reads the books but is such a good cook the Muffs let it go, even though Quinn and I find it annoying. Before she got married she worked in the corporate offices of Williams-Sonoma. Now she and Nate are down to one income and they're in debt—always a problem but one that's only compounded during a recession.

Rachel Baker (32)
rachelbakerart@mac.com

Single, never married, no children. Rachel has a wild pile of blonde wavy hair and a very funky, trendy way of dressing. She's Protestant by birth but practices

Kabbalah—at the moment anyway. She's an artist whose passion is painting male nudes in acrylic, and she makes a modest living at it. She recently found real love after painting Hank, a gaffer in the film biz who found her on Facebook. She reads a lot and likes to push her book choices on other Muffs.

Kiki Glazer (41)
<u>kookykiki@hotmail.com</u>

Married, one child (Troy, 13). Kiki's a beautiful Black ex-Catholic woman who's married to Saul, a White Jewish hedge fund manager. She's an actress — or she *was*—who's thinking of changing her life and doing something significant with the rest of it. She's been taking nursing classes and hoping one day to become a nurse practitioner. Recently she's begun acting like a prude as she never has before and we're wondering what's up. She has a great ass and a fantastic shoe collection envied by all.

Paige Von Hoote (38)
<u>vonhooter@gmail.com</u>

Living with significant other (Richard), *two children from previous marriage,* (Carlotta, 6, and Dashielle, 4). Paige teaches tennis and struggles with finances. She's a great entertainer who has an ongoing rivalry with Sarah when it comes to throwing a great party. Though she and Richard have been together for years, she can't decide if she wants to marry him. (There are "issues.") She's on the tall side, very fit with a brown bob that always looks chic and professionally blown out, but which seems to flip up around her face when she gets angry.

Vicki Butler Mendoza (39)
victoriamendoza@mac.com

Divorced, one grown son (Enrique, 17). Vicki's a self-described filmmaker who has made only one film that wasn't very good, but which she likes to talk about whenever the opportunity arises. She also works as a script supervisor when she needs cash. She has short, spiky hair that she likes to dye different colors. She considers herself an expert in Spanish culture, having lived there during her marriage. She usually reads the books and can be high strung.

So that's us: The Muffia—just your average women's book club, really, like so many others in America, this one in the city of angels, created just after the dawn of the twenty- first century and still going strong. We've read historical novels, memoirs (*real* memoirs—not the made-up kind), non-fiction, comedies, chick lit—you name the genre and we've dabbled, and you can count on me to give you our reading list when I'm done with this tale.

As I said, like most book clubs, some of the Muffia don't treat our book club as seriously as others—Sarah, Lauren, and Kiki, for example, view our gatherings as a time to drink and *klatch*, free of the burdens of home, family and other obligations. Then there's the rest of us—Quinn, Rachel, Paige, Vicki, Jelicka and myself—who read the books and actually like talking about them. Despite our differences, we've known each other for so long and like each other so much that it seems wrong to make reading an ongoing requirement for membership. We decided when we started that we'd all just do the best we could when it came to completing the club's reading assignments.

Every four weeks or so, when the date of the next Muff gathering approaches, a flurry of e-mails shoot back and forth—usually about what food we're bringing or how somebody can't come. Back before we all started reading *the* book, the one that headed me down the path that eventually got me to where I am now, we'd all read another book and were about to meet at Sarah's to discuss it. As hostess, she got the net neurosis started:

> SarahPN@connect.net: All right, Clitties. Next week: the 17th, 7 p.m., my place. I'm making something from the sea in honor of the book. Will also make divine Americana dessert. Need veggies, bread, wine. Pls. weigh in. Barely started the book, but what's with the beads in his balls? XO~ S

Sarah lives in Santa Monica and though she's a great cook and can put together a four-course meal faster than it takes me to drive to her house, she insists on potluck. I love our book club but I hate this particular aspect of our meetings. Maybe I'm old school, but I think it's rude to make people drive *and* prepare a dish when most of us are working and raising kids, some of us alone. Lazy and busy, I do my best.

> MSC@MSCMediate.com: Salad and wine here. Can't wait to see you all but can we please keep the beads-in-the-balls discussion to a minimum? Read the book, Sarah.

Rachel is the youngest in the collective and, in case you need a refresher, is the Muff with the voluminous blonde hair—the kind I'd kill for—and a nose ring—which would probably kill me to get. As I said, she's our resident artist and can always be counted on to make something inspired to eat that has nothing to do with the book we just read, but everything to do with who she's dating.

> rachelbakerart@mac.com: I urge all of you to read the book. The beads in his balls are a cancer treatment and we should discuss on this basis. Cancer is everywhere! I'm bringing spanakopita, Rachel.

Uh-oh… I wondered if that spinach phyllo pie meant things had cooled with Hank and she'd started dating a Greek.

Lauren, our "rich" and, I'd say, most *preppy* member, could often be counted on to flake at the last minute. Sometimes she'd get a better offer, like a ticket to the premiere of a George Clooney movie, but I suspected that often her excuses were offered because she hadn't read the book.

> LBSweet@aol.com: Sounds delish—The food, not the cancer. Unfortunately, my sister is coming to town and taking us to the launch of Chelsea Handler's new vodka (A little obvious, I know. But she drinks so much, she had to start making her own). Sound too hip, late night and sleazy for a mom of two toddlers? Yes, but I must go anyway. Love to all xxoo L

Hmmm…Was it unfortunate that her sister was coming to town? That she was being forced to appear at a vodka launch? Unclear…

Paige was the next to make her opinion and online presence known:

> vonhooter@gmail.com: Sorry you're dumping us for Chelsea, Lauren, but we moms have to feel like we're still in the game. Assuming you haven't read the book, or you'd have asked to reschedule? Anyway, have fun. Score us a case of the stuff if you can pry it away from her.
> XX P   P.S. Will bring yummy coconut cake.

Despite Paige's cheery tone, I could almost see the

individual hairs on her head flipping up as a result of Lauren's bailing on us. The only other time Paige's hair isn't perfect is if she's just returned from teaching her tennis clinic, and even then it still flips neatly, albeit a little damply, from under her trendy visor.

I wondered if Paige might be bringing dessert to annoy Sarah who was not only a good cook of the savory, but a wonderful baker. Either that or she hadn't read Sarah's email saying she had dessert covered. Sometimes I think Paige just needs to act out when people cancel—as one of the original members, she takes it very personally when people don't adhere to the rules, free vodka or no free vodka. But she and I have known each other for twenty-five years, having met and become friends in New York when I was in law school and she was an aspiring singer living in the same Greenwich Village building. Our shared misery of that time bonded us for life.

kookykiki@hotmail.com: Count me in for bread and wine, which Rachel can pick up on the way if Troy's flu isn't better. He's been exploding from both ends. You might not want me there to expose you all anyway. Lauren, it's lovely your sister has come out for a visit but don't drink and drive:) ~K

Kiki also goes back to the New York days and is not kooky at all, really. In fact, she's been doing a lot of soul-searching lately, which has pretty much put the kibosh on her last bit of kookiness. Her last acting job was an Equity Waiver play three years ago—and probably the single biggest reason she decided to change her life. *Good for her*, say we who, to a Muff, encourage this nursing degree—if for nothing else than when we can't afford health care, she can draw our blood and send off our pap smears. She and Saul live in "The Valley" (as in San Fernando) with their son, Troy, who apparently has stomach flu. Of course, Troy couldn't help that he had stomach flu, but Paige didn't seem to have much sympathy.

> vonhooter@gmail.com: So, do these latest exchanges mean we're still on for the 17th (minus Lauren and possibly Kiki)? If there's one more out, I opt for another date.

> victoriamendoza@mac.com: Will bring whatever you need, Sarah, if I'm up to coming. Not feeling great myself, but want to come as I've read the book—a real literary nailing of the banal, dontcha think?

Victoria—Vick, or Vicki, as we call her—kind of fell into filmmaking when she was living in Spain with her now ex-husband, Ricardo, whom she married straight out of college to annoy her family who'd never thought him smart enough for her. (Being a bullfighter, he sort of wasn't.) She's been out of the business for years but wants to get back in now that her son, Enrique, is practically grown and—she's sadly realizing—doesn't need her anymore. That said, she hasn't been able to get a new project going. She either hasn't found the right story or hasn't been able to raise the money she needs to commit the story to film—or, more realistically these days, digitized bits. I was hoping she'd rally and get to Sarah's because if we had one more "iffy" Muff, the night wouldn't happen.

> cunningquinn@Talentpool.com: Hope you feel better, V (and happy birthday, BTW). Totally on board for night change since we may be down three; too many missing Muffies! But just in case, the following week I'm good M, Tu, Th but Sarah should weigh in first since she's the crucial ingredient. Let's do this quickly! Before the rains come!

Quinn has a demanding job with all those celebrities, but she rarely misses book club—which is only right as she is another of its founders. She also keeps abreast of all our birthdays (unless it's her assistant that's doing it). Though I haven't known Quinn as long as I have most of the other Muffs, we get along great—probably because we're both single and share a certain and sometimes un-repressed snarkiness. I often find her to be one of the most grounded and practical of the group—even if she is the most jaded. This point will be relevant as the story proceeds, in that I wasn't completely correct in my assessment of her. Just because someone is grounded in one area doesn't mean they are *totally* grounded.

Now where Quinn was *concerned* about Vicki, as well as the possibility of book club moving to another night, Paige finally went off, and she didn't pull her punches. Though the message could have been a bit excessive, it wasn't unusual. Paige usually takes our Tolstoy award for Most Words in an email thread:

vonhooter@gmail.com: Happy B-day V, but sheeesh, this is like the 10 little Indians! Hope the Chelsea's worth it, L, and that you feel better, V, and that Troy feels better, or at least good enough for a sitter. I'll see the rest of you that haven't bailed on the 17th. BTW, in the future? Let's go over some excuses that rate: Immediate family member's leg cut off—excused. Cancer treatments —excused. Child's explosive emissions from both ends—excused if single. From one end—not excused. DINNER AND HOMEWORK???—Not excused. Busy with work and kids—not excused. Giving birth—excused. Husband out of town— not excused. Gallery opening—excused. Mid-terms— not excused. Getting laid by Brad Pitt?— toss-up but I have to land on the side of not being so available that you ditch book club to accom-modate sex. Let it be shown that we are all busy with work, deadlines, some of us with kids, no husbands, only one with a nanny and *everyone* with plumbing. We changed this date to accommodate members that now aren't even

coming!! Please try to at least buy the book and start it so you have some relationship to the discussion. We've been letting this slide but I think we need to re-group and re-commit. Ours is a book club that is exemplary and I have numerous friends who are dying to join. Let's just say that I hope a slot will not be opening up!
Love you all, P

Totally right, I thought. Good for Paige.

OK, that's probably enough for now. You haven't heard from all the Muffs, but it's kind of like sitting in the sun—probably best to limit one's exposure the first time out. Anyway, with this story, the most important thing is to know that these women are there, my friends, backing me up, even if you can't keep straight who's who.

CHAPTER 2

I dashed through the raindrops, across the wet flagstone walkway and up the steps to Sarah's Craftsman-style house in Santa Monica, and took cover under the dark green awning hanging over the front stoop. I pressed the doorbell and took the few moments before the door opened to shake the rain from my jacket and gently push the drops off the Saran-Wrapped salad I'd brought as part of the night's dinner. I was happy, despite the fact that I was wet and in desperate need of assistance for my terminally limp hair.

It rains so rarely in LA, but when it does, it provides a needed respite from the incessant sunshine, which, to some of us residents, can become an unrelenting bore. Being an east coaster by birth and upbringing, I never mind the rain. I'd enjoyed the beautiful and stormy drive to Sarah's. Coming over the Santa Monica Mountains from the San Fernando Valley where I live, through Santa Monica canyon and up to Sarah's house just south of Montana Avenue, I'd felt enclosed and safe in my Prius as the rain clouds enshrouded me.

"Hi," chirped Sarah, her gamine face aglow atop her professional chef's apron as she swung open the green lacquered door. "Come in, come in. It's horrible out there. I hope everyone makes it," she said with grave concern, looking past me into the darkened sky.

"It's just a little water," I said simply, shrugging off Sarah's suggestion of impending cataclysm.

She pushed from her face several strands of richly colored brown hair that had escaped her butterfly clip. Actually more hair than not had shaken loose and the clip now seemed to be balancing on the top of her head. "It's only rain, yes, but it's horrible. You know how people get in LA when there's 'weather.'"

They often lose their minds, I mused—particularly the people driving, though I'd been fortunate enough to avoid the lunatics that evening. I don't know why but it often seems that when it rains in LA it's as if God has appeared and signaled the end is near, so people drive like maniacs to get wherever they were going before the magnitude-eight shaker levels the city. Kind of like the way ants behave when someone steps on their anthill.

"Anyway, I'm glad you made it," she said, ushering me into her charming flea market-appointed foyer. "You look wonderful, Maddie. Is that a new bag? Really pretty. Here, let me take this." She whisked the raindrop-speckled mixed greens from my hands, completely ignoring the still-open door, which I decided to close, shutting out the *horrible* night.

Looking into the hall mirror, I saw that in addition to my mop of hair, which I tried to arrange, my make-up had been destroyed. Surely Sarah had noticed and I wondered what her criteria were for looking wonderful. Perhaps she thought the smudged make-up was intentional. And surely she'd seen the bag I'd owned for two years on at least ten previous occasions. Whatever. Sarah wasn't known for her powers of observation and she was trying to be nice—kind words being the grease that keeps society running, making for pleasant company and all that.

I know I've told you my name but, to repeat, I'm Madelyn—Madelyn Scott-Crane, with the hyphenated ex-husband's last name still attached—but my friends call me Maddie. I don't particularly like that tag because it makes me think of the angry little girl I once was and would rather leave behind. But it's what my friends have always called me, and it's been difficult to get them to change. Basically I've given up. *Why?* Because they're my friends and I love them, I guess. *There—more grease.*

"Vicki and Jelicka are in the den monitoring *Stormwatch*," Sarah jabbered, leading me toward the kitchen and again brushing the hair from her face before lifting the lid off an orange Le Creuset pot. She wore no make-up, not that she needed any. Her complexion wasn't as rosy as mine but, then again, her skin wasn't prone to splotchiness, no matter how much slaving she did over the stove. "*They* think it's dreadful out there, too."

Well of course Jelicka would think it was dreadful. She becomes alarmed when her coffee gets cold—but Vicki?

"Go—I'll be in after I check the soup."

Something fishy was in that pot but I didn't say anything since, to me, fish never smells as good as it tastes.

As mentioned earlier, a Muff hostess always tries to have a meal that is in some way thematically connected to the book we've just read. In the case of Sarah's gathering that night, we'd read a book that was set on the New Jersey shore. What else could you eat that was specifically New Jersey shore besides fish? Fish soup in anyone else's hands might be a thing to avoid, but I was sure that whatever oceanic dish was cooking on Sarah's stove that night would rate at least 27 in Zagat's—not that any of us except Jelicka frequented the high-end restaurants enough to know.

"Did you read the book? I wasn't sure from your email," I said as she set my store-bought, thematically unsuitable dressing on the counter.

Sarah shook her head. "Ran out of time."

"It was a New York Times bestseller, Sarah. We're supposed to make a little more effort with those."

"I don't think the writer did," came her retort. "How can he expect to enthrall his reader when he creates a central character with titanium beads in his balls? I gave him fifty pages. Life's too short."

"His, too, most likely."

"What?"

"His life."

Sarah stared at me. "His life was too short?"

"Never mind. Probably more of a man's book anyway." I sighed and turned away from the smell of the ocean toward the drama of *Stormwatch*.

Sarah gasped and I turned back, concerned that she'd burned herself or dropped something into the soup.

"Did you hear about Vicki?"

"What about her?"

"She has cancer!"

Now it was my turn to gasp. Then I looked at Sarah in disbelief. "What?" *Why was she telling me this? In this way?*

"She has cancer," Sarah repeated.

"I heard that part but why are you—and we sent all those emails back and forth about cancer. Now *this* is horrible."

"Shhhh—she's going to tell everyone, don't worry."

"I wasn't worried until you—Sarah, how can you blurt out things like 'Vicki has cancer,' and expect me not to be at least marginally upset?"

"*Shhhhh—*"

"I should have heard it from her."

"Well, I'm sorry I ruined the surprise. But it's not life threatening."

"I'm relieved it's not life threatening, but still . . ."

Sarah shrugged. Despite being a kind person, she has a habit of making inappropriate—or *I* think they're inappropriate—announcements. Most of the time it's gossip, a pastime she indulges in with great frequency, and which also explains her not being able to find much time to read, what with a husband, a child, a house and an extensive gossip mill to care for.

I headed in the general direction of the den, toward the din of the TV. It was on so loud that while still in the kitchen, I'd heard commercials for Sit 'n Sleep mattresses, Proactiv skincare and a new anti-erectile dysfunction product that warned a man he should become alarmed only if his erection lasts more than twelve hours. *Twelve—wasn't four alarming enough?*

If I were being honest with myself, I hadn't *embraced* this month's book selection either, though I'd slogged through it in sisterhood. Certainly *that* wasn't worth having a tiff over with the chef. I knew this intellectually, but my happy mood had started to wane—probably due to peri-menopausal mood swings put in motion by the news that a good friend has cancer.

Lately I'd been feeling old, just like the guy in the book. As a single mom of a fourteen-year-old girl, with no real romantic prospects, I'd been wondering *again*, what life was really about. Was I seriously meant to be spending my days mediating other people's disputes? What was I supposed to be doing with my nights, not to mention my vacation time? Reading about Frank Bascomb's travels around New Jersey hadn't given me any greater insight into humanity. In fact, I was probably even more lost. Books need to either entertain or to clarify life, one way or another. And if they don't, well, they've failed.

Vicki got out of her chair and brushed my cheeks with her own as I entered the den. I wasn't sure if I should keep her from standing, given her condition, but of course I was not supposed to know about her condition so I accepted her gesture without comment.

"You made it," said Jelicka, surprised.

"Yeah, who would have thought?" I smiled.

"We were worried," Vicki offered. She didn't appear to be affected by the cancer, though I wasn't sure what I should be looking for. In fact, she seemed fine. She seemed like Vicki; thinner maybe. Her spiky hair was bright red this month and she'd added some blonde streaks.

"Seriously, Maddie, for you to drive that far, in this torrent... What *are* you doing living in Agoura Hills, anyway?" Jelicka demanded. "It's to hell and gone, there are no men and they've just closed the coast highway for its annual mudslide. You couldn't get back now if you wanted to."

Following Jelicka's gaze, I took in *Stormwatch*, wondering if I could also be drawn into the hyped-up fear of an impending flood, but I was immediately caught up in the host's appearance. I don't watch much local TV, getting most of my news from NPR while driving. So seeing this weather guy with a "faux-hawk"—a fake Mohawk hairstyle on the widescreen TV—talking about precipitation levels in a robotic sing-song voice, was an out-of-body experience. Was he even real? Robot technology had come a long way but could Faux-hawk be an actual robot? Whoever he was, it didn't matter to Jelicka. The guy knew his Doppler radar.

"Global warming has yet to cut the valley off from the Westside," I announced. "I'll just take the freeway."

Once again I was put in the position of having to defend my choice of living twenty-five miles from Muff central, the mid-point of the rest of the Cliterati. As anyone who's chosen to live outside the center of any major city in the world can attest, it takes more effort to get to where the action is but one puts up with it for things like proximity to the country (or the appearance of country), reduced crime and cheaper housing—and plenty of convenient street parking.

In the case of the Muffs and Los Angeles, our bullseye is roughly at the intersection of Doheny Drive and Olympic Boulevard, on the south side of Beverly Hills and miles from where any one of us actually lives. Los Angeles is, after all, the definition of sprawl. This means that we are scattered in all directions and each of us has to drive (burning up precious fossil fuels in the process) to talk about whatever book is up for discussion that night. It seems to be lost on those with Westside zip codes that it takes the Muff in Venice longer to reach the Muff in Hollywood to the east than it does for the Clittie in Studio City to get to Agoura. Though book club meets at my house only once a year—like the mudslides, an annual event—the Muffs love to complain about my being geographically undesirable. This is despite the fact that when they come to *my* house, I take care of everything—no pot lucking required. I suppose it's always hard to change an entrenched mindset no matter what the issue— acceptable neighborhoods, universal health care, globalization. It all comes from the same place in the human brain that makes it hard for us to change. Sadly, my geographic unavailability is also the cause of my being left out of a lot of the girl talk I actually cherish, even if it also makes me crazy sometimes. It's a flaw in my character that I both want to be included and, at the same time wish to retain the right not to be.

"And there *are* men in Agoura, Jel," I said. "There are men everywhere. I just don't meet any guys who make me want to—you know... "

I'd been married. I have a child. And though I like the idea of having a man around, I know I don't want another one like the one I had. Unfortunately, that knowledge can keep me from seeking out any new partner for fear of making the same unsuitable choice.

Jelicka shrugged. "Well, I've offered to set you up."

"Yes, you have and I appreciate it," I said. "I'll let you know."

Jelicka's older husband Roscoe is a successful

entertainment lawyer with lots of divorced partner attorneys and associates she wanted me to meet. But as a member of the legal profession myself, I believe one lawyer is plenty for any household. She is the Muff with the most clothes, busiest social life and the firmest grip on the ever-shortening news cycle and the timely information that people want, even if she does make things up just to get a rise out of people. Celebrity break-ups, cloned super-humans and three-eyed alien babies are among the many topics she keeps herself abreast of.

"You can stay with me tonight if you don't have to rush back. Roscoe's in Argentina fishing 'til Sunday. I'd actually love the company," Jelicka said, her eyes still on the *Stormwatch* host. "In fact, after we're done here, anyone who doesn't want to drive home can stay at my house. It'll be like summer camp, listening to the storm and telling ghost stories."

"Boo," I said. They both turned and looked at me blankly. Jelicka seemed to have forgotten it was still fifteen miles to her house in Holmby Hills near the UCLA campus and, driving there, we were bound to encounter more *weather*.

"So, did you read the book?" I asked. Their expressions didn't change.

"Most of it," they said in unison, exchanging a glance at each other.

"We might want to shift to a bi-monthly format," I suggested. "Some of us seem to have trouble finishing. Perhaps people need more time."

"That won't help. Especially if it's a bad book." She had a point. It was just that what she considers a good book is limited at best. Jelicka is all about characters and plot. It doesn't matter to her if a book is billed as literary and high-minded—the story has to grab her. Give her a compelling heroine she can relate to and she's happy.

"I couldn't even listen to it on CD," Vicki said. "It

seemed like the guy, what's-his-name, Frank, kept driving around and around feeling sorry for himself because his life wasn't working out. Well, hey, I feel so sorry for you with your nice house and car and people to have sex with. And did he have to keep talking about his balls? Who picked this book anyway?"

Considering that Vicki was the Muff who'd said the book was a literary nailing of the banal in her email, she was getting awfully worked up. Maybe she was sicker than Sarah knew.

"Rachel—" started Jelicka. "I mean I love Rachel, but she reads way too much and, frankly, influences weaker people when it's their turn to choose a book."

"None of us is weak, Jel," Vicki said.

"But that's not the point," I found myself saying. "Rachel is very well-read and very smart—"

"Yeah, well," said Jelicka, "if she'd read this one more carefully, she wouldn't have picked it."

"She also has more time to read than some of us but the point is, the hostess should pick the book," I continued. "And she should have read it before she picks it."

"She could have read it years ago," Vicki added.

"Right. The trouble is, Sarah doesn't read. I don't know if she ever did. So what's *she* supposed to do?"

"She can read the hell out of a recipe." Jelicka smiled. "Listen, we're not going to kick her out of the group. Besides, we get together to share our lives. The book is secondary."

True enough, I thought, not understanding why we couldn't do both Then the doorbell rang.

"That's the carpoolers," called Sarah. "Could somebody get it?"

Jelicka's head swung back to *Stormwatch* in order to catch an urgent update from Mohawk man, and Vicki flopped down into her chair.

Guess it was going to be me. Leaving the den, I almost collided with Nate, Sarah's husband, coming down the stairs. He clutched my arm and spoke in a whisper that included some spit.

"Maddie—I've been banished. You have to get me a couple o' beers."

The doorbell sounded again.

"I've got it," I called out to Sarah before turning back to Nate. "I think you've already had a couple of beers."

Nate isn't conventionally handsome, but he's compelling in a Jack Black/Adam Sandler kind of way—his sex appeal is hard to deny.

"Ah come on, Mad. Look at it this way: I'm not driving." Then he winked.

"Where's Nate Jr.?"

"Playing 'Grand Theft Auto.'"

"What?" I stared at him. Nate Jr. was four.

"It's a joke, Maddie. He's watching *Land Before Time*, the dinosaur series that won't die. I was pushing for *Gortimer Gibbon's Life on Normal Street* but he would have none of it. Kids today..."

Nate was always charming but at that point he was clearly drunk. "I'll see what I can do," I told him. "Check the stairs in fifteen."

Then Nate pulled me to him and kissed me on the lips. I want to say I pushed him away immediately but I was stunned and slow to react. It had also been awhile, months actually, since anyone had kissed me. But I recovered and reacted as I should have considering he was my friend's husband.

"What are you doing?"

He looked at me, gave me his crooked grin then shrugged before dashing upstairs.

Clearly there was something going on. One thing was for sure: I wouldn't be getting him any beer.

I pulled the door open to reveal Kiki and Quinn, both slightly damp under the awning, while Rachel, dry as crisp bread with her blonde hair cascading magnificently, strolled up the walk under a golf umbrella, Paige flanking her.

"So, Lauren did in fact blow us off for an alcoholic beverage?" I asked as they made their way inside.

"She promised to get us each a bottle," Paige confirmed.

"I couldn't believe Chelsea Handler vodka was a real excuse. I just thought she hadn't read the book again," I said, plucking the spanakopita from Rachel's grasp.

"She read the first sixty pages," offered Kiki "Then she realized she preferred picking up her dogs' poop to slogging through that thing."

"When has Lauren ever picked up dog poop?" I asked in disbelief.

"I *know*, right?" Kiki said, as if channeling a Nuyorican poetess. She looked hot and cool at the same time—the raindrops rolling miraculously off her hair as she took off her white patent-leather trench coat. Kiki's husband, Saul the hedge-fund manager, made gobs of money, which probably meant she's had a pretty easy life too. Lately, though, as I said, the chinks were beginning to show.

"The vodka launch was actually earlier, but then she had to go home to get ready for her trip or something," said Quinn. Per usual, her hair was piled up on top of her head and she was wearing one of her dozen or so miniskirts. Quinn claims that, in her line of work, a pair of decent legs, open or closed, is an asset to be flaunted for maximum effect.

"That's also not a legitimate excuse," Paige said, moving out from under the umbrella, her bob perfect as always, while Rachel closed the umbrella and shook it off before stepping onto Sarah's minimally waxed oak floors.

"Lying on a beach in Jamaica is not an excuse," Paige went on. "I mean, my *in-laws* are coming for two weeks! I should be home vacuuming but nope—I'm here. *And* I read the book."

Of course we'd all received Paige's email tirade the

week before but none of us wanted to indulge her on the subject of whether or not we were taking book club seriously enough. That would only get ugly. Instead, as each Muff entered—carrying assorted culinary delights and bottles of wine and exchanging a double kiss in greeting—we made the effort to shake free of our daily lives and the rainy evening outside, and looked forward to basking in each others' company, conversation and friendship.

With the carpoolers' arrival, we'd reached our quorum for the evening—eight instead of our usual nine. Out of the corner of my eye I spotted the stairs and wondered if Nate was still waiting for his beer? After that bizarre kiss, he'd be waiting all night and he only had himself to blame. What kind of friend gets her friend's husband alcohol after he sticks his tongue down her throat? What kind of husband sticks his tongue down his wife's friend's throat? A girl doesn't need either one.

But as I closed the door and made my way into the kitchen, I wondered if my hard and fast rules about human behavior weren't just a little too harsh.

CHAPTER 3

"This looks amazing," Jelicka said, her bowl brimming with fish, fennel and mussels, as she sat down with the rest of us in Sarah's dark red dining room.

The food was laid out buffet-style on a sideboard positioned under an *Edwin Landseer* knock-off purchased at the Pasadena Flea Market, as were most of Sarah's belongings. White antique drapes lifted slightly from the warm air coming up through the floor grates. Combined with the weather outside, the ambience seemed more Conan Doyle than SoCal. Sarah finally took the butterfly clip from her head and the rest of her hair fell around her oval face in bangs and wisps that made her look about eighteen.

"It's delicious," I said, slurping another mussel from its shell. Murmurs of agreement broke the silence of the collective concentrated consumption.

Sarah smiled. "Aoli—butter, cream, garlic. You can't go wrong."

"It's a sauce! Lauren would approve," Quinn said, dribbling slightly onto her Armani blouse. "Shit."

Lauren, the absent Muff, thinks everything can be improved with one of her sauces. She makes them for meat, vegetables, pasta, dessert; to marinate, to mix in, to dip in, to pour on. She's even brought her sauces to other Clitties' homes unsolicited, which is often a source of contention—especially with Paige.

"I guess I shouldn't worry about how fattening it is when it tastes this great," Rachel said, finishing her bowl.

"No*oooo*."

"Can't think about that."

"Why worry?"

We were all in agreement.

"Besides, it's all about portion control," Rachel went on. "Not what you eat."

"So size matters?" Jelicka asked, licking her lips.

We Muffs are all pretty good cooks with the exception perhaps of Vicki who overcooks meats to the point of unrecognizability, and steams her vegetables so far past *al dente* one needs a spoon. We discovered one evening, however, that she can cook a mean paella. It was the one recipe she must have ground into her brain while living in Spain. Whenever it's Vicki's turn to host, we ask her to make paella due to the dread of any alternative, even though paella usually has no relationship with the book we've just read.

We all sort of have our own signature dishes. Paige is the baker, specializing in pies and buttery Apple Brown Betty, a delicious, if oddly named, dessert. Kiki never seems to mind all the Brown Betty Paige makes, even though it's a dish created by slaves during colonial times. Instead Kiki chooses to view Paige's ongoing efforts trying to improve her Brown Betty as cute, and as acknowledgment that black women were superior cooks even way back when.

Jelicka, on the other hand, loves to *sear* things— fish, steak, vegetables—anything she gets her hands on. It must suit her often-caustic moods. I imagine her standing at the stove and, as she sears, mentally causing pain to someone who's wronged her. She has a personalized stovetop pan with iron strips and a decorative "JG" forged into the bottom to brand her initials into whatever's tossed into it. She brands things with such enthusiasm that, from time to time, it makes me wonder about the Gelmans' bedroom activities.

"This reminds me of the summer I spent in the south of France," Vicki said, her face aglow in the soupy steam. "I practically *lived* on bouillabaisse."

"This isn't bouillabaisse," Sarah responded.

"Tastes like it."

Sarah shook her head. "Champagne is only Champagne if it comes from the Champagne region of France. Bouillabaisse is from Marseille and dates to about six hundred B.C. when the ancient Greeks showed up and taught the French how to cook. In *Marseille*, people practically kill each other over who makes the most authentic bouillabaisse. It's also supposed to be the soup that Venus fed to Vulcan to lull him to sleep so she could cavort with Mars."

We looked at her blankly. Paige feigned boredom.

"You know, the God," said Sarah.

Apparently she did read after all, when it suited her. Collectively we were lulled speechless by her little lecture, though I could tell by her sigh that Paige was less than impressed.

"So you see, this couldn't possibly be bouillabaisse," Sarah finished.

"So what is it?" asked Jelicka.

"Fish Soup."

"Needs a new name," Jelicka said. "But I'm getting more anyway." She rose from her chair, followed by Rachel who'd clearly abandoned portion control for the evening and was headed into the kitchen.

"Whatevs—" Paige said, her cute little bob swinging. "It's *like* bouillabaisse."

Sarah shrugged. "A lot of things are like a lot of other things. But things *are* what they *are*."

Well that was certainly the truth. No matter how much any of us might want things to be different— whether it's what things are called or the fact that your life isn't what you want it to be—things are what they are and we should probably try to accept that. To deny what's really happening is like cutting out a little piece of yourself—like part of a vital organ. Eventually the hole inside you where that missing part used to be can get infected and make you sick. Things could get so bad that the sickness might even take down the whole organism—you! All right, fine, maybe this is an odd tangent to go off on when we've just been talking about soup but I find everything is related when you're paying attention.

"When were you in the south of France, Vick?" I asked with longing.

"Oh my God, probably fifteen years ago now—right after Ricardo and I split. It was when I had money."

"I went to Cannes one year for the film festival," Quinn said, dabbing at her ruined shirt. "The food was amazing except that I didn't have time to get to the best restaurants. That was the year I signed Vince Vaughn to a series of ads for Japanese tractors. We had to go out to a field to see how he looked sitting on one."

"And?" asked Jelicka, returning to her seat. "Was he shirtless?"

Quinn frowned. "In Japan? Please. But he's nice. Huge forehead."

Jelicka was slurping. "Huge what?"

"Forehead." Quinn rolled her eyes.

"I was gonna say... How'd you get to see it? Anyway, I like Vince Vaughn. But I *love* this, whatever it is, Sarah. I *need* this recipe and, while I'm at it, whatever you're cooking for dessert smells unreal and I think I need that recipe too."

This happened every time Sarah was hostess. "Sure," she said. "But you know Paige brought a dessert that looks great, too," she added graciously. Everyone pretty much always said they wanted everyone else's recipes—including those from dinners years ago—and the conversation turned nostalgic for remembered red velvet cakes and fried chicken.

"Let's talk about the book," Paige said finally. "We agreed last time that we were going to start with the book and do the 'what's-happening roundy-round' afterward in the interests of time."

The change in topic prompted Sarah to go into the kitchen, clearing away some of the empty bowls as she went. I questioned Paige's motivation for shifting the topic so abruptly, but I've noticed that Paige often has trouble when Sarah's cooking gets attention.

Personally, I thought it would be better to get dessert out of the way before we started talking about this month's selection because I feared we might be headed for a nasty, contentious bake-off showdown and we'd need the book to take refuge in, such as it was. Paige had brought coconut cake for a change and, as we all could attest, the delicious aroma of Sarah's pie had almost overwhelmed that of the fish soup.

Sarah slipped in from the kitchen carrying Paige's cake in one hand and her mixed berry pie with crumble crust in the other, smartly avoiding drawing attention to herself. Sarah *could* be smart when she wanted to be. She put down the desserts with no ceremony whatsoever and said, "Yes, let's talk about the book, but I think we need to start reading books *by* women *about* women. After all, we *are* a women's book club."

"Would you have read this book if it was about a woman by a woman?" I asked, ignoring the desserts.

She gave me a blank stare. "That's not the point."

"This book would have pissed me off even more if a *woman* wrote it," Jelicka said. "A woman would have known better. How can a book called *The Lay of the Land* not have a single scene where somebody gets *laid?* Bait and switch if you ask me. Yes, our protagonist *wanted* to get laid. He *wanted* to find the waitress who he *thought* had looked at him suggestively one day way back whenever it was—

maybe she did, maybe she didn't—but the restaurant where she worked was closed and he never got that booty call did he? He just kept driving around in that gas-guzzler, getting more and more desperate, ruminating about that funeral home and then watching the building implode with the crazy geezer. I mean, you think he's going to get laid and it turns out to be a book about driving around New Jersey."

Vicki looked at Jelicka. "You told me you didn't read it."

Rachel, having suggested the book, subtly screwed up her face and chomped down on a second, possibly third, piece of garlic bread.

"I did and I didn't," Jelicka said. "I skimmed it for sex scenes but there were none. I guess I just picked up a little of the storyline along the way."

"Well, you got the gist of it. Like you said in your email, Vicki, a literary nailing of the banal." Kiki pronounced banal so it rhymed with *anal*. She looked at the two desserts. "Those sweeties look yummy but I can't eat another thing."

"Didn't the author win a Pulitzer?" asked Sarah. "How does that happen if it's not a good book?"

"More to the point," said Quinn, "how did it become a *New York Times* bestseller?"

"Frank Bascomb is a character whom we are all more like than not, regardless of whether you care to admit it." Rachel now looked smug, casually chasing down the garlic bread with a gulp of wine. "Ford's other books in which Frank appears are transformational."

"There are others?" I asked, sorry to crowd another useless piece of information into my overcrowded brain.

"*Sports Writer, Independence Day*," Rachel said. "Truly wonderful."

"Transformational?" The only thing I knew was that I'd been transformed into a person who'd never read another Frank Bascomb book.

"Sorry, Rachel," Quinn agreed, "I tried getting through *Sports Writer* a couple of years ago and it wasn't much better."

"It was well-written," offered Paige. "I just didn't care about the guy."

Rachel had risen to her feet and was over at the sideboard, opening another bottle of wine. "What Ford is writing about in his books—and, yes, there's an aspect of the banal (pronounced the usual way)—but the character of Frank Bascomb represents the everyman who is simply trying to sanely exist in a world that he believes has gone crazy. It's a form that goes back to, well... England. Many of Dickens' characters or Trollope's—people who function within the society of the day, replete with its many absurdities."

"Well, that's a noble goal," said Vicki, "but isn't it equally important that people want to read your book so you can to actually communicate that and enrich readers' lives?"

"My point exactly," said Jelicka. "It needed sex."

"I do think that's important," said Rachel. "And I think he's done that."

I whispered to Jelicka. "*Sportswriter* has some sex in it—not a lot, but..."

"I see what everyone's saying," said Paige. "My problem is I didn't relate to the guy—not as brother, father, uncle, husband. But does everything always have to be about getting laid, Jelicka? You don't strike any of us as having a problem with that."

"What does that mean?" Jelicka's demanded, a bit harshly.

"Just that you're a beautiful woman and I see you as spending too much time worrying about sex."

"Oh, you do?" Jelicka flicked her double-processed blonde hair with a gel-manicured hand. "And what makes you think I'm *worried?*"

"Alright, listen," Rachel interrupted. "My bad; I'm sorry for pushing a book on you all when I seem to be the only one who got something out of it. But the fact that it's generated strong feelings is a good thing."

"I'm sorry I didn't read it now," said Sarah. "I just couldn't get past the thing about his balls. I mean, can someone tell me if that was necessary? He didn't strike me as the kind of guy who'd do something like that to, I don't know, turn on his girlfriend or intensify his orgasms or—"

"He had cancer, Sarah," Vicki snapped, returning from the kitchen with a little bottle of Perrier. "So the doctors put titanium beads in his gonads."

"Oh," Sarah said, humbled.

The conversation was taking a turn and I needed to use my mediation skills to smooth things over. I was always looking for an opportunity to practice mediating since I couldn't find many paid ways to do it. "I think what we're saying here, or at least some of us are saying, is that all books have *some* value, even if, as in the case of Ann Coulter's books, their only value is as firestarter. Ford writes fiction but he has a truthful view of the world. Bascomb's life is so boring it reminds people of their own boring lives, hence Rachel's point and the one about how banal it was, though Sarah and Vicki's point about the titanium beads in his balls may suggest something different. As Paige said, Ford does put words together beautifully. That quote about Thanksgiving being 'a celebration of the slaughter of the righteous and deserving' probably justified the purchase."

"I'm glad I missed that," mumbled Sarah. "I like Thanksgiving."

Undeterred, I pressed on. "As for you, Jelicka, you're a beautiful woman and give off the impression of great sexual awareness and confidence. Of course that doesn't always mean you or any of us *feel* the way we might *look* to others. What I'm saying is that how a book is received is often out of the control of the person who wrote it."

"That was interesting critiques, Maddie," Quinn said once I'd finally stopped talking.

"She wants to be called Madelyn," Paige said.

"That was interesting, *Madelyn.*" Quinn turned to Jelicka. "And you're just 'hot,' that's all I can say. Hot and married so what are you whining about? You *get* sex."

Jelicka rolled her eyes and sighed.

Meanwhile Quinn was still talking. "As opposed to *Madelyn,* who's pretty hot herself but hasn't had sex in a year and a half."

Actually it had been twenty-two months. And if I didn't meet anyone I wanted to have sex with, that twenty-two months would stretch to twenty-three, then twenty-four then, well, there was no end in sight until death did me part from this life. Sad that Islamic women don't get 1000 sexy guys when they die defending their honor—I'd consider converting. I just find there's a dearth of desirable men who might put an end to my self-imposed dry spell.

"What was with his wife who left him and went to Mull?" Kiki asked. "And where the hell is Mull?"

"Way up in the north of Scotland," Rachel said. "Rough landscape, very remote."

"Like Agoura," Jelicka teased.

"Yeah. What *was* that?" asked Quinn. "His wife goes to Mull to *mull* over the crackpot fat slob her *ex-*husband had become. Meanwhile, her current husband who *hadn't* abandoned her is sick in New Jersey—granted, his ridiculous wife could have been the reason he was sick. But didn't *he* need her more? What's the nobler path here?"

I glanced at Vicki, sitting quietly, looking out the window where darkness and rain prevailed.

"Maybe she didn't like driving around New Jersey," Paige offered.

"Frank must've been a real loser to make her want to go as far away as she could, with the possible exception of Antarctica, to be with a guy who barely registered her existence."

Sometimes I wondered whether our standards for books and relationships were just too high.

"Look," said Rachel, "not every character is going to be a cheerful, positive person whose character arc ends with him or her being better off than when the story started. Think of *The Hours,* or *Line of Beauty,* or *Madame Bovary.* Sometimes we have to accept the flaws in people. Frank Bascomb captures the nobility of carrying on no matter what."

"I agree," said Vicki, suddenly. "We're all flawed. And I hate how our popular culture glorifies only healthy, sane, loveable thin people. Remember how, in my movie, the central character was overweight and crazy? Audiences warmed up to her because she kept trying to make something of herself. That never happened with Frank. I also think Ford was socially irresponsible. In an age of global warming and disaffection, he has his protagonist driving around New Jersey in a Suburban that gets ten miles a gallon. Frank is a grumpy consumer who orders clothes from L.L. Bean and complains about everything as he meets unlikable person after unlikable person. And maybe that's the way a lot of white men are but that doesn't mean it's worth cutting down trees to print a book about him." Vicki did not consider reading a book on an electronic device *reading.*

"What was going on with his daughter who might or might not be a lesbian?" I asked. "Was that whole scene in the gay bar supposed to be his coming to terms with his daughter having a boyfriend after years of living with Cookie, or whatever her name was, who Frank wanted to sleep with? I mean that's not right. He's sad because he didn't get to have sex with his daughter's ex-girlfriend before she tried to go straight?"

"Poor guy struck out left and right," said Paige. "To be pitied really—though, as I said, it's well-written pity."

"A hand job might have improved things for poor Frank, though that doesn't exactly qualify as a *lay* of the land," said Quinn.

"Just like oral sex isn't really sex," said Sarah with a wink.

"Hey"—I blurted involuntarily; I *am*, after all, the mother of a fourteen year-old girl and I've been a tad touchy on the subject of oral sex ever since Lila told me that some of her classmates had been caught giving blow jobs to the boys.

"We all need to be able to satisfy ourselves at the end of the day," Jelicka sighed, "however we can."

"Amen," said Kiki. All heads turned. She hadn't used that word since her conversion to Judaism. "What?"

Everyone was still staring at her.

"I'm havin' a little religious crisis, tha's awl. I still love going to temple with Saul and everything but lately I've been missing my Catholic girlhood for some reason."

"You're not going to convert back, are you?" Jelicka asked. Jelicka was Jewish too, but by birth, not marital conversion. "I don't know if you can even do that."

"Of course you can," said Quinn. "You can be whatever religion you want."

"Not in Iraq—not if you want to live," I pointed out. Nobody stepped up to argue with me.

"I have no plans to re-convert," Kiki went on. "Besides, every religion I've dabbled in is flawed. Or maybe I'm just tired."

"Are we done talking about this book?" Paige asked. "I have babysitter issues this evening."

"I am"—this from Vicki. "And to start the roundy-round, I might as well come out and tell everyone unless Sarah has already—yes, I have some sort of growth in my breast, and yes, I'm a little worried because none of these doctors seems to know what the best medical approach is. I might need a lumpectomy, which would leave me lumpless but the proud owner of a breast with a divot. Or I might need radiation, in which case I'll be tired but functional. Or I might need a lumpectomy and radiation, in which case I'd have a bumpy breast *and* I'd be tired but functional. I might, however, need chemo in which case all the above would happen plus my hair will fall out. That said, I will go ballistic if any of you start treating me like some sort of sicko. Until I'm keeling over and losing my hair in fish soup, I don't want you to treat me any differently."

It seemed to me we were all sitting there with our jaws slightly open, the pause growing longer and longer, not sure what Vicki needed or wanted to hear.

"So, whose turn is it to pick the next book?" Sarah asked.

And so, just like that, we found out one of our inner circle was sick with something we all feared terribly we'd get ourselves. I said a prayer and made a private vow to increase my charitable contribution for breast cancer research. Even though we were unsure what to say that night, I knew we'd talk about it and send endless emails back and forth. Together the Clitties would formulate a plan to help Vicki in every way she needed it— from grocery shopping to cleaning to monitoring Enrique to whatever else needed tending to. But that night we honored Vicki by doing as she'd asked, though probably not as she truly wished.

"I think it's Madelyn's turn," said Paige. "That's what I remember from last month."

"Has anyone read the new Jane Smiley?" Rachel asked.

"Rachel, you have to wait until it's your turn again to pick a book," Vicki said. "I think if we've established anything this evening, it's that the hostess picks the book."

"How about *The Poisonwood Bible* by Barbara Kingsolver?" Quinn suggested. "Or is that too obvious a choice?"

"What did she just *say*, Quinn?" Paige asked, rather too pointedly, I thought. "It's Maddie's, I mean Madelyn's turn to pick. But that *was* a great one and loved by book clubs all over the country." Paige tended to like the obvious choices.

"It's seven hundred pages," I said. "I think I should pick something that we, as a group, have a chance of finishing. And it's supposed to be something I've read, right?"

"How about the Calvin Trillin book about the death of his wife Alice?" offered Sarah. "It was only seventy-three pages. Though it *was* by a man."

"Please, Maddie," pleaded Jelicka desperately—too desperately for a woman who *has it all.* "Pick something we'll *want* to read—even juicy trash at this point. Something we won't want to put down."

"It was good!" Sarah protested. "And short."

"No more cancer books," Vicki said. "That's my second wish."

"Of course," said Sarah. "Sorry."

Vicki patted Sarah on the knee. "I agree with Jelicka. Let's just have some fun for a change. If I'm going to die, you know, *soon*—not saying I am, but if I am, I only want to read good, entertaining books that celebrate life."

"How about something erotic?" suggested Quinn. "I think we all could probably use a book with some good sex scenes."

"Can't hurt," Paige concurred. "But it has to be tasteful. My sex life has turned into a chore just a notch above folding laundry—in fact, folding laundry can often be a lot more rewarding."

There was a beat of silence. Apparently none of us wanted to explore the sex-as-laundry metaphor.

Probably because we didn't want to be reminded about the times in our own lives when doing laundry had been more fulfilling than sex.

"Can erotica be well written?" I asked. "It always seems a little, I don't know, cheap and tawdry or something. But maybe I just haven't been exposed."

"Well, *that's* certainly true," Quinn winked.

What did she mean? I wasn't a total novice—how could I be? I'm forty-two and a mother.

"The new Jane Smiley is supposed to be pornographic," Rachel said, not giving up. "The back cover says it's 'R' for ravishing."

"Does it really?" asked Jelicka. "What's it called?"

"*Ten Days in the Valley.* No—hills. *Ten Days in the Hills.*"

It seemed to me that Rachel only pretended not to know the title, dumbing down her large literary brain by acting absent-minded.

"Whatever you decide, Mad, I'll read the whole thing, but I'm also going to read the Jane Smiley book," Jelicka said, explaining. "See, what you don't know is Roscoe had to give up Viagra because it conflicted with his heart medicine. I haven't had sex in two months. I could really use a lover but living vicariously through a few bodice rippers is probably the safer choice."

So that's how my journey to Udi started, I guess—with a mandate to choose a sexy book. It would prove to be a very special book of cliterature that was certain to lift us all into a richer world of lust, sex and maybe even romance—something that appeared to be lacking in *all* our lives.

CHAPTER 4

What Quinn had said about me was sadly true—even if I chose to avoid thinking about why exactly it *was* true. The reality was I *hadn't* been with a man in almost two years and it had been far longer since I'd felt a passionate fluttering for any of their ilk. Not since my marriage had ended—died out, really—not unlike a mammalian body whose lungs and heart had ceased operating.

As a mammal myself, I don't *feel* dead most of the time. In fact, I'm alive enough to still seek connection with someone who will take me as I am, flaws included, but that's always proved difficult. As I've gotten older, men seem more like aliens to me. And when I feel those flickers of physical desire, they are quickly squelched by the fear I might end up as the feeding tube in yet another relationship.

But enough of the self-analysis—my quest at this point was to choose a book that was both sexy and satisfying; a book that would appeal to Jelicka's need for lust and Rachel's for literary mastery. It had to be easier than finding Mr. Right but where was I to get my hands on such a book?

The last erotica I'd read was *Delta of Venus* back in my twenties and, when I was even younger, the juiciest parts of *Fanny Hill*. I'd flipped through *The G Spot:And Other Discoveries about Human Sexuality* carefully enough to discover my own—not that I was clear about what to do after that—but had dismissed this choice as too clinical. It might even insulting to the Muffs, since I knew we were all orgasmically aware, or at least claimed to be. Erica Jong's *Fear of Flying* was a possibility, despite the fact it was a book my mother might have read. It could be that Ms. Jong's "zipless fuck" hadn't held up over the years, though it still sounded tantalizing to this Muff. I nixed two collections of erotic literature I already owned because short stories about sex were really too short for the extended read we craved, like foreplay that doesn't quite get a girl to the point of no return. None of these choices did I consider worthy of the Cliterati.

Finding and reading a story that might get my libido going enough to forget my fear of relationships appealed to my dormant prurient, albeit neglected self, but after an hour perusing titles like *Princess Desire*, *Blind Obedience* and *Hard Candy*, at the Powell's website, I was discouraged. Most of the titles seemed to be about bimbos meeting princes in foreign countries, who either tied them up and spanked them for long periods or rescued them from horrible husbands, but more likely rescued them from themselves. I wanted a story about a normal woman, maybe between thirty and fifty, who just wants to connect with another human being and have great sex without subsequent fallout.

Perhaps the characters would find love in the process, but that would be of secondary importance. Giving the Muffs a vicarious experience of better living through sex was what the book needed to do—what *Lay of the Land* might have been if it was by a woman about a woman with people getting laid, minimal driving and a satisfying ending.

Unfortunately, as I read the excerpts, there just didn't seem to be anything that spoke to the particular brand of female angst I sought solace for. I took this to mean that either no one had written such a book, or that connection and love were not valued commodities in a novel with a lot of sex scenes. That alone posed an interesting thesis on whether sex and love could coexist in life if they were unable to in art, but that was a topic for Rachel and Vicki, the intellectuals in the group, to argue about, not me.

So one Tuesday when I had no cases to mediate and no consultations for potential cases to mediate in the future (unfortunately not an unusual circumstance for a Tuesday or any other day, for that matter), I got into my car after sending Lila off to school and headed into Los Angeles—Sunset Boulevard, to be exact, and Book Soup, one of those intimate, personalized-service bookstores that still exist in big cities. Shops like Book Soup were one of the only things I missed since moving to the suburbs—that and the anonymity of being able to do or wear pretty much anything without risk of being spotted by someone I knew. Here I could spend hours reading without being bothered or, if I wanted, seek knowledgeable assistance without so much as a raised eyebrow, searching for just the right book.

As I entered the Soup, a startlingly good-looking man with dark brown hair, light stubble and the deliberately casual, frumpy style of dress I've always liked in a man, passed me on his way out. He just walked right by me, making me feel as inconsequential as FOD, which is airport lingo for "foreign object debris." You've seen the stuff. It's all the bits of lint and crud that collects around baggage carousels, which can often be seen tumbling over the linoleum but which most people never notice as they hustle their bags to the curb. Were my jeans and long-sleeved T-shirt so last season I didn't even merit a glance?

I knew my libido was low but my self-esteem was even lower. I felt like I hadn't even registered to this guy as a person. Was he gay? How could he ignore me so egregiously? If I'd been a guy, I'd probably tell myself that a member of the opposite sex failing to acknowledge my presence *must* be gay. Herein lies a fundamental distinction between men (the heterosexual kind) and women, according to me: women can admit failure and men like to put a spin on things so their self-image doesn't take a hit.

Now, I absolutely do not have a problem with gay men. My *problem*, if it's a problem at all, is that I really *like* gay men. I've had a few crushes on gay men, in fact, which, duh, never end well. Gay men are generally sensitive and caring; they usually have some aesthetic sense (or at least an awareness that style matters) and they aren't averse to housework. In most of the ways that matter, a gay man is the perfect life partner for a woman who prefers brunch with friends and shopping or a movie to NASCAR and the Final Four. If such a woman, say *me*, were to become half a couple with such a man, the only issue would be for both parties to find outside penises to play with that aren't attached to men, or god forbid, the same man who might disrupt the relationship I was having with my gay partner. *On second thought, it's too complicated.*

It's very sad that women don't arouse, in gay men, the kind of love and passion we crave. How could we? They're gay. As far as I'm concerned, the only trouble with gay men is that homosexuality shrinks the field of eligible partners.

Let it go, I said to myself as I moved further into the Soup, shaking free of my intellectual response to the handsome *déshabillé* of the sexy stranger. What was left in its place was a slight tingling at the top of my thighs, which I took as a good omen for the Cliterati and finding our next book.

"Justine felt her vulva opening and closing, throbbing in anticipation. She was not a virgin—far from it—but she'd not had a worthy lover in months.

So when Antonio began to unbutton her blouse, cupping her breast in his strong swimmer's hand, her body began to respond without hesitation, her skin pulsing with electricity. She felt a moistness between her legs and every time his fingertips graced her forearm, her ankle, her neck—she groaned—not only for the pleasure she was experiencing as he touched her, but for those pleasures she knew would come. She'd imagined a lover like this, patient, sensual, and of unquestionable beauty; but to have finally found him in Antonio, a man ten years younger than she, was beyond her wildest fantasies. Justine's hands drifted slowly, sensually down his back, over his muscular frame and taut skin, still moist from the swim from which she'd disturbed him. He inhaled suddenly, closing his eyes. Then, with more purpose, his hand reached down, finding the hem of her dress, and lifting it gently, he slid his warm palm up her thigh to her buttocks, which he held tightly in his grasp, pulling her body against his sex.

'I want you,' he said—

'Take me,' Justine murmured. 'Please, I can't'—"

"Are you finding what you're looking for?"

I looked up to find a man staring down at me as I sat slack-jawed and cross-legged on the carpeted floor of the Soup. It took me a few seconds to get Antonio out of my head and focus on the man looking at me, a few seconds before I realized he was the guy I'd seen earlier—the good-looking one who'd treated me like I was FOD. He'd come back. *Maybe he wasn't gay.* Maybe he was just metrosexual, whatever that was. Or maybe he worked here, in which case he'd know what I was reading—I mean, really *know.* He wouldn't be fooled by the fact that I'd carried the books over to the children's section in an effort to avoid detection. I quickly closed the book, and lay it face down in my lap.

It was then that I noticed that the tingling I'd felt

earlier at the top of my thighs had turned to flat out creaming. My vulva was throbbing, just like I imagined Justine's must have been, and I was glad I'd covered it because I was pretty sure the throbbing was noticeable through my jeans. This, in turn, caused my cheeks to flush and my breath to quicken even more. Only a blind person would fail to see what was going on with me.

Over an hour had passed since I'd entered the store, and this man, who'd previously walked right by me, and who couldn't have been older than thirty-four, now seemed to be looking at me with Bambi eyes, waiting for me to speak. Had I changed? Can one get over libido-loss so quickly? Was I giving off some kind of pheromones after my erotic read? I wasn't completely sure what pheromones were or if I was emitting any but I liked the idea that I had some to which I could attribute the cute man's return.

"Yes, I am. Thank you," I said, trying to appear nonplussed. But then feeling the need to elaborate. "See it's my turn to pick the next book for my book club so I'm checking out a few things."

"In the children's' section." One side of his mouth was lifting, which told me he wasn't buying it.

"Well," I proceeded confidently, "I found myself in the children's section but I have books from several sections, actually. Don't worry. I'll put them back."

"I'm not worried." Now he was smiling at me. "That was a good one." He was pointing to *Justine in Paradise*, still shielding my throbbing vulva. Clearly he must have been watching me for some time.

"Oh? Well, I'm supposed to pick something sexy." I casually tossed *Justine* into my shopping basket with the other titles whereupon I stood up so as to appear in control of the situation.

He eyed my stash. So far I'd perused the classics, *The Story of O* (too much bondage) and *100 Strokes of the Brush Before Bed* (needs 101?). Both had contributed nicely to getting my fantasy juices flowing but neither was quite right for the Muffia. Nor was *Fifty Shades of Silly* because, well, that book was so silly it didn't even seem relevant to anyone over 24. "Oh My!" Says heroine Anastasia Steele about 300 times. That book did help me realize, however, that though my search continued it was no longer necessary for a book to possess artful syntax and word selection to make a girl feel horny.

"Ah, that explains it," he said, returning his gaze to my face. "Those are all good. I think I've read most of them, at one time or another, but it's been years of course."

"Of course." *Weren't these books for women? Maybe he was gay after all. But he seemed to be making a pass, though it had been so long I wasn't sure if I'd recognize a pass unless it was labeled. My own flirting techniques were decidedly rusty.*

"So, are there any newer titles you can recommend?"

"Sorry, but I've been into political non-fiction pretty exclusively for the past seven or eight years. If you wanted to get the latest take on religion in politics or swine flu as a means of mind control, I'm your man. But I think you'd be making a good choice with any one of those."

"I just thought you might have heard something, you know, since you work here."

"Actually, I don't work here."

"Oh." I didn't know what else to say. *Had he been watching me?*

"My name's Steve." He offered his hand.

I took it. "Hi, Steve."

"I don't want to appear too forward but would you like to get a cup of coffee?"

Why was he paying attention to me now when I hadn't existed before? Was it the books in my basket? Did it matter? I wondered if his fingertips would send electrical charges across *my* skin, what his hands would be like on *my* buttocks. Could he be my zipless fuck—an erotic encounter with a stranger that renews a woman's faith in the satisfaction of her abject lust?

He gazed out at me through soulful brown eyes, his hair falling around his face most appealingly. I could feel his animal intensity boring into me, which alone probably could have made me come if I'd looked into those big browns long enough, but I broke contact when I found myself wondering what his penis looked like—beautiful to be sure, in the way penises *are* beautiful, except of course when one notices that they're completely ridiculous.

"Listen, Steve," I heard myself say before I could change my mind, "I live way out in the valley and I'm a single mom. I don't really think—much as I'd like to..."

"Just coffee," he said.

"It sounds nice, really." *This was the truth.* "But I have to get home to pick up my daughter and take her to ballet." *This was only partly true. I actually had hours before I needed to pick Lila up.*

The fact was I was terrified—he was a lot younger than I was. Maybe Justine would be all right with that kind of age difference but I was nervous about his seeing my naked aging body. I'd need to work out every day for a month first. Yes, I realize he was only asking me for coffee and I'd already made the leap to the bedroom, but what *was* he thinking? He must have gotten the wrong impression, surely— that I was a repressed housewife from Sherman Oaks who spent her lonely days and nights reading erotica and therefore be easy pickin's.

But, oh, those sleepy brown eyes! Did he want something, anything beyond the coffee? Did he imagine wild flights of sexual abandon? I recognize now this is exactly what I needed. I didn't need any coffee. I needed to fuck this guy. And, after thinking about it, having a fling with Book Soup Steve might have kept me from ever going to Berggren's dinner party. Steve and I might have been together that Saturday night having fantastic sex while Lila was safe at her dad's or at a friend's house. But of course, how could I have known that then, when I stood like an idiot in a bookstore holding a bunch of erotic books— mere surrogates for the real thing— talking to a gorgeous guy who I might have had a good time with if only I hadn't been such an idiot.

But once again, I get ahead of myself.

CHAPTER 5

Deliciously Disturbed and Distracted turned out to be the novel I chose for the next gathering of the Cliterati. Both finalists under consideration were sexy *and* well written so, in the end, unable to decide for myself on the merits, I'd tossed a coin. *Deliciously Disturbed* beat out *The Opposite of Dead* ten tosses to nine.

As far as I could tell, Molly Wanamaker, *Disturbed*'s author, had selected her tasty title as a reference to what was going on inside her protagonist, though her clandestine rendezvous over miscellaneous delectable ethnic meals seemed to carry a plot of their own. The title might also have been a reference to the swath this unnamed thirty-five-year-old married woman, whom I called "Lucky Girl," cut across New York City as she flitted from one lover to the next with seemingly zero negative repercussions. All that said, *Deliciously Disturbed* was beginning to cause disturbances of its own although, in the big scheme of things, it probably wouldn't have mattered what book we read. The ices were melting, the seed had been sown, the lava was leaping and that horse was already out of the barn.

I grew hornier with every page, more and more disturbed because I had no immediate way of satisfying the increasing lust I felt, generated by Lucky Girl and her paramours. I mean, duh, yes, there was always masturbation and I could have gone to a bar or a hotel lobby and scored with the first lonely traveling businessman I encountered but that wasn't going to do it for me. Stupidly, I'd scuttled Book Soup Steve, who after the fact, in my head, I'd turned into a love-God rivaling Michelango's David come to life.

One chapter into the book, after Lucky Girl had enjoyed unimaginably great sex with a swarthy Italian type she'd noticed noticing her on the lat machine at Club Equinox—someone she referred to as "the Hit Man"—I decided to take action. Returning to Book Soup on another slow Tuesday I hoped to find Steve who might, once again, be hanging around, waiting for women perusing erotic books. I planned on taking him up on his offer this time, belated as it was—possibly making him an offer of my own, one he couldn't and wouldn't refuse. In my head I had a very precise idea of what "getting together" would look like. It wouldn't exactly be zipless because he wasn't technically a stranger. After all, he'd watched me cream my jeans while reading *Justine in Paradise*. He knew I had a daughter and lived in the Valley. But it would still be sudden, thrilling and... safe? Oh yeah, condoms. Shit. Well, somehow you get the condom on but that wasn't part of my fantasy. I tried to look busy in Book Soup for three hours, going in and out of the Peet's Coffee across the street a few times, but Steve didn't show. I concluded that he must have found a more willing book-clubber to boff.

It didn't seem fair that Lucky Girl was having sex with three men whom she *wanted* to have sex with, including her husband, and I wasn't getting any sex at all. Looking in the mirror, I couldn't figure it out. Objectively speaking, I'm better looking and in better shape than a lot of women my age—women who have husbands who seem to adore them and who claim to share quality lovemaking at least twice a month. Of course I could also be going down that big river in Egypt.

Either I'd never met my perfect mate or I've been

too particular about what I'm looking for. Or perhaps it was those damned pheromones again—they didn't work. But most likely all three things were true.

I've never been much of a bar hopper, even back in the day when a husband was what we were all looking for. At least I think that's what we were doing. Now it's as if I'm not sure I really want a husband—only a lover or two or three. I'm too old, at forty-two, to attract the eye of the type of man I have both an intellectual and visceral response to because that guy is usually looking for someone younger. There have been men I could have had—fifty-five and sixty-year-olds with well-established waistlines and an overdeveloped sense of entitlement—but I didn't find those guys attractive. There'd been no one I really wanted and I was getting desperate. My throbbing crotch was even starting to interfere when I conducted my alternate dispute resolutions.

In one of my easier divorce cases, not too long ago, I became aware of an attraction I was feeling toward the man whose divorce I was mediating. He was very kind to his soon-to-be ex-wife, and that probably had something to do with it, but he also had a strong, masculine chin, petulant lips, and his shoulders filled out his beautifully tailored shirts as only a well-muscled, body-conscious male physique can do.

He gave me the impression that he'd be able to toss me onto a bed and ravage me while still retaining enough energetic ardor for twenty more rounds. I felt an attraction issuing from him in return. But obviously, in order to conduct the mediation without the appearance of bias, I had to ignore—or, more specifically, repress—these feelings. It would be highly unethical for me to act on them—at least until the passage of a respectable time period after the marital settlement agreement had been filed.

I was actually happy that I'd met someone other than Book Soup Steve whom I was attracted to because that *had* been a problem before: no one got me going except the shirtless teenage hotties in ads for male underwear and that was sort of frightening for a woman old enough to be the mother of one of them.

In truth, I could only praise myself for acknowledging how I felt and commit myself to dealing with the situation: Madelyn needed to get laid. Not just a quick fuck but *laid*—the kind of can't walk, can't think straight, last-through-the-next-dry-spell kind of laid. (Dealing with myself and my problems in the third person always seems to make the situation crystal clear, as if I were dealing with someone else's).

It was about three weeks after I emailed the group to assign the book that I noticed a relative hush had come over the Clitterati—kind of like the lull in conversation when you're out to dinner and people start eating, as if they're too consumed with eating to talk. Was this the usual lull between Muff meetings? Or was something else going on? I wondered if *Delightfully Disturbed and Distracted* mightn't have been causing disturbances—delicious or otherwise—in the lives of my fellow Clitties. I was about to start an email exchange when Lauren, just returning from her week away, beat me to it:

LBSweet@aol.com: Hey all...just back from Jamaica. After being peed on twice and thrown up on one humongous time on the plane, I couldn't be happier to be home. It was brutally hot and there were so many mosquitoes—all of which enjoyed making my family their favorite meal. Can someone please email me the name of the best small pocket battery-less vibrator I should be buying? Must order one online ASAP. And would possibly consider buying the one that Jelicka raved about with batteries. Please send brands and website. Love to all. xxxx - L
PS—Juicy book choice, Maddie

Hmmmm . . . vibrators. . . Lauren gets back from a sunny Jamaican vacation with her loving husband and two kids and upon her return immediately sends out a request for vibrator info? Seems to me like there's a minor disturbance going on there.

Lauren had been married to George Busch for seven years. His given names were actually Sebastian George and when he was growing up, long before the Texas Bushes invaded our consciousness, everyone had called him Georgie. It was unfortunate when Bush II came around, that Lauren, a lifelong Democrat, found herself having to endure the ribbing that came with being George and Lauren Busch—can't help whom you fall in love with, I guess. She made an all-out effort to get people to call him Sebastian, or 'Bastian, a name she'd loved ever since developing a crush on Anthony Andrews while watching her mother's stash of *Brideshead Revisited* videos, but just like me trying to get people to call me Madelyn, it didn't stick.

What *was* most excellent for Lauren, and what probably made her willing to withstand any marital disturbance, was that Sebastian George Busch was a member of the Busches of Milwaukee, great grandson to the scion August Busch, creator of the hops empire, Budweiser and equine promoter of Clydesdales—a breed of horses once known for plough-work, now lifted from obscurity to Super Bowl status as they parade their feathery fetlocks in the most expensive commercials on television.

This is all to say that Lauren didn't worry about money. No one wanted to say anything publicly about what might *not* be going on between Lauren and Georgie in private, but I was thankful she'd brought up the subject of outside mechanical stimulation. That's what I needed—a vibrator. I'd always wanted one, sort of, but had never gotten around to making the actual purchase. A vibrator was the perfect solution to relieve my immediate horniness. This was going to be an email exchange I'd read with great interest. Paige responded first:

> vonhooter@gmail.com: The one I raved about is neither pocket sized nor battery-less. It's the infamous Rabbit that even Oprah swears by, but not what I'd call travel friendly (embarrassing at x-ray). Don't know any others. Sorry about the mozzies. And V, what's going on? No seeds in your sac I trust. ~xx P

> cunningquinn@Talentpool.com: I don't yet own a vibrator but I've been shopping (it's what I *do*). Really a drag not being able to try out the merchandise first. Shit, they let you try on shoes!! So far I like the *Accuvibe*—a carefully disguised mainstream massage instrument sold at stores you wouldn't be embarrassed being seen in, like Relax-The-Back. And guaranteed not to trigger a bag search at x-ray. The joy (and big "O") comes when you add the attachments (carefully stowed under the plane for travel) and available at Babeland. BTW: Seeds in the sac? Didn't we put that book to bed?

Then Rachel weighed in, which kind of surprised me. I suspected she might own a vibrator, but somehow I thought she wouldn't talk about it. She was younger and, well... younger:

> rachelbakerart@mac.com: Hitachi magic wand. I repeat: Hitachi magic wand. If you find a good source let me know. Mine's old. Fun book, M. Am feeling deliciously disturbed and distracted. So glad no seeds in your sac, V.

Vicki didn't have a sac and I didn't think it appropriate to keep going on about it, considering her condition. I was about to shoot off a reply when

Jelicka's email hit. We all believed her to have the most sexual experience in the group. She had to know a lot about vibrators and wouldn't be shy talking about this kind of thing, so I opened her message with excitement.

missjelickag@aol.com: Hitachi magic wand? That's one I *don't* know which doesn't mean anything. There're a lot of good ones, depends on what you need and like. In fact, I've never met one I didn't like. Vick-- great news being spared Chemo. Though you would have been fab in any number of wigs. What's the female equivalent of scrotal seeds anyway?

rachelbakerart@mac.com: Hmmm...sac   o' seeds? Ovaries? Eggs? Dunno. I still say, Hitachi magic wand, Hitachi magic wand . . . Can't wait to see you all next BC.

All the talk about sacs and seeds was our way of coping: we were all aware of the tumor Vicki had growing inside of her, as well as the reality that it could have developed in any one of us. We chose to use humor to deal with the situation. I know Vicki appreciated our effort to remain light and optimistic, but it couldn't have been cheery to be reminded of her condition in our emails, even if it was by way of discussing a fictional character. The truth was, we didn't really know what to do, short of letting her know we were there for her and asking her if she needed anything, probably too often. Sharing emails about vibrators was probably a welcome distraction, even if she wasn't in the mood to use one. I certainly wasn't going to be the one to put a kibosh on the thread.

victoriamendoza@mac.com:I love *this* book, Maddie. Almost counteracts the daily zap, which is probably comparable to Frank's titanium beads. I'm likely to set off airport x-ray machines all by myself. Therefore I will smuggle in any vibrators on said radioactive body for any of you ladies that may need. But for God's sake, can't you go a week without diddling yourself Lauren? (Just a soon-to-be-estrogenless woman asking.) Anyway, doing it myself takes longer than I have the energy for these days. Have new idea for film project—this is the one! Will tell all when I see you.

LBSweet@aol.com: Thank all you Muffs for all the advice...will order a couple now so I have back up. Anyone got a good website for this kind of thing?

But she wasn't done.

LBSweet@aol.com: OK, one more question. Can you use it just as a vibrator for clitoral stimulation or do you have to put the thing in. Not as into fake penises inside me as others seem to be. ~Lauren   p.s. what's the project V? p.p.s.... love our book club!

vonhooter@gmail.com: You guys are funny, but I have to agree, after 9 volts, the old school manual method does take a bit of patience... I always hope for a hotel with a handheld shower attachment, a personal favorite. xxP

kookykiki@hotmail.com: Could you Muffs leave me off this vibrator thread? I don't get it. Thanks, K

She doesn't get it? Kiki had something up her butt—*that* was the problem. I'm speculating here, but she and Saul must be into a tough patch. I just hoped they'd make the right choice for Troy's sake. Whether you stay with someone or not is such a personal decision and never one to take lightly when there's a child involved. Though of course, in my own case, I chose not to stay married even though there was a child involved, thinking it would be better for her not to witness a bad relationship with so little love exchanged. But as I said, this was speculation and I wasn't going to bring up Kiki's behavior via mass email.

sapizz11@connect.net: OK, K's off this one. BTW--You can get a handheld shower at home you know. Also, for environmental reasons, it's better to use the plug-ins v. the batteries. Go for green O's. xxS

MissJelickaG@aol.com: I was a little concerned about the loss of power when I moved from the outdoor Jacuzzi, with vibro-jet action, to the less powerful indoor bath Jacuzzi, but none of you need worry about me, it's all good! ~xo JG

Quinn was clearly right about me. I hadn't been exposed. And never having owned a vibrator or used a handheld shower attachment or Jacuzzi jet in this way, I still had nothing to add. And even if I had, there was so much information coming in from everyone else, I wanted to keep reading.

LBSweet@aol.com: My time spent online at all these women's sex aid sites has been very educational. I suspect that some time in the future, books will come with their own vibrators. Given all the all female book clubs out there, I see tremendous market potential. Am putting it on the list for Vegas Book Club Convention idea...I have a hand held in my shower and have never used it. I am such an orgasm virgin. Off to try...xxL

cunningquinn@Talentpool.com: I found the jackrabbit at a major discount (reg. $59.95 – sale $18.95). We can save on shipping if we bulk order. Who's in? You can also go to www.healthyandactive.com and use coupon code Mailer 56 for an extra 10% off. I would love to hear anybody's recommendations. I collect them.

PS I have to pick a new LA doctor and was hoping some of you might have a doctor (internist, gyne, family doctor, whatever) who you think is great.

vonhooter@gmail.com: I'm not sure what the jackrabbit is, same species but different breed is my guess—or faster jacking? The original orgasmic rabbit retails for $120 or so. Go the extra mile girls. The site that Quinn sent may have it discounted but beware of Shanghai knock-offs. Happy trails! xP
PS I use Mr. Rabbit for quickies (exterior only) probably about 75% of the time, but when the mood hits, the whole enchilada is a beautiful thing. But you're talking to a girl who lost her virginity to a self-imposed broom handle... xP
PPS Lauren, if you're strictly interested in exterior work, the Rabbit would be too clumsy for you.

rachelbakerart@mac.com: Who wants clumsy? For exterior there's no better than Hitachi magic wand. I know you're all wary of my book choices, but trust me on this one. HMW!

sarapizz@connect.net: So whoozy, I can't even think about sticking something called a jackrabbit up my cookie at the moment... :) S

See, in between the last book club at her house and midway to the next at mine, Sarah had announced she was pregnant, which accounted for why she didn't want anything up her cookie. But it might also explain Nate's behavior and that sloppy kiss he gave me. They'd been disturbed even before we started reading *Deliciously Disturbed.*

I considered calling another Muff for more information. One of us had all the details; in fact, they probably all did—as I mentioned at the beginning, I'm usually the one who's slightly out of the loop. Most of the other Muffs talked on the phone with each other a lot—a fact that I should have remembered, and which will come up again and again as time and this story goes on. In the end, I decided to hold off. Instead, as the flurry of vibrator-related emails dwindled to nothing, I decided I needed to stop thinking about vibrators and actually buy one, probably the erstwhile Rabbit—jack or regular.

I didn't want to place an order online fearing that Big Brother, Homeland Security and any number of other savvy data-miners would know what I was doing alone at night. Worse, I might find myself on all sorts of lists, receiving more than the usual amount of unwanted ads for sexual performance-enhancing drugs and paraphernalia. The truth was, since the Griswold case was still the law of the land, I had a legal right to keep my dildo private—which is not to say the authorities respect this privilege one hundred percent of the time. But I would do everything in my power to ensure the information didn't leak out to where it might hurt me, which would begin with shopping for a dildo at a brick & mortar store and paying cash.

Even though I'm no longer practicing law, clearly I still think like a lawyer most of the time. It's just that when I decided to go back to law after my divorce, I chose to be an "alternative" dispute resolver, rather than spending my days slugging out one side of a battle in court. Only it turns out, most people in our society would *rather* fight—or at least start fighting—until they finally get the message that litigation is an expensive zero-sum game and that it makes more sense to avoid court entirely and come to a mediated settlement that saves everyone time and money.

The trouble was, having been out of the work force for so long, it was hard getting people to trust me enough to hire me. I was on a list of mediators—kind of like those lists HMOs send out with all the doctors "in your plan." I had to be pretty close to the bottom because I rarely got called and when I did, it was often neighbors with fights over fence height, or to be the arbiter between a dating service and a guy who hadn't found his soul mate after paying his sign-up fee. To me, "can't buy me love" is a rule just like "love hurts" is a rule. But once again, what do I know? It seems that "hope springs eternal" and that hope ensures the continued survival of the dating industry and a mediation job for me from time to time.

I'd been trying to network with everyone I knew, searching for an ombudsman job with a corporation— an international corporation, so I could travel the world. Better yet, though a long shot, was a position with a group—a panel, as mediation jargon would have it—that dealt with international issues like the U.N. or the World Anti-Doping Organization or even the International Criminal Court. The idea was that in four years, when Lila turned eighteen and I lost her child support, I'd have a job that took me to far-off, fascinating places. Travel had been on my "to do" list for the past fourteen years, during which time the farthest I'd ventured from California was Miami for the death of my Grandma Evie.

Around this time, long after I finished reading *Deliciously Disturbed and Distracted* and started in on *Ten Days in the Hills* (which I found sexy but not as ravishing as advertised), it seemed like my networking was about to get me somewhere. After three years of being a sporadic mediator of all manner of disputes, I'd managed to land an interview with the U.S. Olympic Committee. See, things were gearing up for the London games, and at one time, I'd been a short-listed Olympic swimmer. I never got to compete—repetitive-motion shoulder problems can really mess up a girl's butterfly—but I'd been a *cause celebre* to some extent with my disavowal of steroid shots and drugs to get me to the starting block. At any rate, the Olympic Committee thought my background as a female athlete, lawyer and steroid-shunner might serve their needs, and they called me to come in for a meeting.

On the day I was scheduled to drive downtown for my interview, Quinn and I made a plan to hook up afterward for a little sex-aid shopping, no matter the outcome of my meeting.

"I can meet you at about five-thirty for about half an hour. Then I'm meeting a guy for drinks," she whispered into the phone, barely audible.

"Who's the guy?" I asked, slightly wounded that Quinn hadn't told me she was interested in someone.

"Ugh," she uttered, less than thrilled. "Actually, he's another actor but he seems grounded, comparatively."

"What does grounded comparatively mean?"

"You know. He's over five-nine and seems less self-absorbed than your average climber."

This was always Quinn's rationalization when she resorted to dating a client or wanna-be client. I suppose it was a mutual, almost literal, "I'll scratch your pussy/career if you scratch my penis/ego." Whatever. The point was Quinn and I made a plan to meet.

CHAPTER 6

The day was gorgeous—seventy degrees, clear and sunny—the main reason people live in southern California to begin with. I located a parking space, walked a block and a half to Melrose Avenue and was safely within the hot pink, vagina-like confines of Babeland when my cell phone rang.

"Are you there yet?" Quinn asked, in a hushed voice.

"I'm inside," I said, looking around. "It's very . . . pink."

"Good. How'd the interview go?"

"Also good. They said they'll call me in for some role plays next week."

"If you move to Geneva, make sure you get an apartment with an extra bedroom."

"Let me jump through their hoops and not trip before we figure out what country I might be moving to. Besides, I'd need a place big enough for all the Muffs."

"Valid point. Listen, I wanted to make sure you were in the store before I told you I'm not going to make it."

I felt my throat tighten. "Quinn, how can you leave me to do this on my own when you know I don't have any experience in this area."

"And you think I'm an expert?"

"You've done the research."

"I haven't made a purchase. I have no actual insertion experience." She was whispering as loud as she could.

Walking to the least-busy section of the store I whispered back, "But you've been window shopping and at least have a working knowledge of the whole vibrator/sexual-aid marketplace. Not to mention, you've blown me off for a *guy*—an actor. Isn't that against Muffia rules?"

A door closed at the other end of the line and Quinn started speaking louder. "I do feel bad about it, Maddie, but I can't get away from work yet. If it makes you feel better, I'm going to be late for my date, too."

I took a deep breath and sighed it out. "At least your actor's human," I reasoned aloud in her defense. "If I make a purchase I'll have a booty call with a chunk of plasticized rubber."

"You might be better off," she said. "From what I understand, with the Rabbit you're *guaranteed* an orgasm. That's more than I can predict about Frank Lassiter."

"Who?"

"My date—not his real name. You'll be happy to know I'm wearing flats."

"Good for you," I said, knowing this was a huge concession for Quinn, who is 5'10" and loves heels. Her height is a condition that has been known to emasculate a guy or two, so she was hedging her bets.

"Listen, I'm sorry. I owe you. Just ask the owners for some direction. They're lesbians and know all there is to know about pleasuring women."

"I guess they would be since, *post hoc ergo propter hoc*, they don't have a real cock between 'em."

I felt it vibrate against me before I heard it—a low *purrr* set to a frequency designed *not* to blend with street noise. I must have taken a funny step as I left the store and hit the "on" switch somehow. What had possessed me to buy a wearable pulsating pussy pleasurer? *Not to panic.* I just needed to be able to work the thing, and remember never to wear it during a mediation session where I might send it humming at an inappropriate moment. It did feel nice—stimulating, yet soothing—just like the package promised.

What did the salesgirl say? "Hold on with your labial lips and then cock your hips to return your brand new vibrating genital massager to the 'off' position." I'd probably made an error in judgment letting her convince me to wear it out of the store, though she was the sexiest lesbian I'd ever seen and I'm pretty sure she was flirting with me. I kind of liked it, and spent a couple of minutes imagining the life shared by Ellen DeGeneres and Portia De Rossi in ritzy Montecito, languishing at their villa with their view of the ocean, their dogs and sex toys. But the idea didn't get me there. I still preferred guys.

So there I was on the sidewalk wearing my brand-new *Aphroditty—the woman's constant friend—*an amoeba-shaped gizmo that was buzzing between my panties and pussy. I considered turning around and heading back into the store, where I would not be able to return the item, but as I hadn't drawn attention with my mildly vibrating pelvis, nor with what must have been my peculiar expression, I swiveled my hips from left to right, squeezed my twat together in a Hollywood sidewalk version of a kegel and voila—Aphroditty purred no more. Now all I could hear was the incessant whoosh of cars, busses and the collective whine of the second most over-populated motion picture capital of the world.

Just to test my abilities with my new toy, I squeezed hard again, shifted my hips back in the other direction and the stimulating, pulsing buzz began again. It seemed I would soon become mistress of my own bi-labially-dexterous destiny, ensuring silence or vibrating vaginal transcendence, depending on the mood. No one was watching and I felt confident no one suspected that anything unusual was going on *down there.*

"I heard you," said the attractive dark-haired, dark-eyed man in line ahead of me at the cup o' joe joint four doors down from where I'd been doing my retail therapy—the mature woman's kind, when a new pair of shoes just won't cut it.

"Excuse me?" I responded, immediately flustered by the intensity of his gaze and, just like Book Soup Steve, dark pink lips that were fuller than what should be legal for a man. He wore a crinkled rust-colored linen shirt and, I noticed, no jewelry. "Oh, you mean my phone," I said, scrambling. "I really have to change the ring tone."

His teeth were perfect and his tongue danced in his mouth as he let out a laugh. Then he leaned in toward me. "I mean, I *heard* you . . . *You know . . .*"

I could smell him. *All man,* yet no unappealing body odor. I found myself more turned-on than embarrassed by this tall, artist-handsome ruffian of indeterminate age and racial makeup, but I wasn't sure I wanted *him* to know that. *Who am I kidding? I'd probably give it up to this guy if he blinks at me right.*

"I thought you'd noticed me, too," he continued, his laugh gone now. "But maybe not. I was in there about ten minutes ago and I saw you looking around. In . . . Babeland?"

"Are you following me?" I asked with mock defensiveness. "You better watch that. I'm a lawyer—mediator, actually."

"You don't look like a lawyer. Besides, I'm the one who might need one. You came in here after I did. So who's stalking whom?"

He'd caught me up in a number of ways already and we hadn't officially met. I considered summoning up some   legitimate-sounding   shock   at   all   his presumption—something that gave the impression of control. But my resolve left me as I became aware of the moistening between my legs. The creamery that had kicked into production while shopping in Babeland was now operating full tilt and the product began to slip silently by my new tiny twat titillator, moving down to the flesh throbbing wildly at the top of my thighs without any mechanical assistance.

What was I thinking going into that place for coffee? Did I really need *more* stimulation? I should have gone home, pulled out the other purchase I'd made—my very own purple *Rabbit* in translucently-cast elastomer with twirling dildo and built-on simultaneous vibrator-plastic "G" spot jiggler—and gotten to work. Going anywhere I might meet a real human man after gazing at all the many-fibered, multi-textured penile substitutes had been risky to say the least.

I was so wet I almost swooned when he leaned in again and whispered, "My ex used to walk around with hers buzzing all the time, and not just when she was some place loud, either. I prefer your modesty."

Looking around for rescue, for diversion, I realized the two of us were still a few customers away from ordering, and the caffeine junkies were engaged in antics of their own, unaware of the mating game being played out in front of them.

His right hand—beautiful elegant fingers and skin the color of mocha—came up to sweep the brush of dark hair (with a few perfectly placed strands of gray) off his brow and suddenly I remembered him. His were the hands I'd seen holding the *Fleshlight*—a toy I would have wanted if I'd had a cock. The Fleshlight, like its illuminating brother, the flashlight, is a metal encased cylinder—only in the case of the three-and-one-half-inch-diameter Fleshlight, it's filled with silicone gel parted by a vulva-like slit down its center, long enough to accommodate any man's member, and topped with smiley, welcoming pink lips. I couldn't fault him for wanting it. After all, I'd been shopping for toys in Babeland, too.~

"I'm looking for the *Darling Pink Penetrator*," I had said *sotto voce* to the cute gay salesgirl who was Babeland's part owner. "I read about it online and I've been looking for something hands-free."

"Of course," she replied, a bit too loudly, as she walked me toward the back of the store. "The *Darling Pink* has super savvy suction. It grabs onto a shower wall or mirror so a girl can just back her booty right up to it, allowing for total, hands-free satisfaction. We also have several others," she said, gesturing toward the wide selection of different shaped and colored self-satisfying dildos, their suction cups affixed to a glass shelf. "I'll leave you to play with them," she continued, with a voice so specific to natives of the San Fernando Valley she might have been born inside the Sherman Oaks Galleria. Then she winked and dashed off to help a young couple that was having a bit of difficulty with a strap-on assemblage.

Shy at first, I began grabbing each of the suction cup dongs in turn, pulling and pushing on the pretend penises in an attempt to simulate what I might do to it with my pussy once I got it home and stuck it on the shower wall. I was mildly traumatized to find that none remained fixed to the glass shelf, with even the tiniest of touches. Did this mean my brand of sex had too much movement for suction cup dildos? I'd always considered myself relatively tame, yet it was obvious the suction just wasn't there. In fact, the *Darling Pink Penetrator* showed particularly poor performance, despite its attractive and enticing (and triple-patented) cocoa-colored cyberskin exterior. The anticipated disruption of my self-induced sexual bliss was enough to make me give up on the whole hands-free idea and seek another way to indulge my hypo-active libido.

In an effort to avoid drawing attention to myself, I

quietly began to examine *Mr. Bendy*, with his sumptuously soft, bendable core, which his promoters assured would-be purchasers was " firm, not floppy," but decided that, unfortunately for me, Mr. Bendy bent the wrong way.

As I continued to look around the very pink store, noticeably void of Hitachi Magic Wands, I had a thought that cheered me in a sort of melancholy way: If I never met another guy who I want to have sex with, I could go the rest of my life with the variety provided by the ever-increasing number of sex toys. The sadness came when I admitted to myself that what I really craved was a variety of sexy boys. I'd even settle for one kind-of sexy one and that long-lost feeling of connection —however fleeting, however delusional—with the *real thing*.

"I could tell you weren't finding what you were looking for," said the man who'd heard my Aphroditty, snapping me back to the Java Joint. I freaked at the thought of him seeing me push and pull on *Doc Johnson's Girthquake Vibrating Dong-Along* and I inhaled, trying to blunt the sharpness of the intake.

"Is this what you do?" I asked him. "Watch the women going in and out of Babeland, then try to score when they're at their most vulnerable?"

Across his face, a small hurt appeared. "If that was my style, I don't think I would have bought this," he said with a wry smile, holding up the bag that presumably held his new Fleshlight.

He actually was sort of charming. He had a cultured, cosmopolitan air about him—sex toy in bag notwithstanding. No university sweatshirts for this guy. He wore a linen shirt and sports jacket. I'd already sabotaged Book Soup Steve. Did I need to do it again? After all, this man and I had something in common.

"I made a purchase, so I couldn't have been *that*

disappointed." I held up my own Babeland bag containing not only my new Rabbit but an assortment of Japanese Kimono ultra-thin micro-fiber condoms as well. Some part of me must have felt enough optimism to wager that by buying them, I might actually find someone with whom to use them.

"I'm glad. I wouldn't have wanted you to go home alone." He flashed his eyes and I let my own glitter back.

"I'm Cullen," he said, offering his hand.

"Hello, Cullen. I'm Madelyn," I said, after a fleeting second's thought about giving him a different name. I mean, what if I got offered the international mediation job? I didn't like the headline: *Women's World Cup Figure Skating Hearing Delayed by Mediator's Tricks Off the Ice.* His fingers felt both warm and cool in my hand—smooth, not sweaty—with a heat that extended from his heart.

"Actually," I said, "it's because of my purchases that I'm able to go home alone."

From the way he was looking at me, I could tell he had a better idea.

"Did you really want coffee, Madelyn?"

We'd reached the front of the line and the barista stared, bored, waiting for our order. "Because there's a cute little tapas place around the corner on La Brea. Would you let me buy you a glass of wine?"

On the one hand, there was something sordid about even having a drink with someone you meet at a place like Babeland. It somehow suggested pre-meditation and repeat offenders. On the other hand, it seemed immature and too coy, frankly, to pretend that I wasn't attracted to this man, nor interested in what he might offer. Could it be possible that he also longed for sex with somebody who could eventually become more than just an in-and-out girl? Most people do want something more than just a sex partner, but they settle because the "something more" is harder to find, to recognize and to maintain.

What was the danger in a glass of wine? Perhaps I'd been kidding myself. This had to be what women my age do. Maybe every age—I'm just slow. They simply meet a man they're attracted to and have sex. Isn't that what I'd been saying I wanted?

I rationalized that the first interview with the Olympic Committee had gone well and I'd be moving to the next level of interviews and role plays—cause for minor celebration. And I didn't need to be home for hours—Lila was at a friend's house.

"I'm going to have to help the next people if you can't decide what you want," barked the ballsy barista girl with the giant golden-rimmed holes in her ears.

Cullen was still looking at me when I smiled up at him, doing my best to be perceived as "*available—not desperate.*" He had about three inches on me. *He seemed perfect.*

"I'd love a glass of wine," I said.

"We don't have—" the barista began, looking at me oddly.

"Thank you," Cullen said, never taking his eyes from me as he tossed a few coins in the tip jar. "And you."

CHAPTER 7

Dark-shaded sconces diffused the ambient lighting and cast a shimmering glow over the ochre-colored faux-marble walls of the Andalucia Tapas and Wine bar. Placed at decorative intervals above plushly upholstered booths, they made the mood one of orchestrated romance. Contemporary paintings I could barely make out in the low light hung in every available spot, all affixed with tasteful labels indicating artist and sales price. A mahogany bar, which might have been rescued from a previous existence in old Hollywood, extended along one side of the restaurant with a chalkboard menu above it featuring wine and sherry tastings of the day. At six PM, the restaurant was almost empty, with only a scattering of the beautiful people who would appear later in droves, laughing, drinking and looking to hook up.

Cullen took off his sports jacket then raised his wine glass to me in toast, and I found myself wondering if he'd brought other women to the Andalucia. This was the kind of thought I didn't want to be having, one of those thoughts that create obstacles to experience. It didn't really matter if he had and I had no reason to think he had, other than, of course, the obvious one. But at that moment, he seemed completely focused on the wine.

"I wish they'd just call it Bordeaux," he said, swirling his California Claret. "They're not doing themselves any favors by calling it Claret unless they think by recycling an old word people *these days* probably only know from Shakespeare—that's if they read—that the marketers can pass it off as something new everyone will want. It only fools the sycophants who are always trying to keep up with the next new thing. And like I said, in this case, it's a new old thing. People are crazy."

He glanced over at me, appearing more nervous than he had in the Java Joint. "I'm rambling."

"No, that's fine. And people are crazy, I agree. At least we're entertaining."

He smiled. "How's your wine?"

I was drinking a Santa Barbara County Grenache, which someone had told me once was like Chateauneuf-du-Pape for one-eighth the price, so I ordered it whenever I saw it on the wine list, assured it would make me appear knowledgeable to my companions. "Not bad."

Cullen explained that he was kind of nervous, which was obvious, but I liked that he could tell me that without somehow feeling like he wasn't being *guy* enough or something. I confessed that I was nervous, too, but I didn't tell him just *how* nervous I was, which was about a nine on a ten-point scale. I hadn't been on a date with anyone I liked in almost two years.

"Babeland is the first sex shop I've ever been in," I volunteered after making sure my hand wasn't shaking as I lifted my glass.

"Really?" he asked. "At the risk of offending you, today's my third time. My ex took me twice before. She said she just wanted to look, but I think she was trying to give me a not-too-subtle hint that something was lacking in our sex life and that we needed to consider some 'aids.'"

"Did she ever come out and say that?"

"No. She just left one day. Took the cock, too."

"What?"

"Took the cockatoo. Our bird."

"Ah."

He hesitated, as if considering whether to amend what it was she'd taken, but then switched tracks. This was his first time going in alone, he told me, and definitely the first time talking and having wine with a woman he'd met inside the store. He said that today's visit was actually research for a book he wanted to write—a whole series of books that would break the rules of mainstream detective fiction and create a new genre he called "Cop Erotica."

I had no idea if such a thing was possible, but I wanted to take every word he said as the truth; I'd been lied to so often, however, my defenses were on high alert. At some point, I just decided to go with it, to just *be* with this man who seemed to care what I thought, who spoke about himself not like a typical LA narcissist in need of an audience but as a way to engage me, then listened intently to what I said in return.

As he spoke, I watched his lips, almost unable to take my eyes from them. They reminded me of the wedges of a perfectly ripe blood orange—plump, red . . . *succulent* was the word. And as I imagined tasting them, he leaned across the booth and kissed me— quickly, high up on my cheek just below the ear. Then he sat back to watch my reaction.

A swell of emotion danced the flamenco between my brain and groin. "Well," I said, hoping something witty would come to me. "That was . . . quick." *Duh.*

He leaned in again, his blood orange lips meeting my own soft pink ones for   one . . . two . . . five . . . seconds. The brain/groin connection sped up and intensified, flitting back and forth like a Geiger counter when it's right on top of radioactivity. I was shocked at how my brain went into lockdown mode, as if I was operating off my throbbing groin alone. It was almost as if it didn't matter who the guy was once that shift occurred. With my eyes closed, he could be anybody. I could be anywhere. When I pulled away from him, the lust overwhelming, I found him looking back at me with the same ferocity.

"This is completely nuts," I said.

"Do you not want to?"

"No. I do . . . I mean I do, and I don't. You know. It's . . . "

He moved to my side of the booth and kissed me again.

"Nice," I said breathlessly. Our tongues became disengaged from propriety and engaged with each other, pulling the rest of our unresisting bodies along.

"Very nice." His arm came behind me and his left hand, which up to this point had been holding his wine glass, moved around my shoulders, and pressed me closer. My own hand reached behind his back to feel strength and a welcome absence of back fat. *Now, if I were really into him, would I have even noticed back fat?* Still—we'd have to get a room if this went much further, and I found myself thrilled at the prospect.

The management, whether by established practice or simply because they were happy to have people to serve in a down economy, thankfully left us alone in our dark corner booth. Everything was going so well, but I wanted to talk more. Though I thought I'd wanted a *zipless fuck*, when the opportunity presented itself, I realized I didn't. Or I didn't want it with Cullen. After all, it had been so long since I'd had a lover, I needed a little more preamble for my first time back in the saddle.

He knew somehow that I wanted to slow down and gently took my hand in his, caressing it, kissing me only with his eyes. He told me about living in France and Italy, where he'd learned about wine and worked in a few good restaurants; how he'd returned to Oregon, where he'd grown up and started a restaurant of his own; how he'd then sold the restaurant when an offer came along that he couldn't refuse. He told me how he'd always written stories and how he'd moved to LA a year earlier, at forty-five, with his then-girlfriend to explore the idea of making a living at writing, but how, once he'd been here a couple of months, he'd discovered it was more difficult than he'd thought. Then he told me how his girlfriend, an LA native, had left him a couple of months earlier for an actor who'd landed a T.V. series, telling Cullen he and his writing were going nowhere and that he should move back to Oregon.

He said it was for the best that she'd left, that they weren't compatible really. But he missed her anyway, and even missed the bird. LA's so spread out, he complained, with everyone so busy chasing something not everyone can attain, that it's hard to connect on anything more than a superficial level. He was lonely and to him, despite how many people lived here, it was the loneliest place he'd ever been. Now he was at that proverbial fork in the road and it was taking him longer than he would have thought to decide which direction to go.

As he spoke, I found myself agreeing with the things he said, and I started feeling more comfortable and less like a harlot, though feeling like a harlot hadn't been all bad. I agreed with him about being alone, but that feeling alone when you're with someone else was actually worse—to see that person every day and lie next to him every night and realize that whatever connection you might have once had was now gone—and the choice of whether to stay or go was a mutual decision that never seemed to be made together without one person getting defensive.

I was telling him my story when a couple came into the restaurant with their lips locked together. I couldn't see them clearly—the place was too dark—but I detected a familiarity about the man.

Cullen turned, following my gaze.

"Somebody I know, maybe," I said. "Not sure." The

guy kept leaning down to suck face with the woman. *How gauche.*

A server led the couple in our direction and as they got closer, it was clear to me the man was Nate, as in Sarah and Nate, but the woman was definitely not Sarah. This woman had cleavage where Sarah was prone to good coverage. This woman wore a skirt and heels where Sarah wore Patagonia pants and flip-flops. His hands groping the woman's ass made it pretty clear what was going on, and it at least partially explained the kiss in the stairwell at the last Muffia gathering. But now Sarah was pregnant. *This sucks.*

Should I confront Nate? No. He'd just ask me not to tell Sarah. I could screw up his date, but that seemed like an immature thing to do as well. What I needed to do was report the sighting to someone in book club— *not* Sarah—and come up with a plan.

The worst thing about Nate and his paramour's arrival was that it took me out of the tryst I was looking forward to having with Cullen. In fact, I got very angry with Cullen for no reason at all.

But timing's everything, isn't it? And the timing's always going to be wrong to have sex with someone you've just met, to whom you're legitimately attracted, after seeing a pregnant friend's husband dry-humping another woman when he thought no one was looking. For that moment, I had a bad taste in my mouth about all men—including Cullen. I turned to face him.

"I'm sorry, but I have to go. Thanks for the wine and for the conversation and, well . . . thanks for the possibility."

CHAPTER 8

"It's not our problem, Maddie," Quinn said into the phone from her talent agency the following day.

"But I can help them," I said. "That's what I do—help people work out problems." *At least that's what I try to do when I get a job.*

I was sitting in front of my computer in my home office where I'd been unsuccessfully trying to drum up mediation business for a few hours.

"*Sarah* and *Nate* need to work it out," said Quinn. "And there's something else you should know—Sarah told Lauren so it's probably OK that I tell you—she's not sure Nate is the father."

"She's not sure if—how long have you known this?" All right, I did sound a tad petulant, but I felt hurt, considering it seemed like I was the last Muff to find this out. Further proof that I was being punished for living outside the geographical Muff hub.

"A few days. We didn't think everyone needed to know right away."

"*Weee*—?" I was annoyed now. "I wish I'd *known* I didn't need to know right away *before* I was having a really good time with the first guy I've been attracted to in years who was also attracted to me—whom I left in the Andalucia Tapas and Wine Bar because I thought my friend's husband was screwing around on her. If I'd known they were screwing around on *each other*, then I could have said, 'Hello, Nate. How are you? Nice to meet your paramour; Sarah's isn't half as nice,' then continued kissing the man I was with instead of creeping out of there."

"You were already kissing him?"

"Yes, we were kissing."

"That doesn't sound like you, Maddie. You usually have your prospective partners' DNA analyzed first."

"Well, maybe it doesn't sound like me, but we were kissing and I was . . . it was great." It sort of blew me away that Quinn wasn't horrified about Nate and Sarah, but intrigued instead with my kissing Cullen. "Did you know about Nate?"

I heard her sigh. "Not exactly. But he's always been a dog—and a doggy-dog, too."

When I reflected on it, Quinn was right. Nate was a dog. But that didn't mean I had to like it. I suppose I have an idealized view of what a marriage should be even if it's none of my business. "That's too bad," I said. "But I guess if Sarah doesn't care . . . does she *really* not care?"

"No . . . I mean, she *says* no, but how could she not care? Of course, I could be projecting—I'd mind. But maybe I'm just less evolved."

"You know . . ." I began. "I have a theory about ugly guys. Not that Nate's ugly. He has a certain geeky charm. But he's not really good looking, so the theory still applies. I find that if guys are attractive and women look at them a lot, they have more confidence. If Nate were better looking, he wouldn't need to try so hard to get attention, ya know? I mean, that's my theory, anyway."

As a mediator I try to understand the entire range and dimension of human behavior—mostly other peoples', not my own—however odd or inexplicable it might be. But my *job* is to work out disputes—not to accept or justify the things people do that land them in the dispute in the first place; regardless of my acknowledgment that we're all flawed and make mistakes that we know we shouldn't, I'm still constantly astounded by the things we do.

"How was I supposed to know you'd run into Nate?" Quinn went on, still defensive. "I couldn't tell you before. It was private. It's still private. Don't tell anyone I told you."

"You knew. You *and* Lauren, which probably means everyone and I'm talking way beyond the Muffs."

"Lauren is getting much better about keeping a secret."

"Right."

"Can't you find this guy? What's his name?"

"His name's Cullen and he gave me his card but it's just kind of weird how we met, you know, and to know in graphic detail what he could be doing right now with his Fleshlight."

"His *what?* Where'd you meet this guy?" She gasped. "Wait. You met him in—"

"I met him in Babeland. Well, not *in* Babeland— next door. But I saw him in Babeland and I know what he bought."

"A *Fleshlight?*"

"It's one of those metal-encased silicone cylinder things that guys put over their erect cocks."

"Whoa. Watch out for guys you meet in sex shops, right?"

Quinn had gone all prim and proper on me. It was like all the sex talk was exotic and fun when it was *over there*, but when it was affecting her or someone she knew personally, she turned into a priss.

"You were the one who told me to go there in the first place *and* you were the one who told me I had to loosen up and now you're telling me to watch out after failing to tell me something that might have made at least my evening turn out a little better."

"*Sheesh*, I'm teasing, OK? Maybe you should go unwind with your own new toy."

"I might," I said, still annoyed with her. She didn't need to know that I'd brought myself to climax three or four times already today with that new toy.

"If it's any consolation, I didn't go home with Frank Lassiter—whose real name is Orin Footlick, by the way. He's very cute, but we barely got through dinner before he started quizzing me on which celebrities I represented who might have parts for him in their movies, and I had to remind him that I book *commercials*."

"How'd that go over?"

"It didn't matter. He then tells me how he sees himself as a young William Shatner, only *he's* more talented, and that he'll be starring as the next Priceline spokesman, completely disregarding Shatner's history as Captain Kirk, pretty much the star of the most successful television show of all time. *Please*."

I'd taken the opportunity to Google Frank Lassiter, and his artificial persona's web page came up. He looked remarkably like Ted Haggard, the defrocked evangelical male prostitute patron—perfectly coiffed with a toothy grin and a canned tan.

"He asked me what I thought he could make if I were to negotiate a deal for him in traditional as well as new media platforms, and what I thought about crossover Twitter synergy. I couldn't wait to get out of there," Quinn said sadly. "I'm giving up on meeting men the traditional way. If we lived in another culture, we could hire marriage brokers, but we're on our own and LA's not a warm, fuzzy world for the female serial dater over thirty. Hey, how about I come over on Friday and we compose profiles for Match.com?"

"Can't," I said. "I'm going to a dinner party at Berggren's."

"Another dinner party? That woman has too much energy. Doesn't she ever get tired of entertaining?"

To say Berggren has too much energy is an

understatement. Berggren isn't a member of the Muffia, as you've no doubt picked up, though she's been dying to become one. Unfortunately, unless one of *us* were to die, that wasn't going to happen. In the five years our Ladies' Cliterature Club has been meeting, we've kicked out only one person—the inappropriately named Honor—who never read a single book and who none of us really liked. No one actually remembers how or why Honor attended any of the meetings in the first place—sort of a collective denial thing. At any rate, once she was gone we decided we didn't want anyone else.

Berggren has a dinner party just about every other week. She loves putting people together and, kind person that she is, usually invites me. We've been good friends since our days in New York, when I was in law school, struggling away against my better judgment. She'd been an actor back then and had changed her name from Elizabeth to her mother's surname of Berggren—like when Susan Weaver changed her name to Sigourney, only Susan/Sigourney did it first.

Berggren and I have weathered feuds and the death of a friend, and when we found ourselves single moms in Los Angeles, we discovered we had even more in common. She's far better than I am, however, at socializing—making the effort at both going out and meeting people, as well as staying home and inviting people to come to her. As an independent producer of small, successful Sundance-type films, she always has interesting types swarming around her—great writers, celebrity actors and an endless supply of beautiful young interns of both sexes. She's also had the energy and fortitude to keep her dream of making small, quality films going. While most people who start out in their early twenties producing films for love more than money begin to grow tired of the constant struggle, Berggren still seems to thrive on it. I envied her energy.

"Well," said Quinn, "have fun. But let it be known that I was willing to come see you in Agoura Hills."

I hesitated before I spoke again. I'd never met anyone I wanted to sleep with at Berggren's house and Berggren herself was always too busy to have a satisfying conversation with anyone in her effort to entertain everyone. Perhaps signing up for Match.com *would* be a better way to spend my Saturday night . . . *Not.*

"Duly noted," I said, finally, with optimism. *Maybe this would be the dinner party that shattered my no go status quo.*

CHAPTER 9

Before Friday rolled around, and with it the promise of Berggren's dinner party, another onslaught of e-mails bounced off satellites and streamed through cables and modems to land on the computers of the members of the Muffia. As usual there was a delay from the time one person would send out a request for information and when all the responses came in. In the meantime, other questions would get asked, some answered, and pretty soon you didn't know if you were commenting on Jelicka's sister's husband's rug company, what florist in NY we should use to send an arrangement for Rachel's gallery opening, or what Paige should do about being stalked by the dad of one of her tennis pupils. It wasn't necessary for everybody to "Reply All," but that's what everybody did. When weeding through emails, I was always glad that we hadn't signed up any new members—nine was enough, even if some of them didn't even weigh in on some subjects, like Kiki whenever the topic was sex. I knew she *had* sex, but, like me, she didn't enjoy discussing it via the Internet.

Because of geography, I miss out on a lot of the in-person communication that goes on between the Muffs who live in closer proximity to each other. Consequently, I get most of my Muffia news by e-mail, usually long after most of the others know about it—

Sarah's fooling around and possibly getting pregnant by a guy other than her husband, for example. This little fling of hers had apparently begun a few weeks *before* I picked *Deliciously Disturbed and Distracted* as our next read.

If Sarah was disturbed *before* I assigned that book— a fact clearly not in dispute— and I had become deliciously disturbed as soon as I cracked the book open, it hadn't taken long for the rest of the Muffs to get disturbed in ways of their very own:

MissJelickaG@aol.com: I just read an article about a woman who's become a porn star at 50! What do you think? Might take my mind off my soon-to-be-ex-husband. I'd send the article but I can't figure out how. Quinn, help! How do you do the link thing again? Signed, Luddite on Lantana Lane.

vonhooter@gmail.com: What do you mean what do we think? Are we supposed to support your going porno? It could ruin your life!

kookykiki@hotmail.com: Nothing surprises me anymore.

vonhooter@gmail.com: BTW I was KIDDING. What do I know about porn? Just sounds scary. What does Roscoe say?

victoriamendoza@mac.com: I don't think she cares what Roscoe thinks. I think that's the point. Kiki we need to get you a surprise or two.

MissJelickaG@aol.com: BTW I'm NOT kidding, though I'd change my name to Mia Vanta Mann so if anyone's life gets wrecked, it's hers.

cunningQuinn@Talentpool.com: If I were you, Jel, I'd just call one of those guys from the *Geek Squad* to help you with your computer . . .and other things. There's gotta be some value added.

Nerd Herders might be cuter though. I'll check online to see if there's a blog that'll tell us for sure.

victoriamendoza@mac.com: Go for it. Why not? Whatever. Life's too short not to do porno. Especially if it pays well.

cunningQuinn@Talentpool.com: Can I come to the set?

LBSweet@aol.com: Does anyone know anyone who's had that little "tightening" procedure? And I don't mean on the face.

MissJelickaG@aol.com: You mean vaginal rejuve? Don't get your twat tightened, Lauren. I looked into it. You can't have sex for like ten weeks and then it stretches out again in a year or two.

MDCMediate.com: I kind of like the idea of porno for older people. You'd probably be good at it, Jel.

MissJelickaG@aol.com: Thanks, M—I think. The woman's kids and husband are cool with it and she's really enjoying herself. The market's growing and they're looking for people. I'm not going to find a job with the geeks and nerds, that's for sure.

Sapizz11@connect.net: Just have an affair, Jel. It's easier and less pressure. Think of the HiDef display of your bod, fine as it is, for all to see. Every hair, vein; every wrinkle (not that you have any).

kookykiki@hotmail.com: Can't believe you're saying have an affair Sarah, after what's been going on with you and STDs and everything! But if you're looking for a career, nurses are still in demand.

vonhooter@gmail.com: Are you speaking from experience when you say it's easier, Sarah? What part would that be?

It had been my idea to do a sort of pseudo-reverse intervention on Sarah at a centrally located Starbucks one mid-week morning on my way to another role-play for the Olympic committee. I confronted her about the mess her life was in and how she needed to deal with it. She still hadn't told Nate that he might not be the father of the baby, and soon she might lose some of her choices.

"Nate was spotted with another woman," I told her. "I saw him."

She made a grimace then let out a resigned sigh. I was proud of her for taking it so calmly and not overreacting. If she had, she would have been a hypocrite. She went on to say something I didn't expect—that after reading *Disturbed* (the whole book for a change), she actually felt more of a sense of belonging with other women and peace with her own choices; that, until then, she thought having sexual desires for many men at once wasn't normal.

"It's not that it's normal or not normal," I said. "It's that sometimes we need to keep our desires in check. Lucky girl wasn't able to do that but maybe you need to try harder. You have kids—Nate Jr. and now this new little person."

"I know it's irresponsible of me, Maddie, but I've come to accept that even though I love Nate, he's never going to be everything for me—nor am I for him, apparently. That's too much pressure anyway. So instead of bemoaning the fact, I'll just have to fill my needs in other ways and if he does the same, so be it. We aren't going to talk about it though."

"Why not?"

"Because it would destroy the illusion."

The illusion of what? That everything was fine? That she and Nate are "happy"? Well, news flash: It's pretty obvious they're *not* happy, so keeping up the illusion isn't working. Besides, in a marriage, if you've got to pretend to be happy, how happy can you possibly be? I'm all for sticking it out, weathering the tides and all that, but not at the expense of your health and sanity. Generally my *modus operandi* in life has been geared more toward breaking down illusions. That's because a lot of people who build illusions can be dangerous. They often operate like members of religious extremist groups who concentrate so hard on what they see as the truth about God, upcoming Raptures, second comings, everlasting virgin fucking, future lives and things like that, that they're totally missing what's happening in front of them at that very moment—things like polar melt, the decline of democracy, corporate greed, poverty, even that their spouses doesn't love them, circumstances that people might actually be able to do something about if they made an effort and didn't shut themselves off in protective bubbles with the similarly fantasy-minded.

Then again, perhaps I'm just envious that I can't look at things through those proverbial rose-tinted glasses. Sarah seemed content with her illusions. But I find it too difficult to shake the knowledge of what actually *is* or *isn't so* only to focus on what I *wish* were true. *Whatever.* No one was listening to me, least of all Sarah. who was, at that moment, washing Nate's underwear.

CHAPTER 10

Berggren Wolfe lives, along with her identical twin daughters, in a terrific house in a section of Greater Los Angeles called Mar Vista. Mar Vista is bordered on the west and south by Venice and its famous beach, by Santa Monica to the north and Palms to the east. The words *Mar* and *Vista* are Spanish for something like sea-view but every time I hear them together, I think of something *ruining* that view—as in marring my vista. I realize it may seem a little odd, but I can't help sub-consciously thinking this every time I go to Berggren's house.

This particular Friday night was no different. I saw the mental hurdle looming before me as I started up my fuel-efficient automobile and headed to Berggren's sleek and lovely home, which offers guests a *poquito* peek at the Pacific from her roof deck. That night, however, I was determined to remain positive—about the view, the guests, everything. I would remain open, available, and not let anything mar the evening.

If I'd never actually met anyone I wanted to sleep with at any of Berggren's parties that was probably just as much my fault as that of her guests. The root of my concern could be the fear that if I ever get coital with someone too close to any of my inner circle of friends and acquaintances, I'd find out he was once sexually involved with someone with whom I'd rather not have shared a penis.

This almost happened once when Ben, a guy I knew through Paige, kept making passes at me at her house while I, and he, were still married. I was even more disgusted when I found out he did this on a regular basis to many women we both knew, regardless of their marital status, and he did it in front of his wife! Worse than his flirtatious, obnoxiously persistent harassment was that I thought he was a complete idiot for being so coarse about everything. His wife surely had to know he was making a play for countless women, many of whom his wife counted among her friends. And he had to know that all the women he hit on would talk to each other and realize he perceived all of them as prey. He was attractive enough, I guess, but even if I were desperately horny, I draw the line at extra-marital coitus with people in my regular planetary rotation, and this guy was in too many of my friends' concentric orbits. To sleep with him could disrupt all our lives. Luckily I had safely avoided him, and all like him. Though the fear of sharing a penis was still real, it was now tempered by my desire to get laid.

I arrived at Berggren's right on time at 7 PM and was just stepping up to the open door and over the threshold, when I heard an odd shuffling of feet on the driveway behind me.

"'Allo there. Make way, please," said a strapping young blonde man with a ponytail and Scandinavian accent. This must have been one of Berggren's new assistants. He was rolling her table enlarger—a ten-foot diameter piece of particleboard—toward the front door and me. "Are you Madelyn?"

I nodded my head.

"I saw your picture, yah. I am Thor. So excuse me, Madelyn. Coming through vith the big round piece of vood." *Thor had one very cute accent.* He looked to be about twenty. Seducing him would be a shade short of cradle-robbing, so I made myself content watching him with the big wood.

Perhaps the table enlarger requires a little explanation. When one enters Berggren's house on a typical evening, one sees a smallish round piece of glass resting on an architecturally striking pedestal in the dining area. But when she has dinner parties with a head count over fourteen, the glass table can't handle the bodies. So voilà, Berggren created the table enlarger to place on top of the glass. With this *big piece of vood* in place, she can accommodate the cast of a play, film or perhaps a small orchestra. The only drawback was that when everyone was seated and talking, anyone on the opposite "side" of the table was completely inaudible.

"Yah, could I get a hand here?" An older male guest I didn't recognize stepped in to help Thor lift the big vood and fit it snugly on top of the glass. Thor pushed on the enlarger, making sure it was balanced and wouldn't fall off if somebody leaned on it wrong.

"OK, Berggren—I'm off, yah?" *What a shame, handsome Thor is taking off.*

Still in the foyer, I looked beyond the table to the sunken living room with vintage 1960s furniture and a grand piano framed by the vista—marred by nothing. Berggren stepped up and gave Thor a hug goodbye before turning to me.

"Maddie. I'm *so* glad you could make it. We're going to have so much fun. But I'm running late, what else is new? And Carl just left with the girls." She gestured toward the kitchen. "I've got to finish getting dressed. So go introduce yourself. There are people you know."

I watched her walk down the hallway then glanced into the kitchen where I saw about six people munching on appetizers and sipping wine. Two of them I thought I'd met before—at Berggren's, of course— but the rest were new faces. I didn't see anyone who immediately attracted me on any level, but I reminded myself of my commitment to remain open-minded; Berggren's friends and acquaintances were *all* interesting and every one of them had something to say if I'd give them a chance.

I entered the kitchen and started chatting and pretty soon I began not to care that even though I'd come to the dinner party seeking *exciting* and *moving*, I was now extremely pleased to talk with individuals who were simply *interesting*. The wine certainly didn't hurt. Wine can make anyone seem more interesting.

People kept arriving and eventually we sat down to eat, conversation flowing freely and loudly. On my left sat a gorgeous man named Christian who'd recently arrived in California from Italy to make his name in production design. He'd come with Berggren's mother's husband's sister, Petra, and was off limits because he was married with a wife socked away in some charming hillside village on the Italian coast. But since it was hard to hear anyone who wasn't right next to me, he and I struck up an easy Italian-English exchange under the watchful eye of Petra.

At one point in the evening, I considered suspending my "no married men" rule for at least an hour after he informed me *sotto voce* that he and his wife have an open relationship. It's not for me to judge what other couples do, especially Europeans, I reasoned, even if I wouldn't have wanted that lifestyle myself. I was fantasizing about what sex would be like with Christian in a gauzily decorated bedroom with a sea breeze drifting over our naked bodies in a villa on a Sardinian mountain top, when I saw Petra glaring at me. So I pretended to busy myself with my napkin.

There was an empty chair on my right and I noticed another empty chair across the table next to ZsaZsi, Berggren's new producing partner on an English-American collaboration. I waved to her over the yellow table-clothed expanse between us, and we had a brief, semi-audible conversation about their upcoming film project, which it sounded like they hoped to shoot in I-think-New Mexico in I-couldn't-hear-how-many months. I like ZsaZsi. She's a smart girl—smarter for having hooked up with Berggren. She yelled to me that her fiancée was expected at any moment, pointing to the empty chair next to her. I also had an empty chair next to *me* but had no idea if there was someone else coming who would fill it.

Dinner was going along—salmon, pasta, salad, plenty more wine—and conversation was flowing smoothly. Berggren was in her element, breaking the ice and getting us all to talk about ourselves by answering the question, "What would we do to make the world a better place?" It was like the Miss America pageant only we were all too old and jaded to suggest we could end world hunger.

It was just coming up on my turn and I was debating if I should fold and suggest something innocuous about planting trees and flowers, or if I should rant about impeaching elected officials and enforced ball removal for convicted pedophiles, when the doorbell rang and spared me the decision.

ZsaZsi's fiancé came in, along with another guy. Introductions were made, but I wasn't paying a lot of attention because I was using the opportunity, and Petra's well-timed visit to the bathroom, to gaze at Christian and ask him questions about his Italian hillside village.

During all this, I was faintly aware that ZsaZsi's fiancé, Nissim, and his friend had sat down and, I assume, started to eat. I remember seeing Petra come out of the bathroom and, when she spotted me monopolizing Christian again, glowering at me even more harshly than before. At that point, I turned to my right to find Nissim's friend looking at me, probably thinking me rude for not at least acknowledging his presence and including him in my conversation with Christian. But he smiled an unreal smile, which caused his entire face to light up and his green-gold eyes to sparkle. His hair was very close-cropped and his cheekbones were those of a model, though thankfully a model older than the ones in the Abercrombie & Fitch catalogue. He said something and I thought I heard an accent, but I was so entranced by his eyes, I couldn't be sure of what he'd said, let alone in what language he'd said it.

"Excuse me?" I asked.

"Would you pass the pepper?"

"The pepper?" I remember mumbling, still mesmerized. He *did* have an accent. *Middle Eastern maybe?* His eyes were penetrating, making me feel completely naked with my clothes on.

"The pepper. Of course—*pepper.*"

On my left, Christian was talking to the American costume designer on *his* left who'd recently returned from shooting a *Lifetime* movie in Bulgaria and who'd said she thought she could improve the world by dressing people in colorful clothes, thereby making it more difficult for them to be sad and depressed.

I reached for the pepper without so much as a glance from Christian and handed it to my new dinner companion. Our hands touched as I gave it to him and I swear I felt electricity. He said his name was Udi—*Udi Hamoudi*—like *OOOO-dee*, rhymes with *BOOO-tee.* Udi with the most beautiful, intoxicating eyes I'd ever seen. How had I not noticed him when he walked in? Christian seemed like wine dregs in comparison to this fine glass of Syrah.

Was it the fourteen point five percent alcohol acting on me? Possibly. But I didn't care. All I was aware of was having a deep physical connection to my new dinner partner. I remember feeling warm and turned on as I gazed into those eyes. It felt as if we were alone instead of surrounded by eighteen other people; I was aware of only myself and Udi. Everyone else had been banished to Berggren's roof deck.

He said he was from Israel—he and Nissim both—where they'd met in the army at the age of seventeen. That explained his sexy accent. He told me he'd come for a visit because he hadn't seen Nissim since his friend had moved to LA five years earlier. I could have listened to Udi talk forever with his Israeli accent and imperfect grammar. Grammar *shwammer*. I hung on every word.

More and more he drew me to him as he told me, between mouthfuls of salmon and salad, that he'd wanted to meet ZsaZsi before she and Nissim got married. He liked her, he said, and was happy for his friend. It turned out Nissim was now selling real estate in California and, by his own account anyway, doing very well. I could tell Udi was a little disoriented. Understandable. I would be too if I'd been in his place—foreign country and all, unfamiliar language, jet lag and a bunch of new people all at once. But he didn't seem nervous. I was the nervous one. Heart racing, mouth dry.

Udi was charming, with lots of smiles and eyes that just kept sparkling. He was younger than I, I could tell, which kind of turned me on and made me self-conscious at the same time. I was trying to remember the last time I'd worked out, when he put down his fork and out of nowhere said, "You are beautiful."

My breath caught and my heart beat even faster. Emotions darted around my body, making me weak. And my face flushed—all of which combined to make me speechless. *I'm beautiful? When had anyone told me that when I believed it? My dad when I was sixteen, going to the prom? And yet I believed Udi.*

He smiled, picked up his fork again and resumed eating. He'd said it so simply—it couldn't have been a line. He had me at shalom. My bullshit detector was working, but the batteries were obviously fading. Still, I believed he'd said it without agenda, plan or design, perhaps because he thought he'd never see me again so it didn't matter what we said to each other. But he was at least convincing.

"Oh, thanks, but, no, that's, well . . . thanks," I said, or something inane like that, not wanting to dwell on whether I was or wasn't beautiful—a topic on which reasonable people might differ.

"You are. You know this, I think."

I remember shaking my head and blushing again. It all really sounds kind of trivial now, trite to even mention it, but I was so stunned. He disarmed me of not only the barriers I'd put up, but of my fear. He just had this way of looking at me that made me feel completely exposed—emotionally stripped and vulnerable and helpless to resist. And I had the sensation that he was, too. Through his eyes, I felt like I could see inside him, and that I'd be safe there.

I hadn't fallen in love in a long time, and I'm not even sure that was what was happening, but I was falling into something with Udi. What was also immediately apparent and attractive about him was that he had no obvious baggage—Berggren had met him for the first time that night, too. I just thought he was the sexiest man I'd ever laid eyes on and the perfect zipless foreign fuck.

At some point, I had an awareness of people slowly beginning to get up to leave the party. Meanwhile, I'd been energized. After the two recent experiences at Book Soup and Babeland, both of which could have gone somewhere, I wasn't going to strike out three times.

After saying our goodbyes to Berggren, Nissim and ZsaZsi walked behind Udi and me as he began walking me to my car. He took my hand and, after a couple of steps, put his arm around me as we continued for the twenty or so yards left. I fell into him, like we'd been walking like that for years. We fit.

Udi didn't know which car was mine—how could he? As we reached the Prius, we slowed and I reached for the door. But he placed his hand on top of mine, keeping me from opening it, instead turning me to face him. Then he leaned down, gently kissing me on my lips. The electricity I felt during dinner now had to be visible to anyone watching. Slowly, his lips pulled away from mine and he raised his head. He clasped my hand in his and looked into my eyes with such passion I became unsteady.

"Wow. That was—" I began, but before I could complete the sentence, he was kissing me again and I was kissing him—lips, longing, lust, his body hard against me and me pressing into him.

What I'd hoped he would taste like, smell like, kiss like turned out to be the reality of him; such a wonderful thing—not to be disappointed. If he'd pulled my dress up right there on the dimly lit Mar Vista street, I would not have resisted. Without a doubt, we could have provided the neighborhood with triple-X viewing that evening, which I'm sure would have improved a few peoples' view.

"Come back to my hotel," he whispered.

CHAPTER 11

So I did. After all my prudery, whether put on or real, with both Book Soup Steve and Cullen of tapas and *Fleshlight* fame, I decided it was the most *mature* thing to do. I couldn't see what would be gained by holding myself out as some ultra-valuable commodity that needed to be left in the store until full payment was made.

The truth was, I didn't want to deny myself, because I'd probably lose the opportunity to be with him *ever*. Despite the connection we had—his honest smile, masculinity, and eyes that told me so much about his innate goodness—there was no guarantee he'd: (a) keep my number, (b) dial my number even if he didn't lose it, or (c) ever come to the U.S. again. So I decided to go with the bird-in-hand principle, though the idea of a bird in my hand wasn't something I particularly relished. Birds often leave unpleasant surprises behind and I wanted Udi to leave me only with joy.

Udi's hotel was close to Berggren's house and, like a day when you go down your "to-do" list checking things off as fast as an airline pilot before take-off, everything clicked. It was like we were meant to be. Parking the Prius at his hotel, located in an area of Santa Monica known for parking hassles, was, on this evening, no hassle at all. A block away, a spot appeared and we swept into it. He ran around the car, opening the door for me, and lifted me up into his arms and began kissing me again. No one stumbled, nothing dropped. He was eager but not sloppy or in a hurry.

I was struck again by how neatly we fit together. My soft protrusions melded into his firmer ones and his hard cock pressed into my groin. Our respective heights served to allow our arms to gather each other comfortably and our lips to meet without neck strain. We were like that yin-yang poster, peas in a pod, water into soil, sugar into butter—so, so sweet.

Sometimes I think we endure the truth that we don't always fit together very well because it's easier than admitting the other person is not the right key for our lock. Finding that special key can be the challenge of a lifetime and some of us never find it. We settle—which kind of gets us back to that whole *being in denial/believing in illusions* thing. But let's not wreck the mood.

Udi and I managed to walk the distance from the front door to the elevator demurely holding hands, but once inside, he looked at me again as if he intended to devour me. It felt like his eyes were boring holes through my body into my heated inner core. We were like radioactive isotopes seeking their purpose. I knew I was wet—in fact, I was past ready. The desperation of wanting him inside me at that precise moment made my legs feel as wobbly as a two-wheeled tricycle. I was swooning and he grabbed me again—this time to hold me up. His mouth came to my ear, my neck. Then it was his tongue and teeth, gently tugging on my earlobes.

Oh, my God, thank you, Berggren, I remember saying to myself. I will never say or let anything bad be said about your dinner parties ever again. *Ev-er.* You are the queen, the goddess, the shepherdess and I shall not want.

Udi . . . Udi . . . I whispered to him as he pushed me up against the dark paneled wall of the elevator, lifting me slightly. I felt his hand under my dress, his fingers grazing the outside of my panties, touching my engorged pussy through the silk, making me feel like a tea kettle just before it starts howling and sending up steam. I was oh so close to coming—remember, it had been a long time since I'd had an orgasm except with the Rabbit—when the elevator settled, dinged and the door opened. It was late, past midnight, and it was unlikely anyone would be on the landing waiting for the lift—at least not anyone who'd consider what we were doing to be odd. Clearly neither of us cared if anyone was there to see us like that anyway.

Fumbling to get the card key out of his jacket pocket, he inserted it into the door and *boom*—we burst into the room. The door closed and, still clenched to me, he flicked the lock.

"I want to make you see the stars," he murmured in between kisses, then stopped to look at me. "Look at yourself. Unbelievable." *That accent again.*

"Wow," I sputtered incoherently, not believing I'd actually found a gorgeous man who I wanted desperately, who wanted to give me pleasures of a celestial variety. He didn't say, "I want you, I've got to have you," or any other thing that would have demonstrated his own desire. He was concerned with making *me* see the Milky Way. Besides, he didn't have to tell me he wanted me—that part was obvious. His cock was rock hard against me, but he was content to let it be—so refreshing after some of the premature grinding I could recall from earlier in my sexual prime. He seemed content to let everything take whatever course it would take.

In between the kisses he would say only how he wanted me to feel, what he wanted to do for me. I couldn't remember that happening before. I mean, I'm sure at one time my ex-husband had cared if he moved me or not, but this guy seemed all-consumed with giving me pleasure and watching how he affected me, rather than taking any pleasure for himself. Udi was into the process, whereas the other men I'd been with focused on the result—the orgasm, the big "O" and the first coming. Fitting, I thought, that Udi was from a different culture. Non-Americans could still be goal-oriented, but the process of getting to a goal—whether it was the Olympics, orgasms or the Olympics of orgasms, was of at least equal consequence.

He nuzzled my neck and breathed into my ear, warm and strong. "I'm going to make you scream," he whispered.

I sighed him my wish that he would.

Gently turning me, he tugged at the zipper on my dress. As he pulled down on it, his mouth followed its track—from neck all the way down to the small of my back. Taking the shoulders of the dress, he lowered it, still following its descent with his mouth—a gentle nip on my butt, a kiss between my legs, which threatened to remove my remaining strength.

He lowered the dress to the floor and lifted one high-heeled leg at a time—fondling each as he did so— gently assisting me to step out of it. And in one swift gesture he'd lain it over a chair. Slowly coming to stand behind me, he ran one hand up to my belly, palming it before taking my breasts in both hands and letting me feel his cock, hard against my ass. I pressed back with equal force, so obvious I wanted him inside me, my body begging for it. My hand reached behind me, feeling his balls, so hard from the engorged blood, no titanium beads to be found, but soft to the touch and smooth.

"What can I do for you, Baby?" he asked so sweetly. I almost laughed. *What did I want? How about a grande latte?* I didn't want my answer to sound as silly. "I want you inside me," I begged, pressing my wet pussy up against him, only my flimsy panties between us.

I reached for my bag, for the condoms I'd purchased at Babeland. He seemed to know and took over the task. Thank God. I hated the things and had never mastered the art of putting one on elegantly. And even if I'd once been good at it, I was out of practice.

"Please, Udi. I can't wait to feel you." The panties were off now. Explosions were going off in my head, no stars quite yet, just the need for sex—driving, Formula-One style, in the frantic rush to consummate. Even now, I don't recall ever having felt the way I did that night—not before or since—with the exception of that day in my solarium, of course, when Udi . . . But we're not there yet.

He turned me around to face him and smiled at me with such tenderness I almost cried. He steadied me, then lifted me up and laid me onto the crisp white-sheeted bed, tossing the oversized pillows off with ease. He moved into me gently and we both gasped—it was that good. And I did see the stars. And he did make me scream, and scream and scream. If anyone was bothered by my screaming, we didn't know or care. We fucked, and fucked, and then fucked some more. Like we'd never see each other again, which is probably what we both thought.

What I kept feeling was how lucky I was to have a one-night stand. It was the kind of thing I probably feared when I was nineteen—I honestly can't remember—because of some idea that the guy wouldn't respect me, or something. It was so liberating to just operate on desire and adrenaline, not caring what anyone thought. *What a relief!*

Maybe the whole event shouldn't have been so shocking to me. I suppose an argument could be made that the possibility of having a romantic sexual encounter with one of the hundreds of thousands of people who move through Los Angeles on their way to somewhere else in any given month should be one of the frequent perks of being a city girl. There were plenty of prospective sex partners. So why had it taken so long for me to find one? *Was* he special? Or was I kidding myself?

At any rate, I never expected to see Udi after that incredible night, even though I certainly wanted to. After all, he was only thirty-six—way too young for me. And I'd been disappointed by men for so long that when he said he'd be back in LA in a month, I smiled and nodded like an Asian comfort woman and said, "I would love to see you," to which he replied in that intoxicating voice, "I will call you when I know the dates. I have to see you again soon."

If my friends had been there, listening, they probably would have said, "Maddie, don't sabotage this. He's nuts about you; of course he wants to see you again." To which I would have demurred, "Yes, but it's just physical."

See, it was only normal for me to protect myself from potential emotional devastation. And at the ripe old age of forty-two, I've begun to cultivate the Buddhist philosophy that if I have few expectations, I won't be disappointed.

I had no idea what was going to happen with Udi— I mean, how could I, given that we'd started with the classic characteristics of the one-night stand? The truth was that no matter what happened next, this time I wouldn't be disappointed. I couldn't be. I'd just had the best night of physical connection I'd had in years. And if I never saw nor heard from him again, the way we had been together had given me back my faith that such a thing was possible.

CHAPTER 12

When Udi called me on my cell from Tel Aviv a few days after he and I had shared multiple concurrent orgasms in his Santa Monica hotel room, I almost drove my hybrid under a Hummer.

"I will be there on Thursday," I heard him say. "I know you are busy, Baby, but I cannot stop thinking about you. I hope you can make me some time."

Some guys sound stupid when they say 'baby'—politicians, for example. Well, maybe not Bill Clinton or JFK. But Udi made it sound like it was my rightful name.

I was about to respond with, "I can't stop thinking about you either. My body's aching and I can't stop fantasizing about us in bed"—which was the truth—but Lila was in the backseat hyperventilating after the close call we'd had with the Hummer. I didn't want to upset her further with the kind of breathless sex talk she'd hopefully only heard on television. She'd only be confused, if not flat out disgusted.

Up to this point, I hadn't seen the need to tell her about the man that Mom met a few nights before. Nor was it appropriate to tell her, given that the extent of my relationship with Udi was hotel sex. Great hotel sex, but hotel sex nonetheless.

"I want to see you, too," I whispered loudly into the phone with as much longing as I dared. It was an understatement in the same way saying it's time Angelina Jolie stopped adopting children is an understatement. The truth was I'd been thinking about Udi incessantly and those thoughts had led to frequent practice sessions and complete mastery over my purple Rabbit. I could make myself come with very little effort in just under two minutes.

"How long will you be here?" I asked.

"Three days."

Three days, I thought dreamily, swerving to avoid a semi, which prompted a frightened gasp from Lila. "God, Mom. Drive us into a truck, why don't you? Hang up the phone."

But I didn't want to hang up the phone. I wanted to reach through the line and touch him, pull him to me.

On our night together, somewhere between flights of passionate sexual bonding, he'd told me he was a sky marshal and that he never stayed anywhere for very long. I had to figure out how I'd get clear to see him. *Three days. If only we could spend them all in bed.* I'd drop whatever wasn't critical. Shit, did Lila have a ballet concert? Or a volleyball game? *Please, no.* There was the Muff meeting at my house but that wasn't until the end of the week. Udi would be gone and I'd be flushed from ravishing by then.

The biggest hurdle to getting deliciously disturbed and distracted with Udi was the possibility of starting a job with the Olympic Sports Mediation panel. It was looking very promising after four interviews, intense scrutiny and a series of role plays negotiating resolutions between jostling speed skaters, some weight lifters accused of spiking each others' power shakes with testosterone, and a bribe-taking dressage judge. I successfully resolved these disputes, but—and this is typical for mediation—nobody really got what they wanted.

They say mediation is win-win. But if you're being honest, it's also lose-lose. As a practitioner, I'm a fan—

the process generally saves people time and money that would otherwise go to courts and lawyers. Still, we live in an adversarial society and no one can take away the glory of winning in court, or anywhere else for that matter. In any event, I still hoped I'd get the job, but also that I could postpone the start of it so I could see Udi.

"Do you want to come to my house? It's nice, private. You might like seeing another part of LA," I suggested.

"I would like to do this very much, *daahhling*," he murmured to me over the crisp connection. "You are in the countryside?"

"Not exactly," I said. "But close." *Not that we'd have a lot of time for hiking.*

"Mmmm. You're so sexy, Baby. I want you so much. I had such a good time with you."

Just hearing him talk sent another wave of desire pulsing through me. He kept starting me up, but my driving was suffering. The things he said . . . Yeah, they were kind of cornball but he was so sweet and sincere his words seemed to go straight from my brain to my nether regions, sending warm tingles throughout my body on their way. I was about to tell him the same, how much I'd been thinking about him, how much I wanted to kiss him, peal off his clothes and lick him, when I once again spotted Lila in the rearview mirror. She was looking out the window. *Was she listening?* I ventured not.

"Udi, you've made me feel things I never thought I'd feel again and—"

"Mom, would you concentrate on the road, please?" Lila stared at me in the mirror and I smiled guiltily.

"That was your daughter?" he asked.

"Yes . . . Lila. I just picked her up from school." It was hard to leave that warm, sexy world we'd created over the phone and across the time zones that separated us, but it was probably safer.

"Be with her," he said. "I just want to tell you how much I look forward to seeing you. I want to kiss you all over. As soon as the plane lands, I will come to you."

Glancing into the rearview mirror again, I saw Lila had her headphones plugged into her ears, at least trying to make it appear that she wasn't paying attention to the conversation Mom was having.

"I can't wait to kiss you either. I'm so happy I met you. You have awakened me from some—"

"Mom," came Lila's voice—crisp and insistent. Clearly I'd let myself get swept away.

"Uh—sorry. Hold on," I said into the phone, once again pointing the Prius away from danger. "Yes, honey?"

"That's like really gross. Who are you talking to?"

"Just a second, sweetie. Hi," I said back into the phone. "I'll email you my address and directions. I'm so excited to see you."

"OK, Baby," he said. "I cannot wait to be kissing you. I will kiss you all over and make you see the stars again and again. You saw them the last time, yes?"

"Yes, thanks to you." I was beaming and Lila was rolling her eyes in the back seat, her index finger thrust down her throat.

"Bye," I said.

"Bye, Baby."

"Bye."

It was one of those "you hang up first" scenarios one usually outgrows at eighteen. I finally just hung up. I knew I was blushing—in front of my daughter, no less.

"OK, Mom, are you going to tell me who that was?"

"I don't know."

"That's what you always ask *me*: 'Are you going to tell me who that was?'"

I didn't whine like that, did I? "Yes, I do ask that, but I'm your mother and so that entitles me to a certain . . . "

"A certain what?"

Where was my diplomacy when I needed it? "He's a friend. His name is Udi and we met a couple of weeks ago at Berggren's house."

"Berggren's weird. And what kind of a name is Udi? Is he your boyfriend?"

"Listen to me, young lady. Berggren is not weird and I am entitled to have dates with men. I'm a grown-up. When you're a grown-up you won't have to explain yourself to me, or to any children *you* might have, OK? He's Mom's special friend and right now, that's enough. If we see each other a few more times and things get serious, I definitely want you to meet him and—"

"Are you sleeping with him?"

"Lila—"

"I'm fourteen, Mom. I had sex education, like, three years ago. I know what's going on. And you're old. Old people do it a lot."

"That's enough." I steered the car toward the off ramp. "You *know* I haven't had a boyfriend or even dated a man since your father and I separated. I deserve to have a little fun, young lady."

"Well, you better make the guy wear a condom, that's all I can say."

"Don't be rude."

"Well… you should. *Do-oh!*"

My daughter was more sexually aware than I cared to admit. I suspected, from what other moms had told me about their own fourteen-year-old daughters, that Lila may have already dabbled in that non-sex type of sex—the oral kind—despite her protestations to the contrary. I knew I couldn't keep her from experimenting so I'd done what I could to prepare her—warning her about the perils of going unprotected and buying her condoms which I hoped she'd be better at using than I was. I'd tried to let her know that I wouldn't judge her when it came to her own budding sexuality, difficult as that was proving to be, and that when she was ready, I'd help her with birth control. I actually felt lucky she and I could talk about the subject—though I'm sure she was selective in what she told me. I know I'm a hypocrite about all this, and even though I hate hypocrites I wasn't ready to share stories of my own sexual experiences with her.

"I just want to make sure he's good enough for you, Mom," Lila said, interrupting the righteous blathering in my head. It's the kind of thing I would have said to her. But from her, it was pure sweetness. Our eyes met in the rearview mirror.

"Thank you, honey." I smiled. "So far, so good."

CHAPTER 13

Quinn was going to be thrilled at the news that I'd gotten laid after all this time—so happy it might be like she'd gotten laid herself. Though given the state of her own unsatisfied libido, there was no telling how she'd react. It turned out she'd given Frank Lassiter, aka Orin Footlick, the benefit of a second date, but soon discovered he had some unspecified "issues" in the bedroom and was now railing against *all* men.

I'd tell everybody eventually, but Quinn was the one who'd made a mission out of finding me a guy when I was at my most discouraged, telling me, "Shut up with the 'I'll never meet anybody.'" I guess I felt I owed her the titillation.

"You wouldn't believe how strong he is," I told her. "He pushes me onto the bed, gently spreads my legs and goes at me so tenderly. It seems like the only thing on his mind is making me nuts, which he keeps on doing. Then after I come the first time, he puts one arm under my body and lifts me from the bottom of the bed all the way to the top in one smooth motion, laying my head on the pillow—I felt my hair feather out perfectly over the pillowcase—*then* he looks at me and says again, 'Look at yourself. You're so gorgeous,' with this unreal sexy accent."

"Wow, like the movies. I'm swooning." She seemed genuinely happy for me.

"Big time swoon. After he says this he kisses me, another movie kiss—gentle, but firm, you know? Strong but soft, the kind of kiss you can't explain. Then he pulls back and stares at me. It sounds funny, but he says, 'You are the most beautiful woman in the world,' and he makes me believe it. He's either a great actor or . . ."

"Don't start. Why wouldn't he think that?"

"Well, the main reason is it's not true."

"You are a very well-preserved woman, Mad— Madelyn."

"Yeah, for my age I'm OK, but he could have a twenty-year-old."

"But he chose you, so shut up and enjoy it. Besides, he's not American so he accepts what real women look like. Not to mention there aren't many twenty-year-olds who have it goin' on yet. That doesn't usually happen 'til a woman is thirty-five at the earliest."

I sighed, ignoring the backhanded compliment. "I'm so thankful to you and Jelicka and everyone for getting me to choose an erotic book. That's what started it. The whole process has done wonders for my outlook on life. I almost feel like if I never have sex again, I'm good."

"Don't say that!" she warned. "You've got lots of years left."

"I live in hope."

"So is he coming back?"

"As a matter of fact, yes. Next week," I gushed.

"Lucky thing. Does he have a friend?"

Quinn was one thing, but I wasn't sure how I would share the good news with the rest of the group. Ultimately I decided that since everyone else tooted their own horns, I'd give mine a honk, even if it meant discussing sex online:

MSC@MSCMediate.com: Ladies, I hope the reading is going well. I credit *Disturbed* with shaking up my life enough to get me laid for the first time in 22 months (not that I was keeping track). I am now officially more sexually satisfied than I have *ever* been. He's the gift that keeps on giving, appearing to me in waves, leading me to conclude, it is *never* too late to change your life. And he's coming back. Yeah!!!

LBSweet@aol.com: Go on Maddie! What kind of vibrator did you buy again? ~xo Lauren

MSC@MSCMediate.com: Rabbit   and Aphroditty twat stimulator but I swear, it was the book that really got me going. Book Club's next week and I'll tell all then.

SarahPN@connect.net: Things shaking up here too, but will wait for Book Club to tell. Miss all your faces. What can I bring, Maddie?

MSC@MSCMediate.com: I'm the no potluck lady, remember? Just bring yourself, Sarah, along with the story. Am slightly concerned. Sure you want to wait to tell?

kookykiki@hotmail.com: How sexy, Mad. Can't wait to hear about this guy. (hope you were careful) If he's coming back, he must be more than a one-nighter, right? Hate to wait 'til book club (which is what day again?)

MSC@MSCMediate.com: He's sort of an enigma. I really don't know much. He's a friend of a friend of a close friend. Is that too many steps away from safety? I don't care. He's an Israeli sky marshal for El Al and 14 years younger than I am. He's very dangerous and very sexy.

vonhooter@gmail.com: Yeah. You gotta watch that and I hope you used a condom.

> rachelbakerart@mac.com: Whooo-hooo. I bet he's really a spy, Maddie. That sky Marshal stuff is probably just a cover. What does the friend do? Does he/she have more friends?

> MSC@MSCMediate.com: The spy who loved me. I like that...

I didn't need to tell them we used about twenty condoms. Not that leaving that out would increase the chances of Kiki contributing to the thread.

> victoriamendoza@mac.com: I thought you were only with him one night.

> cunningquinn@Talentpool.com: She was. She's gloating. But maybe she deserves it since she hadn't been gettin' any in so long.

> MSC@MSCMediate.com: Don't mean to gloat but the dearth of sex up to meeting him kind of warrants gloating over the plethora that night. The whole last two years confirms the title of my autobiography, "The Plethora and the Dearth: The Sex Life of the LA Woman."

> MissJelickaG@aol.com: If you moved closer, you'd get more plethora ;). Anyway, happy for you, Maddie. Really. Wish I didn't have to bust the love-bubble, but I have some bad news that can't wait. The book drove me to a sexual frustration I couldn't handle so I confronted Roscoe about the whole going off Viagra issue. I told him I needed sex and wanted his input on how I was supposed to do that, considering I'm married to him and he isn't interested. Well... shocker... Ready? Turns out he *is* interested in sex... just not with me. He's been having an affair with a more age-appropriate 60 year-old woman in his firm. Am devastated. Love you all.

After Jelicka's email, there was a flurry of phone calling. She sobbed to each of us in turn. She told me she wasn't going to mediate her divorce, not that I could have helped her since I had intimate knowledge of her life—both their lives actually, all the way down to their desire to sear food.

What struck me as particularly sad, though, was that she admitted one of the reasons she'd married an older guy in the first place was because she thought she'd always look pretty good next to him. And she did. So it was a shock to her that Roscoe would now choose to be with someone closer to his own age. But I guess it proves that age is one of those relative things and not every older man wants a younger woman. After all, sexual thrills only last so long and take up a tiny portion of each twenty-four-hour period—that is, if you're lucky to have sex that often. At the end of the day, you gotta like each other and I suspected Jelicka and Roscoe just didn't have a lot to talk about. He and his secretary were the same age and had a lot in common. Why wouldn't they choose each other?

Then there was Udi and me. Rules didn't apply. Young Israeli, older shiksa. What did we have in common other than the need to put our bodies together? It might be a fantasy to think it could be more, but it was a fantasy I was willing to indulge, even if he broke my heart in the end. The sex was just too good not to.

CHAPTER 14

I opened the door and there he stood—my God of Eros. Even after sixteen hours in the air, which in another century would be akin to killing a buffalo or scaling a low mountain range to get to me, he lifted me into his arms and planted kisses all over my face, head and neck.

"Baby, Baby," he whispered, warm and urgent.

I glimpsed us bound to each other in the hall mirror, the arrangement of white tulips he'd sent on the table underneath. We looked like a greeting card.

Holding onto each other, it was as if we were lovers of years standing, reuniting after a divisive civil war that had torn us apart. Or, perhaps, as in a soap opera storyline when one of our so-called "friends" leads one of us to believe the other has cheated; then, upon learning the truth, we rush into each others' arms begging forgiveness. In other words, we clung to each other desperately. We stood in the foyer, hugging for a long time, taking in as much of each other as we could with our clothes on.

"I kept looking out the window," I said, "willing you to drive down the street. I even went outside a few times, watering plants that are set to automatic sprinkler and to the mailbox, which probably looked really ridiculous to anyone watching, considering the mail doesn't come until four."

"Shhh, I'm here now. I missed you so much." He kissed me passionately, then leaned down and gently parted my lips but held his tongue back, withholding it, teasing me, making me want it more. I *loved* that.

He'd been halfway around the world and back since we'd met, keeping the skies safe, and now I was holding him, my big, strong, gun-toting sky marshal with the beautiful bod. How odd and miraculous that we would meet the way we did and connect on this deep physical level—and at Berggren's of all places. Couldn't I have found anyone else to connect with who was a bit more geographically available? Or was Udi attractive and safe precisely *because* he didn't live anywhere near me? What would have happened with Book Soup Steve or Cullen of Babeland if I'd given *them* a chance?

I sighed those thoughts out of my head and came back to Udi. I would have gone for this guy no matter where I'd met him, no matter who he was. He was so *there*. And he was so there *for me.*

The way he smelled…the same cologne, I remembered, I was smelling now. He must have showered somewhere, somehow. He smelled delicious. He tasted delectable. Better than my fantasies. And he was here . . . and holding me. It was overwhelming. My heart—

"Your heart…it is pounding so strong," he said, pulling away gently and placing his hand over the place where my heart beat wildly.

"I know. I've been pacing the house, waiting for you."

He smiled, his eyes looking at me with the same desire I'd felt before. He placed my palm on his own chest and grinned. I felt a beat that matched my own beating heart. "You are so beautiful."

I know I blushed. I wanted to disagree. I just felt embarrassed. It's my own shit, I know. Eighty-year-old women can be beautiful. But I guess I just felt like

I couldn't possibly be that most superlative of descriptions when there were so many younger, more "beautiful" women to compare me to. But the way he was looking at me somehow made me believe him.

"Do other men not tell you that?" His hand felt divine on my cheek. "You have so much power, you do not know. You make me weak and I love it."

Did it matter in the big scheme of things if I had power or if I was or wasn't beautiful? No. Did it matter to me that he felt this way and was confident enough to tell me so without fearing I'd use it against him? Absolutely. I started to cry. I felt like he "got" me. And that was all I had ever wanted. I know our love affair was very new—we were still pre-honeymoon phase—but I couldn't recall any man, in the beginning of any relationship I'd ever had, speaking to me so ingenuously, with what seemed to be absolutely no guile.

He glanced around the living room then lifted me up. "Where do you want to go?"

"Oh my God, anywhere," I moaned. "There." I pointed toward the solarium, which was close, didn't involve stairs and provided privacy, a day bed, beanbag chair and lush light for hours of uninterrupted love-making. He carried me effortlessly and lay me down on the day bed.

I'd worn clothes that could be easily removed, but they just seemed to fall off me. Udi's clothes also seemed to vanish. Or did I rip them off? I can't say for sure, but soon he, too, was naked…moving inside me, answering my every need before I could ask.

I screamed so loud, anyone walking by would surely hear me, but I didn't care. Our fucking transcended all bounds of propriety and we couldn't stop ourselves until, of course, his body stopped.

So this is where you came in. Or, I should say we've caught up to the beginning, where Udi and I were having fantastic sex on the day bed in my solarium. Then he collapsed on top of me, dead as dust. Poor Udi. Poor me.

PART II

CHAPTER 15

Udi's body was still lying peacefully on the day bed, an angelic expression on his face. I seemed to have lost some time in there somewhere, but I did finally manage to get out from under him, using the "push, shift an inch, lift, scooch" method, and to keep myself together long enough to close his beautiful eyes and make a phone call.

I still couldn't get over the fact that we'd been going at each other with wild abandon only a couple of hours before. I'd never had sex like that, except, of course, the first time he and I had sex, and now we'd never have sex like that again. My wonderful new lover was dead. It was horrible. I'd already had one round of crying and I was poised for another.

Over my shoulder, Quinn was staring down at Udi. She'd been the Muff I'd called for assistance because she knew more about him than the others, and she was also the one with the fewest personal responsibilities after four PM.

"Wow," she said. "That must be *some kinda sex* when the guy dies coming."

"Yeah. Some kinda sex," I sighed, my eyes filling.

"I'm really sorry, Maddie. What do you want me to do? Should we call the police?"

"I don't know. Probably. Help me brainstorm first. I don't understand how this whole thing happened so I'm not sure what to do. He must have had a heart attack. That's sort of how it happens, right? Maybe he had a congenital heart defect or something."

"Yeah, maybe. But he's pretty young," Quinn said.

"Maybe he wasn't as healthy as he looks. The sex *was* great and very athletic but I swear, he just died. I mean, he came and then he just . . . *went.*" There was so little one could say.

"I don't want to be unsympathetic, but he sure is a lot better looking than you led me to believe."

"I showed you his picture," I protested, referring to a shot Berggren had forwarded to me from the dinner party, in which Berggren was also featured, and which I had then forwarded to Quinn.

"Pictures lie. His didn't." She took a step closer to him. "And nice...you know, *thing,* too—cock, penis, pink prober."

"That's enough." I blew my nose.

"Sorry. What's his name again?"

"Udi. Udi Hamoudi."

"Udi— he looks really peaceful," she said.

"Hopefully he is. Hopefully he died happy."

"What about Udi's booty? As nice as his fruity?"

"Would you *stop*. I finally find a guy I like and now he's dead. You could be more, I don't know . . . *aware.*"

That's when I started crying again.

Quinn put her arm around my shoulder and leaned into me, brushing the tears from my cheek. I know she was *trying* to make me feel better, but she didn't appreciate the depth of my pain. I was a bit alarmed by the depth of my pain, to tell the truth.

"Maddie, listen to me. He's just the one who reawakened you. You said yourself you didn't think it would last with the guy."

"I know what I *said*. But maybe I didn't really mean it."

I flopped down onto Lila's beanbag chair and got my heel caught on the cream-colored, loosely woven chenille throw I'd bought on sale at Crate & Barrel, suddenly realizing why it had been on sale—it was actually a web. And I was stuck in it.

"Oh, sweetheart, you'll find someone else. You've been meeting a lot of guys lately. There was that bookstore guy and the one you met in Babeland sounded promising, too—even if it is a slightly odd place to meet someone. Then there was Udi and, even though he's no longer with us, things were looking up."

"But I killed him. You said so yourself." By this point I was really sobbing. Luckily Lila had called to ask if she could go home with a friend, so I was free to let the emotions, along with any fluids, rip.

"You didn't kill him, Maddie. He died. He would have died no matter who he was having sex with."

"Thanks," I said as insincerely as I could.

"On the other hand, you shouldn't sell yourself short," she went on. "*You* ended up being the one who fucked him to death. I've never had that kind of sex."

Clearly, she was being insensitive. But I know she was just trying to be practical. After all, he did look like he'd died happy. And it wasn't as if, now that he was dead, I needed to pretend we'd shared an intimate, longtime relationship that demanded a lot of morbid carrying on, as in the ritual people usually act out for dead friends and relatives.

"Did you love him?" she asked me. "You're acting like you loved him. I thought he was just a new friend with excellent benefits."

"Well, he was… but you know, you have great sex with someone and the mind… extrapolates."

"What does the mind do?" Quinn's face twisted into a puzzled frown.

"Sometimes lust starts merging with love. It's unavoidable."

"Tell me again where you met him?"

"At one of Berggren's dinner parties," I replied.

"Right, hence that picture with Berggren and the late great Udi. Does that woman have a dinner party every week?"

I was suddenly reminded that she and Berggren didn't really like each other.

"Just about," I said. "I thought he was vetted because he came with the fiancé of Berggren's producing partner. Yesterday I called to tell her I was seeing him a second time and she got all excited and told me she'd do some snooping for me. But her partner, ZsaZsi, who's engaged to Udi's friend, Nissim, didn't know much about him and Nissim wasn't around to talk to. He was supposed to call back but he didn't, which I took to mean that maybe Udi was one of those guys with a woman in every city El Al flies to. Maybe Nissim didn't think he'd be able to hide that and thought I'd figure it out if we talked, but I truthfully didn't care if there were other women because, I mean, I didn't really want a relationship—I don't think." Tears started forming in my eyes again.

Quinn squished in next to me on the beanbag and took my hand. "Are you listening to yourself? You really didn't want a relationship… That's what you said."

"Not knowing if I'm ready for another serious, committed relationship and having your new lover die on top of you are two very different things, Quinn. I wish you would stop treating this so cavalierly."

"It could have been drugs," she suggested. "Or— and I might have just read this—air quality? I think the air in Israel causes health problems."

"No, it doesn't; no more than anywhere else. Plus he said he didn't take drugs because of his job. I thought about asking you for some pot but he told me he gets tested all the time and can't smoke it."

"Too bad," said Quinn, who is the Muffia's connection to premiere Humboldt County Pot. She's always looking to hook people up. "What kind of job does he have?"

"He's a sky marshal for El Al."

She looked stumped. "Did you tell me that?"

"I emailed everyone."

"I guess I just read the word Israeli and thought—*macho, arrogant.* But now I can see how he lifted you into all those positions you were talking about. Did you know El Al is the safest airline in the world?"

"No. I did not know that."

"Jelicka told me that. She's also the one who told me Israeli men have a terrible reputation."

"How would she know?"

"She went to a kibbutz when she was twenty and got date-raped."

"You can get date-raped anywhere."

"Who said you couldn't?"

"Look," I said, getting annoyed at how little progress we were making. "I don't care about Israeli men's reputations. As I've pointed out a couple of times, we weren't having a *relationship*. It was purely physical. So whatever the elements were that went into making him the man he is, or was, don't matter. He treated me like a goddess."

By this point I'd reined myself back from the abyss of tears and was trying to regroup. "So what should I do?"

"First you need to find out more about this fiancé. And then next of kin and stuff like that. I'd start there."

"You wouldn't call the cops."

"Not yet. It's too impersonal. Do you know the friend's—I mean the fiancé's number?"

"I could get it."

Quinn got up and started pacing the length of the solarium. "Have you looked in his pockets?"

"No. I'm sort of afraid to. Aren't you supposed to leave the scene as untouched as possible?" I asked rhetorically.

"You're right. Do you have any gloves?"

"Gloves?" It should have been a clue.

She gave me a dead serious expression. "CSI: Special Victims Unit: Agoura Hills."

I had to smile. "Under the sink."

She headed into the kitchen and returned with pink rubber up to her elbows. I knew exactly what she was onto now. As she picked Udi's pants off the floor, she asked, "Can you think of anything else he might have told you about himself?"

It was then that I truly realized that the only thing, or things, I knew about Udi were the things he'd told me, which amounted to almost nothing. He'd told me his name, his age, that he lived in Tel Aviv and what he did for a living. That's it. And I had no way of knowing if what he'd told me had been the truth.

As a practicing mediator and occasional lawyer, I pride myself on my ability to detect deception—something that doesn't always follow—but I'd been so attracted to this guy that my radar for bullshit got turned off.

"His name's not Udi," Quinn said.

"What? Of course his name's Udi."

"Maybe it's a nickname but this El Al I.D. card says his name is Yehl—Yehlehc—I have no idea how you say this name."

"Let me see," I demanded, extricating myself from the chenille and pulling myself up off the beanbag.

"Yeah—you're right. It's different. But let's call him Udi."

Quinn took a few steps toward Udi then turned back to me with a conspiratorial look on her face. "Did you ever see *Weekend at Bernie's?*"

As it happened, I had seen the movie, but I didn't want to encourage a train of thought that could lead to any more bizarre behavior. "I realize you're a talent agent for a lot of famous movie stars, but life is not a movie."

"No?" she countered. "*Saving Private Ryan*—life and movie, *Sound of Music*— life and movie."

"*Pirates of the Caribbean?*" I said. "Not life. And even though it was based on life, I don't recall anything like this happening in *The Sound of Music.*"

"People died," she said, totally straight-faced. "Movies inspire life, just like life inspires movies. Remember *Natural Born Killers?*"

"I hope killing is not the kind of behavior filmmakers want to inspire."

"You keep missing the point," she insisted.

"Well, what is the point?"

"The point is, we don't need to come forward right away to tell the police there's a dead guy in your house."

"Isn't that sort of prolonging the inevitable? Won't I increase my trouble by waiting?"

"If you didn't have doubts of your own, you would have already called the police. Now you have to explain why you didn't immediately call nine-one-one."

"There was no emergency. He was already dead."

"You don't need to convince *me*," Quinn said.

"I can't call the police."

"Ah, now we're getting somewhere. Why can't you call the police, Madelyn?"

"Because I'm finally close to landing my dream job and I don't want to jeopardize it."

"How would it be jeopardized?" she asked. "You didn't kill him. He just died."

"Yeah, but this doesn't look good. Plus Udi's Israeli, and the job I'm up for is international. They're not going to hire me if there's anything like this on my record. I won't be viewed as unbiased when it comes to, say, mediating with the Israeli rowing team."

"How many Israelis row sculls?"

"The point is, some people will always wonder if I killed him."

That's when the doorbell rang.

Quinn looked at me. I was pretty sure it wasn't Lila or the mother of her playdate. As far as I knew, they were on their way to the movies.

"I have no idea."

"What do you want to do?"

I wanted to crawl away. The whole thing was unbelievably awful. "I thought you were here to help me," I said. "Muffs together through thick and thin."

"I *am* here to help you. You just don't like what I'm offering in the way of help."

The doorbell rang again.

"Should we answer it?"

I had to think. It seemed obvious that whoever was at the door would know that someone was inside. "Tell them I'll be out in a minute, and I'll put his clothes on," I said, springing to action.

"So you like the *Weekend at Bernie's* idea after all."

"It's brilliant," I said. *Weekend at Bernie's* was a late-80s comedy featuring dead Uncle Bernie propped up and acting his part for the whole movie. "You're a genius for thinking of it. Now go answer the door."

"What if it's the cops?"

"Why would it be the cops?"

"Maybe someone heard you screaming but didn't hear the ecstasy in your delivery."

"Go!"

Quinn dashed away toward the front door and I tried to sit Udi up with great difficulty. He was far heavier than what I would have expected, given the agile way he moved around the bedroom, and he didn't want to bend. *Wasn't it too soon for rigor mortis?* Maybe I was just tired and sore from the work out I'd had getting out from under him.

I settled on a position for him that looked more like lounging than actual sitting. At least he wasn't lying flat. I put his sunglasses on him and even though he was dead, I kissed him once more, then covered him with the chenille throw. The overall impression was of peace and contentment.

As an afterthought, I tried to open his mouth with

my fingers, the idea being it might make him look like one of those guys whose mouth fell open while sleeping. But there was no budging it. His jaw was locked. Rigor mortis there, too. I wondered what rigor—discipline and work—had to do with mortis, which derived from the Latin word for death. Well, in *this* case, death was proving to be hard work—at least for me.

CHAPTER 16

"Madelyn? Madelyn, could you come out here, please."

It didn't sound like the girl scouts had arrived selling their cookies. Quinn's tone of voice was one I'd heard her use on the phone while reprimanding her errant movie stars, and she was using my *whole* name. This had to be serious.

Glancing back at Udi who looked so peaceful, if in need of rolfing, I got a waft of sadness once again. I finally meet a guy I like *and* like having sex with and then he dies. Does anyone need this kind of luck?

Heading into the front hallway I saw Quinn smiling a little too brightly, her eyes pressed open as wide as they would go, standing next to three guys dressed in black, who, taken together, gave me the impression of the kind of sound system you see on stage for giant reunion concert tours for bands like *Kiss* or *Deep Purple*, with an enormous center unit flanked by two smaller, but still substantial boxes of indeterminate purpose.

The center guy had a *ginormous* bald head with a few indentations here and there—a refrigerator-with-a-head kind of guy, but with even less animation. One of the side guys with red hair on his head and chin had a bit more of an expression. At least he was chewing gum, even if his eyes were fixed in a stare. The guy on the other side, who had dark hair, a sparkle in his eyes and a very Eurotrash-y, navy blue pin-stripe suit, seemed remarkably familiar. He looked a little like Nissim, the man who'd brought Udi to Berggren's dinner party that fateful night. What was odd was that as I got closer I realized it *was* Nissim from Berggren's dinner party.

"Hello, Madelyn," he said in a voice evocative of Udi's but not nearly as sexy.

"Hello," I ventured. "Nissim? What are you doing here?"

"Is Udi here?"

"Udi? You mean the guy I met at Berggren's?"

He smiled. "Yes. Udi. Udi Hamoudi."

The refrigerator grunted then crossed his arms in front of his expansive chest.

"What makes you ask?" I said.

Quinn excused herself to "use the restroom" and headed back toward the solarium where I hoped she'd improve upon my attempt to turn Udi, or whoever he was, into Bernie.

"I know he was planning on coming to LA to see you. That's why he told me he couldn't see me. He must have got on the flight last minute because he only called me before the plane left Tel Aviv."

"Ah," I nodded my understanding then nodded again while I continued to search for a better response. "Ah," I said again.

"He's here, yes?"

The red-headed guy with a little too much facial hair said something to Nissim in Hebrew and he said something in return. The refrigerator grunted again and uncrossed his arms. Then all three of them looked at me. And I wished Quinn would come back.

"Yes," I said tentatively. "Is that a problem?"

"Can you get him to come out here, please? I need to speak with him."

"Well, actually—the thing is—Quinn? Could you come out here?" *Couldn't Nissim have just called if he needed to talk to Udi? Had Udi given them my address?*

"What is it, Madelyn? Is there some reason to be concerned?"

"No. No concern. It's just Udi's not feeling well," I began. "I mean, you know what that flight is like and being a sky marshal and all, he doesn't get to sleep. He's got to stay vigilant, you know, for the possibility of in-flight altercations."

"Yes," said Nissim, sounding unconvinced.

Quinn reappeared and was able to see and hear the red-haired man say something to big fridge, then the two of them laughed. Nissim said something else to them in Hebrew and they stopped. Then Nissim leveled his gaze at me. "We really need to see him. It's very important."

Quinn threw me a look that I couldn't read, but it gave me courage. I realized it was my house we were all standing in and these guys, even if Nissim was a U.S. citizen, had no business making me feel vulnerable.

"You know, I think you should come back," I said confidently. "I don't want to wake him, but if you tell me what you want him to know, I'll let him know what you said. Or leave a message on his cell phone if you want."

"Say, why were you guys laughing just now?" Quinn asked.

The three of them exchanged looks that I couldn't read, then Nissim said, "Actually, Madelyn, these guys are with El Al and we really must see him."

"Why? He's so tired, Nissim. He needs to rest."

"Yeah," said Quinn. "He's passed out. You couldn't revive him if you tried."

I glared at her.

"If your friend has seen him, perhaps you will permit us to do the same."

"Listen," said Quinn. "I just came to get my makeup, which I'd left here and, well, you know how a girl needs her make up."

Nissim scrunched up his face. Clearly they didn't believe her. I felt like the tension in the entryway was audible, bouncing off the plastered walls so loud it hurt my ears.

"Let me speak to you for a moment, Madelyn," Nissim said.

"Why don't you go into the solarium," Quinn suggested. "He's sleeping peacefully. See for yourself."

I looked at her.

"Go on, Madelyn."

Something about her calling me by my proper name told me she felt confident that we could go back into the solarium and Nissim wouldn't suspect anything.

"Do you need something else?" I asked Quinn, trying to convey my concern.

"Nope. I'll wait out here with these guys while you two have a private chat."

"All right," I said. "We don't want to wake him up, though."

"Understood," said Nissim.

"You see," I said, gesturing toward the daybed. "There he is, sleeping like a, well sleeping quieter than a baby. That saying is simply untrue."

"Yes. Babies are louder than that saying would suggest." Nissim was staring at Udi while he said this, I suppose looking for signs of life. "Udi?"

Nissim took a step closer to the couch and I remember hoping that Quinn had propped Udi securely enough so that he wouldn't keel over if someone pushed him.

"You said you wouldn't wake him," I said stepping between the dead and the living. "So I'll just get him to call you when he wakes up."

"I didn't say that." Nissim walked over and took Udi's wrist, pressing his finger to the vein. The jig was up. What did it matter? I knew I hadn't killed him. That would be evident from any autopsy, I told myself.

"As I thought," Nissim said, taking Udi's sunglasses

off and opening his lids. He let them snap shut and my mind flashed on the other book I'd considered for tomorrow's book club, *The Opposite of Dead*. Oh, how I wished Udi had been the opposite of dead at that moment. However, it was Nissim's coldness, rather than Udi's, that chilled the room. "You should have said something."

"But . . . but . . ." There are times you just can't think what to say.

"I will need to take him with me."

"You can't just take him. Where are you going to take him? And what do you mean, 'as you thought?'"

"We've been monitoring him. There's been no movement for over two hours."

"You've what?"

"We've been monitoring him. He has a chip in his shoulder."

"A chip? Like a bone chip?"

"A silicon chip. A tracking device."

"You mean like those things people put in their pets in case they're stolen?"

"You are an intelligent woman, Madelyn. I'm sure you have seen these Hollywood spy movies. Chips are implanted in people, too."

I cringed at the word implant. It reminded me of my own ruptured prosthetic breasts which I'd finally pulled out during a particularly difficult chapter in my marriage and which might have contributed to Lila's father's affair with a woman whose boobs didn't present such challenges.

"But he's a sky marshal," I said.

Nissim pushed his chintzy jacket aside and rested his hands on his hips, facing me. "Yes, he was. We put chips in them."

What? Was he a cookie?

"Really. You put chips in your sky marshals. Does Virgin?" I loved saying the name of this suggestively named airline. It made me believe that the tedium of modern commercial jet travel could still offer promises of the new and exciting.

"I don't know," he said.

"I just want to understand. You're saying El Al makes its sky marshals get little global positioning chips installed in them."

"Not just the sky marshals, all the employees. Udi has a chip, I have a chip, so do my friends."

"And this is normal?"

"Yes, this is normal. We live in the Middle East. You never know."

"You never know what?"

"You just never know. That's all."

By this point I was thinking that none of this was normal. Three guys showing up at my house, the burly associates that looked like appliances. Something wasn't right, but I kept coming back to the fact that Udi and Nissim were friends and one of *my* closest friends thought Nissim was a good guy.

"No, I guess you're right. You never know what's going to happen. One thing I do know," I went on, "is that the older I get, the less I know about anything."

Nissim wasn't listening. He was sniffing the air. Then a wistful look came over his face.

"We were, you know . . . *at it*, when he just sort of moaned and then collapsed," I offered.

"I suspected this could happen."

"You did? How?" *How could Nissim have suspected this could happen?*

He turned away. "I'm sorry. I know he liked you a lot."

"Well . . ." I didn't want to begin this line of discussion. I'd likely end up crying again. "What do you think killed him?"

"I don't know, perhaps some sort of heart defect. Usually the testing catches these kinds of things during the hiring process, but we will do an autopsy."

"An autopsy?"

"We will need to take him with us, Madelyn," he said.

"No—" I stood protectively next to my dead lover who only a few hours ago had been the polar opposite of a corpse. Something about Nissim taking Udi seemed all wrong. "This should be reported," I protested. It had become clear that I would have to risk losing the international mediation job.

"I'm going to call the police." I moved toward the phone again. Now I really wished I'd called earlier, before I let Quinn stop me.

"Please do not call the police, Madelyn. Udi was an Israeli citizen and this is an internal matter—internal to the state of Israel and El Al Airlines. There is no need for your government to be involved."

"What if this whole thing comes back to haunt me in some way? I mean his fingerprints are here and he's dead."

"This won't happen. Trust me."

"How can I trust you? I don't know you."

"You know I was Udi's friend. And I'm a friend of Berggren's."

"Well, yeah, I guess I know that. But I didn't know Udi very well either. And I just found out his name wasn't really Udi."

Nissim gave me a chilly look. Then he called out to the appliances, "Neve, Josi." He said something in Hebrew that I, of course, couldn't understand, but I knew they'd be rolling in imminently. "Everyone called him Udi," he said to me.

"OK, well, since when do airlines go to such lengths to ensure proper after-death care of their employees? If I'd known they were so generous, I might have considered the industry as a career myself, probably on Virgin."

"El Al cares. I cannot speak for Virgin or any other carrier."

Seconds later Neve and Josi appeared, tailed by

Quinn, who only shrugged and mouthed something in my general direction that was completely obscured by her hand flitting in front of her mouth.

As soon as they spotted Udi, they began speaking quickly in Hebrew. Udi had only taught me the words for kiss and hug so, since there wasn't much of either going on, I recognized nothing of what they were saying. But it seemed like they repeated a couple of words more than twice. One sounded like *katoon* or *kitten* and another, *hassle* or *les hassles*, which was French for lots of hassles, I think, which is what the whole unfortunate event with Udi was turning into.

The guy with the excessive red facial hair, whom I believe was Josi, left the room, almost tripping over the beanbag chair and getting caught up in the chenille throw before narrowly avoiding a collision with Quinn.

"Maddie, what's happening?" Quinn asked, dodging Josi.

"They want to take Udi."

"You're a lawyer. They can't do that . . . can they?"

"Maybe...I don't know Israeli law. And I don't know what the law is on possession or removal of dead Israelis within the contiguous United States." This issue clearly demonstrated how legal specialization limits one's knowledge of areas outside the specialization.

"Well, how can we find out?" Quinn asked.

"Neither the state of California nor your federal government wants to spend money or time on one sky marshal for El Al Airlines when he has died of natural causes," Nissim declared.

Josi returned with a stretcher and a suitcase out of which he pulled two white doctor coats. He and Neve the fridge put on the coats while Nissim laid the stretcher out next to Udi on the floor. Once they'd buttoned the coats, each took an end of Udi and lifted him onto the stretcher.

Poor Udi, I remember thinking. Poor me. *Such a*

waste. We were only getting started and we were destined for a lot more great sex and probably a lot of other fun stuff before he was cut down so young. As I watched Nissim and the other two guys carry him away, I longed for him to get up and say it was all a cruel joke. Of course, he wasn't going to get up. Or get it up ever again.

I was annoyed with myself for feeling relieved at not having to go through what would probably have been a lot of probing questions by overly inquisitive American cops. Once they'd realized we'd been fucking, they would have barraged me with prurient questions that had nothing to do with anything relevant—questions like what position we were in, if this had been the first, second or third time that afternoon, where his penis was and what my hands were doing—all the while perhaps jerking off under the table or behind those one-way mirrors they have in interrogation rooms.

Quinn snapped me out of my gloom. "All I can say is I'm glad the Muffia are meeting tomorrow. This is going to be a show stopper."

CHAPTER 17

At seven o'clock the following evening my doorbell rang. I was still disturbed and distracted by the events of the previous day, but I was determined to serve a delicious meal and put on a brave face that evening, even if I had to paint it on, which is what I ended up doing.

Initially, when I first read *Disturbed,* I'd been turned on by all the connections between food and erotica. Originally I'd planned to prepare some delectable fare inspired by the movie *Tom Jones.* In that fabulous film, Tom, played by Albert Finney, and Mrs. Waters (consummately portrayed by Joyce Redman), share a sumptuous feast at a roadside inn without exchanging a word. Across a rustic table by candlelight they gnaw on a chicken carcass, suck on crab legs and slurp oysters from their shells, letting the flesh slide down their throats before finally burying their faces into juicy ripe pears—all as if they were eating each other's loins. They tug, suck, lap and lick—leaving little to the imagination about what they would later do in the bedroom. Of course, in our case, the Muffs would be talking and not having sex, but the point was to show the food/sex connection.

As might be expected after the event with Udi, I didn't have the same . . . *drive* to cook up a delicious erotic meal. But in keeping with my Muff hostess credo, I hadn't asked people to produce potluck either. The solution was to take half the money I'd made earlier in the week for assisting at the anti-doping arbitration hearing of a well-known bicyclist and put it toward a meal I would call eclectic take-out.

The value-added that evening, and a distraction designed to ensure the pressure to entertain was off yours truly, would be in the person of one Laetitia Verdun, an acquaintance whose pre-nuptual agreement I'd handled. Laetitia made a living going to gatherings of mostly women, but sometimes men, selling items she claimed were guaranteed to improve anyone's sex life.

"Kind of a Tupperware party but with sex toys," she'd told me. There was an endless assortment of sex toys—positioning pillows, an item of sex furniture called "The Liberator," books like "Toygasms" and "Tickle His Pickle," various flavored lubricants, fake fur handcuffs, vibrating thongs as well as a varied selection of vibrators like the "Fukuoko Finger Fun" and the "Talking Head." All would be served up by Laetitia like so many casserole covers. And all of the toys could be handled if not taken upstairs to a bedroom for a full test drive.

"That," she said, "would most definitely *not* be permitted."

Since I was pretty sure there was at least one Muff who hadn't made it to Babeland to purchase a *wascally wubber wabbit*, I thought the sex toy demo would be the best way for everyone to look and take a feel, if not actually enjoy.

Glancing in the hall mirror, I caught sight of the lovely white tulips Udi had given me, now beginning to droop. I also noticed my shirt was stained with coffee, which I'd been drinking too much of. *I'm falling apart.*

Quickly I whisked off the shirt and threw it at the bottom of the hall closet, leaving me clad in a dark spaghetti-strapped camisole when I opened the door.

Standing outside were Jelicka, Vicki, Lauren and

Paige. Quinn had called an hour before, swearing up and down that she hadn't said anything to anybody about Udi and the El Al guys, so I was a little puzzled to find the four of them staring at me. Paranoia stuck. Then I realized I had more makeup on than they'd ever seen me wear, which I'd smeared on in an effort to cover the dark patches under my eyes. That, combined with the low-cut cami, must have created a picture that didn't jibe with what they knew of me.

"Hi," they said in unison a half a second too late.

"Hi!" I replied without missing a beat.

"Is this your impression of 'Lucky Girl?'" asked Paige.

"You'll see," I said, ushering them into the hallway, which looked just as it had when Nissim and his associates had carried Udi out on the stretcher the day before. In fact, the whole house reflected no change at all. Not even Lila had felt a different vibe when she'd come home from the movies last night. It was as if Udi had never happened at all.

Yet I knew that Udi *had* happened and waves of upset kept hitting me. Even though I'd tried to hide my sadness, shock and lack of sleep under makeup, I knew it was just a matter of time before I couldn't keep it up anymore and I'd have to kick them all out.

"What beautiful flowers, Maddie. Are those from the pilot?" Lauren said.

"Sky marshal. Yes."

"Gorgeous. He has good taste."

"He picked Madelyn," said Paige. "That shows he has good taste."

The two-dozen tulips were spilling over the edge of their thick glass vase. A few petals had even become detached from the stems and lay forlornly on the glass side table. I had a nasty visual of Udi's body going through something similar.

"How's it going?" asked Jelicka, her blonded locks swept up in a chignon. "He's really sexy, huh? Israeli men are totally hot, but they're arrogant as hell, I want you to know."

"Well, I don't know many Israeli men, but this one's very attractive and very nice," I said. "I promise I'll tell everyone later." *And more than you can imagine.*

"I've been to Israel. I know from whence I speak," Jelicka said vehemently before backtracking. "Of course, he could be different. I've been wrong before."

"Really?" said Paige.

"Not often," Jelicka shot back.

Vicki, wearing tight jeans and no make up, gave me a kiss, then pushed past us with a large zippered black bag. "I'm going to set up my video camera in the dining room."

"This is the project she was hinting at in the emails," Jelicka whispered. "She's been very good about keeping it a secret, but obviously it's about us. Given her condition, I think we should indulge her."

"I don't feel like being on camera," I said.

"Yeah, you don't look well," said Lauren. "Everything OK?" Lauren was more put together than usual. She was wearing a brown tweed mini-skirt—unheard of for her—but she did have on typically fabulous footwear. The skirt might have been a little *too* short, but she projected such confidence she pulled the look off.

"Well, most things are going all right. Lila's doing well, and I think I got the job with the Sports Mediation panel, but I didn't sleep well last night."

"Just put on more makeup, Maddie," Jelicka said as if she couldn't see that I already had on more makeup than all of us collectively wear in a week. "Plus I doubt Vicki will do many close shots so just punch up the eyes a little and you'll look great."

The doorbell rang again. I was wondering if I'd make it through the evening and if I did, what kind of condition I'd be in at the end of it. Because I didn't think I could feel any worse. In any event, there was no turning back.

CHAPTER 18

Take-out food was presented in various cartons and containers, bowls and trays along the dark maple sideboard in my underused red dining room, which had capacity for twenty at my large, only-looks-expensive dining table. All the candles had been pushed to the two ends and lit, and the group of us occupied the center. I'd made some effort with the table settings at least. Each of us had a pretty new placemat and napkin of gold-threaded burgundy silk made in Laos but purchased at the local Pier One and positioned at decorative intervals.

"Is there a reason why you had this catered, Mad?" Lauren asked. "I mean other than this mysterious 'tough couple of days'?" It's not like you to farm out responsibilities.

It was nice of her to acknowledge this but it was as if she was speaking through a dense fog over a long distance connection on a dying cellphone. Then she was talking again before I could respond.

"Maddie? Are you all right? I didn't want to say this when we came in… but you are *not* all right, are you?" Lauren somehow had come to be standing next to me, holding a tray with her plate piled high with schwarma, garlic naan, Peking duck, and farfalle arrabiata (in honor of the "hit man" from the book), as well as a bowl of steaming tom kah gai. *Nothing wrong with her appetite.*

"I don't know," I said. "I wanted to cook, but I was

too . . . *disturbed?*" I offered a wan smile. I suddenly realized Lauren hadn't brought a sauce or condiment. It was almost shocking.

As the day had turned out, my disturbance had interfered with shopping and cooking. I'd ended up ordering dinner from several local restaurants using my credit cards in an effort to keep up the theme of *eating the book*, as it were. In *Deliciously Disturbed and Distracted*, Lucky Girl conducted many an illicit rendezvous in various and fantastic ethnic restaurants, and since I'd been too discombobulated to cook or to choose one main ethnic restaurant, I'd given up and gone with them all. The only nationality I hadn't been able to find represented locally was Ethiopian. Lauren apparently had been so flummoxed when I told her what I'd be serving, she couldn't even think of a sauce to bring. *That explains it.*

"Maddie?" Lauren repeated through the fog.

"Her name is Mad*elyn*," Vicki said, giving me a wink. She'd had some treatments for the cancer and the latest tests had come back negative, so she'd bleached her short spikey hair white-blonde to celebrate. "I personally think it was inspired to have all this ethnically eclectic food, though if you've had a tough few days, you should have called us to bring things."

I proudly and resistantly, despite recent events, held onto my refusal to hold a potluck. "If the characters in the book had feasted on paella," I responded. "I might have delegated that."

Vicki smiled then pointed her video camera at Lauren's heaping plate. "This looks deliciously disturbing."

"It looks great. I just wish you'd let us know you needed help," Lauren said.

In fact, no one seemed to mind that night that they'd driven in from all the various corners of LA County for such a cobbled-together meal. Everyone had been disturbed—deliciously and in other ways—after reading the book and they all wanted to talk about it.

"Let's start," said Quinn, giving me a smile of encouragement.

"OK," said Paige. "I'm going to start."

Vicki's camera was pointed at Paige who *seemed* normal—for Paige—though her hair wasn't *quite* as perfect as it usually was. "This woman is a real mess and I felt an immediate bond. She could be me," she said, a tone of resignation in her voice.

"Are you stepping out on Richard?" Jelicka asked.

"No, but I'm attracted to her life of adventure."

"If you had her life, you'd be attracted to some other kind of life," said Kiki. "That's life."

"Part of me wishes I could be more like her," Jelicka resumed. "You all think I'm brazen and go after what I want, but when it comes to men, and actually acting on my desires, I'm a chicken." She paused, and despite the fact everyone wanted to talk at once, in our usual fashion, we waited for Jelicka to continue. "That's all I'm willing to say right now."

"Come on," Vicki said, camera still shooting. "That's weak."

Jelicka shrugged. "Sorry." She wasn't apologizing for anything.

"This isn't exactly about the book but the book sort of started it all," said Lauren suggestively. "After I bought the Rabbit, based on all your recommendations, I started practicing and I started getting really good. One evening when I thought George wasn't coming home 'til late, I got it out and started doing some o' that 'exterior work.' Who's line was that?"

Paige raised her hand.

"I love that. So I was doing exterior work, determined to have an orgasm only by playing around on the outside, and I'd been at it for maybe five minutes. Sia's 'Breathe Me' was playing and I started working it a little deeper, you know? That song is so erotic—"

"Sorry, but are we doing the roundy-round or talking about the book?" Rachel asked.

"Shhhhhhh." Everyone except Rachel and me were into Lauren's story. I was only half listening, thinking about how I was going to tell everyone about Udi.

Lauren went on. "I couldn't stand waiting and so, you know, I started working Bugs—"

"Bugs?"

"Shhhhhhhh," said Vicki, capturing it all.

"Calling it 'the *Rabbit*' was too impersonal so I gave it a name. Anyway, I started working Bugs further inside. And each time I did, I must have let out a little groan or something. I don't know how much time had gone by, but the song was still on—maybe it was on a loop. Anyway, I felt the orgasm coming on. I must have been getting loud. That's when George busted through the door and he had a candlestick in his hand, ready to clobber somebody, I guess. When it registered what I was doing, he dropped the candlestick and stared at me… and I couldn't read the expression on his face. He looked angry and hurt and kind of afraid all at once."

"What happened?" Quinn asked, kind of stupidly. Lauren wasn't *not* going to tell us. I was now hooked and even Rachel wanted to hear about Lauren's disturbance.

"I remember being embarrassed that he'd caught me so I said, 'Hi honey,' and he stood there for about a minute before he pulled his pants off and jumped on top of me. He kept saying how hot it was that I was getting myself off and how he never knew I had it in me and then I told him there was a lot of stuff he didn't know about me and that just made him more nuts. He threw Bugs on the ground and started screwing me like mad."

"Wow," most of us chanted collectively, sighing in vicarious pleasure.

"Ugh," said Sarah. "That sounds so . . . I mean, good for you, Lauren. I don't want to take anything away from that, but right now, better you than me. I'm bloated and feel like *Supercunt*. As you've no doubt noticed, you are all fucking and my life is just fucked up. My husband is having an affair, I'm pregnant and reasonably sure the baby is not Nate's and I don't want to know—"

"Shit, I'm sorry Sarah," said Vicki. "Camera roll out. Can you say all that again?"

"V, can you just pick it up from wherever?" I said. "I mean . . ."

She shrugged. Something happens when people get a video camera in their hands. It's like they forget about other peoples' feelings.

"The good news, I guess," Sarah went on, "is that Nate and I have come clean and since we've both been bad, our wrongs have cancelled each other out, in a way, I mean, neither of us can get all high and mighty about the other one's antics."

"So you'll stay together?" Rachel asked.

"Yup. We wanted another kid and after Nate read *Deliciously Disturbed . . .*"

"He read it?"

"Yup," Sarah said again, "and after he read it, he said, 'I didn't realize women go through the same kind of stuff guys do. You know, all the wanting to feel excitement and newness and all that.' He's agreed we will be open with each other from now on and we've talked about a more open marriage, swinging and, you know, things like that to keep our marriage fresh."

"How progressive," Quinn said. "I don't think I could share."

"It's not a bad idea," Jelicka said. "Roscoe never even suggested it."

Kiki wore a tight expression. "I actually found all

the vibrator emails to be a little offensive, if you want to know the truth. People spend too much time worrying about sex, in my opinion, especially for an endeavor that at its best is fleeting and, its worst, just more laundry."

Kiki had never struck me as particularly evolved sexually, certainly not someone who'd condone swinging, for example. But she seemed to be turning into a prude, and I knew she wasn't one. After all, Kiki was the brazen Muff who'd told us that when she was walking around Rome in her early twenties, she had a way of getting rid of all the Italian construction guys following her through the cobbled streets. Her technique was to reach into her underwear and pull out her soiled sanitary pad. Then she would wave it at them like an escaped mental patient, sending them running as fast as their legs could carry them.

But maybe it was all an act. Appearances are deceiving and Kiki was more than capable of secrecy. There could well be something more going on. People do what they think is good for them, after all—things they believe they can get away with.

CHAPTER 19

"OK, Maddie's turn. Oops," Paige said, catching herself. "I mean Madelyn."

"Never mind," I sighed.

Lauren was trying to get comfortable while wearing a miniskirt and balancing a cup of tea. "Why do I keep getting this feeling we should have started with you?"

"Oh, no," I said. "That would have put a damper on the rest of the evening, trust me." I'd postponed it as long as I could. It was my turn for the roundy-round.

Everyone but Quinn turned toward me with anticipation.

Oh boy, where to start . . .

We'd moved into the solarium where we always conduct a portion of our meetings whenever I host. The solarium was also where *it* had happened—only yesterday. On this early May evening the sky was clear, the temperature warm and the day lengthening, but I couldn't stop visualizing Udi lying on the day bed where Jelicka and Lauren were now sitting.

"Rolling," Vicki said. "And action."

"Well," I began uncomfortably, not looking at the camera, "I met a guy." For a second I had the thought that it might not be smart to record what Nissim made clear should be kept hush-hush, but I determined that it was too ridiculous a scenario to be believable so I dropped the thought.

"We all know you met a guy," said Sarah. "Give us the good stuff."

A couple of the Muffs nodded, tittered a little at what they hoped might be the upcoming sexy tale, then got silent with anticipation.

"You emailed us about him," Kiki said. "He's from Israel right?"

Was from Israel, I thought. I don't consider myself an incredible actress able to bury the secrets of her soul, but I thought at least one of my friends would see that something deeper was going on with me. Paige had, sort of, but now the Muffs beamed at me with unequivocal joy in my apparent good fortune. I remember being very impressed with Quinn for not having told anyone that Udi had come and gone so quickly from my life. Funny that this one time—when I almost wished she had told them so I didn't have to—she'd been able to keep a secret.

"We are all ecstatic for you," Jelicka said, her happiness for me sincere. But it felt a little over the top, as if she never thought I'd actually meet a guy I wanted who also wanted me and now had to eat humble pie. "Tell us, tell us," she squealed.

"*Shhhh*," said Quinn. "Let her talk."

"So," I said. "I met a guy. A *real* guy."

"I can't believe what a good idea this book was, Maddie," Vicki said, her eye glued to the camera's eyepiece. "And I'm particularly happy for you. You more than anyone needed to get laid."

I'm glad they all agreed on that point.

"I'll say," said Jelicka. "And she didn't even need to move."

"Would you let her talk?" said Paige.

"Were you one of the Muffs in on the vibrator exchange?" Lauren asked, tossing an apologetic look to Kiki.

"I *read* it with interest," I replied. "But I didn't have anything to add."

"Because that was one of the things that got me going," Lauren went on. "I mean in addition to the book. I just had a feeling that sharing all that vibrator information was going to be good for all of us."

"Good for online vibrator sales, too," Jelicka said. "Not that the Muffs are a critical mass."

"Did you get the Hitachi magic wand?" Rachel, who'd arrived late, was looking at Lauren expectantly.

"No. I mean, it sounded great but I realized I needed more interior work than exterior. I mean—you heard . . . No, I guess—I'll tell you later."

A little flicker of disappointment moved over Rachel's face.

"Can we move on?" Quinn asked.

"Turn your face to me a little." Vicki was speaking, but all I could see was the video camera pointed at me. "So where'd you meet?"

I'm a little camera shy, anyway, and my inclination was to tell her to put the thing away, but we'd apparently agreed at some point, because Vicki needed a creative outlet, that we were going to let her document our meetings—*all* our meetings, every moment of them—which in the case of what I was about to say might be very stupid if Udi's death were to come back to haunt me.

I was aware of music playing from my iPod, lilting in from the kitchen into the solarium. It was set to shuffle and at the moment was finishing up a free download of Imogen Heap.

"Yeah, tell us," Sarah said. "And juice it up. I'll be doing a lot of vicarious living for awhile."

Even Vicki's camera panned to look at Sarah.

"Awhile?" said Kiki with a certain reprimanding tone.

"All right, then, *forever* as far as I know. What's his name?"

The camera panned back to me.

"His name is Udi. He was from Israel."

"We know all that already!" Jelicka exclaimed. "Stop teasing us."

"Was?" I thought I heard Paige say, but I wasn't going to stop at that point. They wanted it? They were going to get it.

"OK…" I looked at each of them before continuing. "Well, we met at a dinner party. We had amazing sex a total of two times—actually, several times on two occasions, the second of which was right there on that day bed where you're sitting—when during our second or third shared orgasm, he died on top of me, after which it took me half an hour of pushing and pulling to get out from under him. And as I was trying to decide what to do, three guys from El Al showed up and took him away."

The members of the Muffia stared at me like they didn't know me. Mouths agape, stunned to silence, all except Quinn, who was watching them watch me, her right leg crossed over her left, swinging to the beat of Pink Martini, which had shuffled into the iTunes playlist. She uncrossed then recrossed her legs in rhythm.

I realize now that I'd kind of blurted out the sequence of events without embellishing them for their listening pleasure, but I hadn't wanted to draw it out. The point was that the wonderful Udi was dead and nothing was going to bring him back. Why prolong the torture?

"You're joking right?" Jelicka finally asked.

"No, I'm not joking."

"He's dead?"

"Yup."

"Mito-cardial infarction?" asked Kiki, the soon-to-be nurse practitioner.

I nodded. "I guess so."

"You're not sure?"

"I've never been with anyone having a heart attack. I'm not sure what it looks like."

"Did he clutch his chest?"

"Sort of but he was mostly clutching me."

"A heart attack—that was always my biggest fear with Roscoe," said Jelicka. "I mean, given our age difference—not that I have to worry anymore now that he's fucking his secretary."

"Saul's older so I worry about that, too," Kiki added. "But did you know that heart attacks kill more women than cancer?"

"Good to know," said Vicki. "My heart's always been much stronger than my breasts."

"The thing is, Udi was only thirty-six," I said.

"Thirty-six? Go on, girl." Jelicka seemed to forget that, despite his youthful vigor, Udi was dead.

"Did he . . . how long did the whole thing take?" Kiki asked.

"How long did what take?" Jelicka was being deliberately obtuse.

"Seconds. Maybe thirty seconds."

"Hmmm. I'm really not sure what the norm is. We haven't studied heart presentations yet."

"And he died on top of you?" Paige asked. "How did you know when it was over?"

I shrugged. "He wasn't breathing?"

"This is shocking and truly amazing," said Rachel in the pause that followed, when no one knew what to say. "I mean . . . life, sex, death—and we just ate. That's all there is, ladies."

It's true, these are life's biggest events and we were sharing them all together. But then, you've probably already figured out this is one hell of a book club.

"I got here just after it happened. It *was* pretty shocking," Quinn said, her jaw dropping in an expression of disbelief just as she said it. But the damage was done. Everyone turned to look at her. She and I had agreed she wouldn't say anything to the Muffs about her knowing for fear someone else in the group would feel slighted, though feeling slighted about not being invited to see a dead body was really kind of silly.

"Well," Quinn went on, glancing at me unsurely, "I sensed something was wrong and I decided to come—"

"To Agoura?" Jelicka asked, stunned. "You usually need a bribe to drive out here."

"No I don't," she protested. "I like it here. It's…" She drifted off, searching for the right word. "Remote."

"Look…I called her," I said, hoping to put the subject of where I lived to bed permanently. "Quinn was the one who'd been pressuring me to get laid and she knew all the details of how Udi and I met. I'm sorry if I didn't tell all of you, but it wasn't really a group event, if you know what I mean. It was my choice to wait until tonight to tell you and I swore Quinn to secrecy."

"He was gorgeous," Quinn said. "You would have loved painting him, Rachel. His body was beautiful."

"You saw him *naked?*" asked Paige.

"Yup."

Vicki was panning the camera back and forth, not wanting to miss anything.

"Oh, Madelyn," Lauren began, "I think I can speak for all of us when I say we're really sorry. We all know how long it's been since you had a man you were attracted to, and then to have this happen? There's really no justice."

"Well, *that's* certainly true. But I didn't really *have* him, you know. I guess I had him once or twice for a few hours, but basically it was just nice to find someone I liked." I felt tears starting to form. "And it took so long to find him."

"That's what we mean." Lauren put her arm around me.

"And then this had to happen," Sarah said, trying to

be sympathetic. "Some of us have multiple lovers and then this has to happen to *you*. It's just not fair."

"Since when is fairness a reason for anything?" I asked, without a hope of any response that would be satisfying.

And I didn't get one. I remember I just wanted to let myself be sad, morose really, hoping the footage would be too awful for Vicki to ever use in whatever little video she was trying to make. Life just isn't fair. And I hadn't even read *When Bad Things Happen to Good People*. I don't think any of us can explain why things happen most of the time, despite our noble attempts to do so. I mean— life's not a toaster where you put in your piece of bread, press *on*, and then a little while later you get browned bread. That would be direct cause and effect. But most of the things that happen to us—car accidents, friends getting cancer— have no explicable reasons for them, no matter how hard we look.

"I can't and won't live my life thinking that there's anything different I could have done to prevent this from happening."

"I'm not saying you could have," said Sarah. "It just that it's so…"

"I know," I said. "Unfair. Well, I'm not going to let this affect what I do. I'm not going to start thinking that if I do a bad thing I should be prepared for something bad to happen; or that I could win the lottery the day I let an old lady go ahead of me in the check out line."

"I know you're upset, but I have to say, Maddie," Kiki said after I'd stopped crying, "that it might not have been a good idea to bring him to your house."

"Shut up, Keek," Quinn said. "Why not have him come here? She's a grown-up and it's a beautiful place to make love."

"What's the beauty of the place got to do with it?"

"Sex in this house would be far nicer than hotel

sex."

"Depends on the hotel," Paige offered.

"They hadn't even made it to the bedroom," Kiki said. "That's not really utilizing the house."

"They hadn't gotten there yet!" Quinn was getting emotional. "And they were attracted to each other, so they didn't have *time* to get to the bedroom. The solarium was closer. They *would* have gotten to the bedroom later on if . . ."

I remember being aware of a pain, right where I thought my heart was. This was a different kind of heart attack.

"I'm saying she didn't know him well enough to bring him here," Kiki went on after a beat. "He could have been a nut job and she was alone with him."

"I did think of that," I said. "But he *was* a sky marshal. It's like if he were a cop. I felt safe."

Kiki *harrumphed*. "Remember the cop in *Pulp Fiction* who raped Ving Rhames?"

"Are you sure he was a sky marshal?" Jelicka asked, suspiciously.

I hesitated. "Yes."

"You must never have seen *The Departed*," Vicki said, from the other side of the camera that was focused on me. "Or the one with Alec Baldwin where he's a crooked cop. Nah, that's a bad example—he's nasty enough in real life." Southern Cal gals all, the Muffs knew their movies.

"He was a friend of a friend of a friend; plus, I'd already spent some quality time with him," I said. "I also think, being a mediator, that I'm a pretty good judge of character."

"That's what all those little boys killed by Jeffrey Dahmer would have said if they were still alive to speak. Ditto Ted Bundy's women."

"Give yourself a break, Maddie, when your emotions are involved, you're not functioning as you normally would," Lauren suggested.

"Crazy people out there," Paige said. "You can't be sure of anyone."

"I agree," said Jelicka. "Crazy people here, in Israel— crazy people everywhere. And you can't make up all the crazy shit those crazy people do."

"Well, that's certainly true," I said. "If I'd known that I was going to screw the first lover I'd had in almost two years *to death*, I might have extended my self-imposed celibacy for another few months."

No one said anything for a few seconds. I took this to mean they concurred.

"You said the El Al guys came to take his body away?" Jelicka had that look on her face that she sometimes gets when she needs all the details.

"He had a chip in his shoulder, so they knew where he was and that's how they knew to come get him."

"A chip?" Rachel asked, recovered from the Hitachi Magic Wand incident.

"Apparently they put chips in all their employees," I said.

"That can't be true." Jelicka had her nose out of joint—probably because I'd suddenly undermined her authority regarding all things Israel.

"OK, it's weird," I agreed. "But it's weird enough that I even met an Israeli. I've never met an Israeli before."

"Jewish guys are great," said Jelicka. "Like I said, Israeli Jewish guys are arrogant and slightly wild, but they're still Jewish, so they're great. But that chip thing—doesn't sound right."

"Let's not generalize," Kiki said. "Remember, I'm married to a Jewish man and he's quite flawed."

"In my experience, they're great . . . except of course when they're assholes."

Kiki was more worked up than I recalled seeing her in recent memory. "Mayor Bloomberg—Jewish— pretty great. Mike Milken—not great. Adam Sandler—*seems* great, might not be great. Barry

Minkow, the carpet king—maybe repentant, not great. Bernie Madoff—great con artist. Andrew Weiner—could have been great, but sending naked pictures of himself on his cell phone? Not as great as he thought, obviously—"

"Alright, I got it," Jelicka said, getting up for a second white-chocolate coconut cupcake from my favorite local bakery. "Geez, I said they were great guys. I didn't say they weren't flawed. We're all *flawed.*"

This was the closest I'd ever come to hearing Jelicka admit she had *issues.*

"Look," Lauren said, "Jewish men are still men. More alike than different."

"Enough male bashing," said Quinn out of nowhere. "This is about Madelyn, remember?"

"OK, OK," Rachel said, louder than necessary. "One thing I think we can all agree on is that *Deliciously Disturbed and Distracted* was exactly what we needed to get us feeling alive again, Madelyn most of all, though, of course, that aliveness was cut short by, well…"

"Yes, it certainly was," Lauren concurred.

There were a few awkward seconds of silence during which they all seemed not to know exactly what to say, though I could feel their collective commiseration.

"I've started a whole new series of paintings that you're all going to go absolutely batty over," Rachel said, apropos of nothing.

Everyone seemed glad of the opportunity to move off the uncomfortable topic, however briefly; me most of all, even if I was having trouble expressing my enthusiasm. The past couple of days had been so emotionally and physically draining, I don't think I could have mustered the energy to go batty over a diamond necklace. It was about that time, as people were talking about Rachel's paintings—something about men missing body parts—that I realized Laetitia had thankfully not shown up with her sex toys. In retrospect, sex toys would have been over the top.

"Listen," I said, picking up my wine glass and tossing back the last bit of Viognier. "I'm really glad you all liked the book. I loved it, too. But at the moment I'm disturbed and distracted for all the wrong reasons. I thought having you Muffs here would be good to take my mind off things, to distract me, as it were. And it worked—for awhile. I love you all, but right now I need to throw away these empty food containers and send you all home."

CHAPTER 20

The following morning, a Saturday, I was slightly hung over—a rarity for me. But it only takes a couple of glasses of wine to do me in and I'd had three. I vaguely remembered a text from Laetitia apologizing for not showing up. She said she'd been waylaid by a group of over-eager bachelors who had somehow managed to rupture a life-sized, blow-up sex doll she'd provided for a party earlier in the evening, and the minor explosion had resulted in injury to the soon-to-be groom. She didn't mention what part of him had been injured, but she didn't really have to.

Lila was still at her sleepover so I could just lie in my bed like a blob until I felt like moving. Stipple's purring at my head could have been a problem, but the sound almost blocked out my neighbor's lawn mower and distant leaf blowers on that sunny morning.

I was well into the double-reverse sleep syndrome—a condition characterized by the second or third time one wakes up after the normal hour of rising, making one woozy and wondering what day it is—when the phone rang. I picked it up, still not awake and not thinking clearly. It was Jelicka sounding like she'd had at least five cups of coffee. I'd need to concentrate and get up to speed quickly if I wanted to follow her rapid-fire delivery.

"Thanks for a great evening," she began. "The food was lovely, inspired and eclectic. And you know I liked the book."

"You're welcome."

"I'm so sorry about what happened with Udi. It's just shocking is what it is, but it was a fascinating night all around."

"Yeah," I sighed. "Fascinating. And now things are back to the dull status quo."

"Hardly," she said. "I couldn't sleep all night, I was so wound up."

"Not about this, I hope. Something happen with Roscoe?"

"Roscoe? God, no. He's with the secretary."

"Does the secretary have a name?"

"Yeah. Old bag."

"Jelicka . . ."

"I think I'm just going to let him divorce me. But listen, I don't want to talk about him or the geriatric hussy. The reason I couldn't sleep was because I couldn't stop thinking about you and Udi."

"Oh, Jelicka, please don't—I mean unless it takes your mind off Roscoe and whatshername. I really don't want to talk about it."

"All right. But I have to tell you, he didn't just die, Maddie. I think he was murdered."

This topic would do nothing to improve my hungover mental state. I'd already considered the murder possibility myself when Nissim showed up so quickly to take Udi's body. But I dismissed it as being ridiculous and against all sane interpretation of events, even if Viagra mixing with heart medication seemed too obvious—or, at the very least, predictable. But then I remembered *the principle*.

"Have you ever heard of Occam's razor?" I asked.

"Whose razor?"

"Occam's. I can't remember who he was exactly, but the principle of Occam's razor says that the simplest, most obvious reason for anything is usually the right one. Murder isn't the simplest answer."

"Pshhht."

"Oh, come on, Jel. I was there. He was coming and going at the same time. Gasp, groan, whimper and sigh. Gone."

"You're missing the point. Listen to me, he was a sky marshal, right?"

"Yeah."

"Well, that's a front."

"A front," I repeated. I could tell I wasn't awake enough to fully defend my point of view.

"Not a front. Wrong word—a *cover*. I mean, he may actually *be* a sky marshal, but he's only a sky marshal so that he can travel surreptitiously from one country to another to conduct his spy business."

Jelicka had once been an aspiring screenwriter and a reader for one of the studios, searching submissions for the next *American Beauty*, or possibly *Shrek*. She sounded like she was pitching me the plot of a movie.

"So you believe he's a sky marshal…but you secretly think he's a *spy*?"

"Not just any spy—Mossad. And he had to serve in the army. All Israelis have to."

"Mossad?" I vaguely recalled hearing the term but wasn't completely clear on what it was. "Tell me what that is again?"

"Mossad is the Israeli version of the CIA, Special Operations, Navy Seals and an elite assassination force rolled into one, only much more secretive and lethal. It also explains his being able to lift you up, throw you around and fuck you like he did."

"I don't remember telling you the details."

"Quinn shared on the way home. I'm telling you, those guys go all over the world and assassinate people their government doesn't like. Imagine if we could've done that with Osama or Saddam."

"Yeah, imagine." I actually didn't want to imagine, though I suppose she had a point. I just wasn't sure what this had to do with his sexual proficiency.

"We might have avoided this ridiculous war we're

in." Jelicka's escalating enthusiasm for her topic had her talking faster and faster. "First thing this morning I called a girl who was on the kibbutz with me twenty years ago who now lives in Tel Aviv and she told me that Mossad agents masquerade as all kinds of things—accountants, carpenters, fry cooks and El Al sky marshals. In fact, that's one of the main, you know, fake personas. They travel as sky marshals to where their missions are and once they get there, they do their spy thing—follow people or kill 'em or whatever."

"Yeah, *whatever*. Jel, I don't know," I said with as cool a head as I could muster. "It's a little far-fetched."

"All right, how 'bout this. You said the guys who took his body away kept saying a word that sounded like hassle or something like that, right?"

"Right, so . . ."

"So, it wasn't *hassle,* but *lechasel.* It means *to terminate* in Hebrew."

Jelicka had the Hebrew pronunciation thing going on pretty well at the back of her throat—remnants of a long ago bat mitzvah. She sounded like Udi and Nissim—at least with that one word, which actually did sound familiar.

"Really?" I asked, wiping my eyes and trying to focus.

"Yes. Really. I wouldn't lie about termination."

"Well, even if *lechasel* means terminate, I don't know if that proves anything. I mean, I could have heard it wrong."

"No," she said definitively, "I think you heard it right."

"And even if it *was* terminate, they were probably referring to something else. Udi was already dead."

"Because they terminated him!"

She had to be on uppers.

"And then there's his name—Quinn told me on the way home last night that the I.D. in his pocket did *not* say Udi *anything*, though she couldn't remember what it *did* say. And, by the way, that name he gave you? Udi Hamoudi? It's totally made up. *Hamoudi* in Hebrew means cute."

"He *was* cute—"

"Maddie, you could be in danger. If he was Mossad, it makes perfect sense that he would give you a fake name for your protection. It also makes sense those three guys would come take his body. If Quinn hadn't been there, they might have terminated you, too!"

"Well, if anything happens to me, Vicki's got the story on tape and you can take it to the authorities."

"I'm serious, now. They might think he told you something, or that he planted something in your house. They don't want publicity. Look out the window right now."

"Nobody there," I said.

"Could just be a matter of time. See, they can't afford to have anyone knowing the real reason he died. No. Something else is definitely going on. We just need to figure out what."

She made some valid points, but I still couldn't go along with her. "Jel, we are not going to figure out anything. Even if what you think is true and he's Mossad, it's not our business. I barely knew Udi, or whatever his real name was. He and I just had this great physical connection and it was what it was, but I don't want to make any trouble by making it more than it was. What if Udi had a family? Poking around and asking questions might cause more problems. And if you *are* right—not saying you are—then we should definitely not make waves. We should watch our asses. Spies is spies. They have guns and they're dangerous. Best stay away."

"That's why you need to figure out what happened before they figure out that you've figured out what happened," Jelicka declared as if it was perfectly clear. "What if the guys who killed—let's just call him Udi—

what if those three guys who killed Udi—"

"They didn't kill—"

"—did it because he'd infiltrated their plot to bring large amounts of radioactive polonium-two-ten into the country, like the stuff that killed that Russian spy in England, and put it in our water supply? Still want to lie in your bed and say nothing?"

"Why would the Israelis want to contaminate our water supply? America is Israel's friend."

"Ah-ha!" she said. "I already thought of that." I could feel her smugness through the phone. "See, Nissim and his buddies are extremists who want to derail the peace process."

I was stunned into speechlessness. "You need to go back to screenwriting 'cuz this is good."

"If they had polonium-two-ten, you could already be contaminated," she went on. "All it takes is, like, a dot of the stuff to—"

"Jel—Jelicka!" I had to stop her, but she was like a ball of string rolling down hill, coming unraveled as she descended.

"But you won't feel it for a couple of weeks," she said, continuing her roll. "And see, they knew Udi was onto them, and they figured out a way to kill him that wouldn't look suspicious. They made it look like a heart attack, with poor little you to agree that's what happened in case anyone asked questions. 'Yes, officer, he died when we were having sex,' you'd say, and they'd believe you. You're a legitimate person. You have a respectable career and, up until a couple of weeks ago, you were pure as the driven snow that's drifted, ever so slightly."

"Stop already." I took a breath and attempted to regroup in order to infuse this out-of-control conversation with a little rational thought. "I met Nissim, one of the guys that came to get Udi, at my friend Berggren's. You've met Berggren. At any rate, he was at the same dinner party where I met Udi and

Berggren told me he's a really good guy. Her dear friend and producing partner is engaged to him, so she would know," I said calmly.

"Yeah, well, not necessarily. What kind of name is Berggren?"

"Swedish." I wanted to go back to bed. "Listen," I began again, "I need to lie here for awhile and be miserable. How 'bout I agree to make a couple of calls to see if I can find out—*sheesh*, I'm not sure how to phrase it. But if all I get is more glowing reports of Nissim, I want you to drop this."

There was a silence. But then she agreed.

"And please, don't go blathering to the other Muffs." Silence again. "Jelicka? Promise me. It's just going to get people upset for no reason, thinking there's a price on my head and that we could all be radioactive."

"All right, fine."

I hung up, not trusting that she would keep her mouth closed, but committed to keeping my end of the bargain. I'd call Berggren and tell her about Udi, which would, of course, shock her. Then I could ask her some questions about Nissim, possibly find out where he lived, or perhaps find out more about ZsaZsi, his fiancée. I could also call some sort of crime person. *Who could that be?* I used to know an FBI agent, the father of one of Lila's friends, but I'd heard he'd gone to jail for child pornography.

And then I remembered Cullen—my would-be Babeland babe. *Would it be weird to call him?* No weirder than anything else about our relationship. He was writing detective fiction. He'd probably done a lot of research and knew about procedures and CSI-type stuff. I could pitch the plot of my relationship with Udi as if it were fiction, adding a few of Jelicka's embellishments, and see what he thought. *What a great idea! I'll find out as much as I can about Udi, then pitch the plot as fiction and see if Cullen thinks it could fly as a believable story. Yeah, that's what I'll do—later, when I feel a little more ambitious and ready to get out of bed.*

I glanced at the clock and decided I could sleep for another hour, when I noticed my purple Rabbit poking out from a drawer in the bedside table. My first reaction was to slam the drawer closed because using it had been the farthest thing from my mind. But it was quite possibly exactly what I needed.

CHAPTER 21

"Berggren Wolfe's office," intoned a deep male Scandinavian voice a few hours later, once I'd pulled myself together enough to call. I recognized the voice of the sexy Dane immediately.

"Hello, Thor. Is she in? It's Madelyn."

"Allo, Madelyn. Good to hear you. But sorry, yah, Berggren's not in. She's in New York. Do you have her new mobile?"

Right—she'd told me she was going to New York. I hadn't had a chance to respond when I heard another phone ringing at Berggren's place and Thor's honeyed tones were telling me to hold on.

Berggren had gone to New York to rehearse a movie she hoped to produce that summer. What a dynamo. I live in awe of her. But finding scripts that actors want to do, then flying all over the place to make them happen while raising her daughters was a challenge I wasn't up to.

It wasn't as if she did *every*thing herself, though. She did have all those cute interns to help her, and at that moment she had Thor. Maybe if I'd had an intern like Thor I could have . . . No. With or without help, it still wasn't my temperament to be the go-go go-getter Berggren was.

While I was on hold waiting for Berggren's new number, my own cell phone rang and it was Kiki. "You need to go somewhere and be tested," she said.

"For what?"

"For radioactivity, of course. Jelicka told me all about it and I think it would be a good idea."

"Udi did not die of radiation poisoning."

"That may be true, but if his death is related to the theft of plutonium or uranium or whatever, then it's possible he was exposed to it. And if *he* was exposed, then you were exposed, which means we were, too. Granted, it's very low-level contamination, but if you're positive, I, for one, would like to know."

Perhaps because Kiki was still in school, merely *hoping* to become a nurse practitioner, she was somewhat alarmist when it came to health concerns, but I would have thought being a nurse practitioner required a bit more sense. Then again, Kiki was less than halfway to earning her degree and you know what they say, "a *little* knowledge is a dangerous thing." And Kiki was positively frightening. Her overreaction could be related to whatever was going on in her personal life but, so far, she hadn't told any of us what that was. Regardless, I wasn't going to accede to her wishes and agree to be tested for radiation poisoning just to settle her down.

"I'm not going to the hospital to be tested for radioactivity, Kiki. That's ridiculous. Besides, Alexander Litvinenko, the Russian spy who died in London—so sick, and in so much pain—came into contact with many, many people after he was exposed—none of whom developed any symptoms."

"Come on, I told Vicki I'd meet her there."

"On a Saturday?"

"The cancer ward is always open."

"That's good to know. But what if I *am* radioactive? I should *not* be around cancer patients," I said.

"Exactly the opposite. If you're radioactive, you might zap the cancer out of those people."

Again—were these the words of a medical professional?

"Madelyn," she said in a different tone.

"What?"

"I'm kidding. I had you going, though, didn't I?"

"Yes, you did."

"It could endanger the lives of hundreds if not thousands if you walked into Cedars to be tested for radioactivity."

"You don't say."

"Actually," she said, "I just wanted to see if I could still act the hell out of a scene. And you bought it."

"You had me, Kiki. You're a great actress. Is that what you want me to say?" I was a little annoyed.

"Sorry if it upset you. It's just that Jelicka is so riled up about this whole thing that I guess I got caught up in it, too.

I supposed it was a harmless ruse she'd perpetrated—not that it didn't contain serious undercurrents. "So why *are* you meeting Vicki at the hospital?"

"She felt another lump."

"Oh, shit."

"I know. She didn't want to get into it last night. But I'm sure you noticed "

"Shit, shit, shit. I thought after they took out the first one and she had the radiation, she was cancer free. How can there be another lump already?"

"I don't know, but she needs us to stay positive—as in *cheerful*, not death sentence. That's what she wants. Anyway, she's having the lumpectomy at one o'clock and we could maybe hang out and have a coffee while she's having it."

I thought Kiki was taking being positive into the realm of denial. But instead of commenting on that, like any trained attorney would—lapsed or otherwise—I went back to my original line of questioning. "Listen, Kiki. Did Jelicka just call you, or did she call everyone about this? I mean about her stolen-nuclear-material idea." It didn't surprise me that

Jelicka had told the Muffs. It just surprised me a little that I'd gone through the ritual of asking her not to talk about it, thinking I might get a different result. Isn't that the definition of an idiot?

"She thought we needed to know in case we wanted to be tested," said Kiki. "But truthfully, it sounded far-fetched to me, too."

Not so far-fetched as to keep her from having some fun at my expense.

Thor came back on the line after what had seemed like an hour.

"I'll call you back," I told Kiki.

"'K. And don't worry—we can always get a tester to come to you if it comes to that." Then she hung up.

Once I'd gotten Berggren's number from Thor, I called, hoping I'd catch her during a break in rehearsals.

"Berggren?"

"Who's this?" Berggren asked, as if speaking through twelve layers of cheesecloth with her lips tangled up in the first layer.

"Berggren, it's Madelyn."

"Madison, how are you?"

"Ma-de-*lyn*," I said louder, glad I was at my house and could talk as loud as I wanted to. "Is this a good time?"

"Mad . . . be . . . long . . . hard."

I think that's what she said. "I just wanted to tell you something, but if you're really busy right now, I can call back."

"It's . . . fff . . . go ahead."

Berggren had a way of being distant and approachable at the exact same time. This was one of those instances when I didn't know if I should continue or just hang up."

"Udi, remember Udi? The guy I met at your house?" I began.

"The Israeli, yes!—very hot. I heard from ZsaZsi

that he's really into you. It was so sexy watching you two that night, and I couldn't be more thrilled. How did the second date go?"

"Not so well."

"What?"

"He's dead, Berggren."

There was no point in leaving that part out. In fact, she might know this already. But anything else I told her I'd have to filter, given that she and Nissim's fiancée were business partners.

"ZsaZsi didn't say...I had no idea...Oh my God. How did he die?"

"I think he had a heart attack."

She gasped. "Oh, you poor thing. Did this just happen? Is he there?"

"No, no. It was a couple of days ago but, well, the thing is, it was just so sudden, you know?" I wanted to see how much information she might provide without my having to ask. "We'd barely gotten started and his death was so sudden. I hardly knew anything about him and now I feel like there's no *closure.*"

I try to avoid using that word whenever possible, particularly in mediations. It has so much pop-cultural baggage attached to it, and it's never been a satisfying word anyway because so few painful events ever receive real closure. You can't just zip-lock the bad chapters in your life away like so many leftovers; they'll still spoil eventually. But in this conversation, *closure* suited my purposes.

"Oh, Madelyn, I'm so sorry. I wish there was something I could say."

"Did ZsaZsi say anything? You know, about him? Anything she may have told you? I just need to know."

"I don't think ZsaZsi knew much about him. She'd only just met him, too. All she told me was that Udi and Nissim met in the Israeli army."

She was breaking up, but I think that's what she said.

"The army?" I asked.

"Because in Israel—"

I don't think she heard my question. But I remember Jelicka telling me that all Israelis had to serve in the army, so it might make sense that that's how Udi and Nissim knew each other.

"Yeah, I remember ZsaZsi saying that's where they met," she said again. "Nissim stayed in for like ten years or something, which I guess is a long time. Maybe Udi did, too, and that's how he got into sky marshaling."

Well, she was trying to give me something, I guess.

"Where are they?" Now she was speaking to someone else, presumably in the rehearsal hall, and she was clearly annoyed. "I needed them here half an hour ago. Call their agent, the little flakes." There was a garbled exchange before she came back to the phone. "Sorry. Where was I?"'

"The army?"

"Oh yeah, the army. Well, here's the thing. I don't think she'd mind if I told you because it's over now, but ZsaZsi told me that Nissim had been an assassin."

Granted, we had a bad connection, but I could have sworn she said *assassin*. "Really?"

"Yes, really. I think it's sexy, though, even if it *is* a little scary and dangerous. I mean James Bond, Jason Bourne, Jack Bauer—"

She *had* said assassin.

Then, without covering the mouthpiece, she yelled in a cheerful voice, "Mary Kate! Ashley! Over here!" Then she returned to the line. "They finally deign to make an appearance. The word contract means nothing to these people."

"The Olsen twins are in your movie?"

"Who knew? But the movie's about twins separated at birth, so I wanted real twins. Anyway, I've gotta rehearse now, babe. I'm so sorry to hear about all this. Let's get together next week when I get home and we can talk about it. Come to my dinner party?"

"I'd love to," I said.

Yay . . . another dinner party at Berggren's house! It was exactly what I'd been hoping for and a surefire opportunity to find out more about Udi. But that would have to wait because I had other pressing concerns—Vicki's lump, Lila's volleyball game, then there was a mixer at Lila's school with me as one of the parent chaperones.   At least Lila's friends would distract her from asking about "Mom's special friend." So far I'd been able to avoid telling her what had happened, but sooner or later she might press me on the subject and I hadn't figured out what I was going to say. I just wanted to present a believable alternative to the truth. Why upset her?

In retrospect, I think I must have been starting to get caught up in Jelicka's plot. Perhaps she wasn't so crazy after all—particularly since some new information had emerged about Nissim—*assassin!* The whole thing could actually turn out to be very serious.

Despite that possibility, however, I didn't thoroughly think through what could happen to us if Jelicka *was* right.

CHAPTER 22

Vicki sat propped up in her hospital bed, a silvery curtain hanging from chains strung from an oval ceiling rod pulled around it, staring wide-eyed at Kiki and me. The anesthesia had kicked in and her eyes, along with her pale skin and spiky blonde hair put me in mind of a teenage drug addict rather than the conscientious filmmaking Muff I knew.

"This is the best *mmmoo*ovie I've ever had an opportunity to be involved in," she said with conviction. "Whatever happens with this l-l-lum-l-l-lummpec-tomy"—

Vicki's anesthesia was making her unable to form words, not to mention the problems it was causing to her synapses.

"—annn-ddd I wanna have Jelly or some*body* shoooot me—"

"Honey, Jelicka's not here."

"OK, OK, OK...then *you* guys shoot me, the *lumcotopeee.* The trunk is my video camera in my car. *Promminisssse* you'll finish me with this film."

Kiki and I exchanged a worried look. Kiki shook her head.

"We promise," I said.

"I wannnna *die* making this Muffie. *Pleeeassse.* It'll be my . . . gift of parting to the world."

Kiki and I each took one of Vicki's hands. "You're

not going to die, Vick," Kiki said. "It's probably a benign fibroid."

"I love you guys. I just, it's just, so *sig-nif-i-cant!*" Vicki belted, startling even herself. She reached for my hand. "Sad Maddie. Are you sad? You're sad, aren't you?"

"I *am* a little sad," I told her.

"All right, ladies," said a Filipino nurse in pale yellow scrubs with a nametag that read: *Gloria P.* "I'll take her now. How are we today, Victoria?"

"I'm so lu-luh-cky," Vicki said as Gloria P. began pushing her down the hall.

"Yes, you are."

"Soooo luuuhcky . . . my *frienddzzs . . .*"

"Mmmmm, hmmm."

"They're the Muff-eeyaa. Ya know what a muffia is—GloriaPee?" It had taken awhile for Vicki to focus on the nametag.

"Ah, no, Vicki. I don't believe I do," Gloria said with some trepidation.

"It's the bush on your twat!" Vicki screamed, then began laughing, turning heads as Gloria P. continued rolling the gurney toward the OR. "I'm a luuuhhhhckkk-eee gurrrlllll . . ."

Then both were gone, beyond the double doors and out of sight.

We were in the new cancer center at Cedars-Sinai, a huge hospital serving most of Los Angeles. We were there to support Vicki and not, as Kiki wished, to have me tested for radiation. Which was preposterous.

The waiting room was scarier than any other hospital I'd ever seen—probably because it was dedicated to advanced-stage cancer patients. Most of the people looked very ill, and many probably didn't have long to live. But I found myself looking at their drawn faces, feeling guilty and so happy I wasn't one of them and, all the while, worried for Vicki. My mind flashed on the Rabbit for no clear reason, and though I felt particularly *not* sexy at that moment, it was still a shocking thought that one could go from orgasm to the nasty realities of the scourge of our age so quickly.

"How long?"

"Couple of hours," Kiki said. "Wanna walk around? Get a coffee?"

"I don't know," I said taking in the fragile souls in the waiting room. "I'm a little afraid of knocking someone over."

I stood and stretched, glancing at the patients, their attendants and loved ones, trying not to dwell on anyone for too long. In some cases it was hard to tell if someone was offspring, parent or paid staff. I decided Jack Kevorkian was not such an evil person after all. If someone wanted to spare himself this end, I reasoned, he should have the right to.

CHAPTER 23

The sliding entrance doors swished open with a ding, and I spotted a cute older woman being pushed toward Kiki and me in a wheelchair. The woman—wearing black and with her hair cut in a chic style—had that pert, defiant look of the cancer fighter.

Letting my eyes drift higher to whoever was pushing the chair, I saw that it was Cullen—as in Babeland/Fleshlight/Andalucia Cullen. He'd spotted me, too, and was smiling broadly, just as handsome as I remembered.

"Hi, there," he said, taking his hands off the wheelchair and standing up to his full height. I hadn't remembered him being over six feet but, then again, I'd been wearing heels and a power suit when we'd met, and now I was clad in sweats and flip-flops. He had on a light blue linen shirt that wrinkled and draped tastefully and, though he probably hadn't put a lot of thought into his appearance, he looked great—far better than I did, that's for sure.

"Hi," I said, glancing at the woman in the wheelchair who suddenly didn't seem quite so cute. This had to be his mother. She was a smaller, shrunken version of him and, to me, didn't look sick at all. She was staring at me with a distinctly hostile expression. I couldn't make out her ancestry any better than I could her son's—Italian, maybe, or Spanish? She had a head of thick black hair and eyebrows to match. I wondered what kind of cancer a woman with hair like that could possibly have. Then I realized she was wearing a wig.

My hands went to my own head, attempting to adjust my own fine, fragile hair into something bordering on a style. I think I've mentioned that I consider my hair to be my worst feature, requiring a lot of daily attention and *product* in order to create the illusion I had hair at all—and I didn't even have cancer. That day it was particularly wispy and I remember wishing I were wearing a hat.

We stood there—except the woman in the wheelchair, obviously—for a couple of uncomfortable seconds, Kiki looking at me oddly while the woman in the chair glared at Cullen, waiting for an explanation.

"This is my mother. Mom, this is Madelyn. She's a lawyer."

"What do we need a lawyer for?" the woman snapped. "I'm sick. I need a doctor."

"She's not *our* lawyer, Mom. She's just *a* lawyer."

"More of a mediator at this point, actually," I said, hoping to clarify.

"I don't believe in meditation," said Cullen's mom.

Kiki's eyes opened wide, I believe in an effort to tell me there was no point in discussing anything with this one.

"This is Kiki," I said. "She's one of the women in the book club I told you about."

"Right, I remember. The *Muffia*."

Mom cleared her throat loudly, again turning around to glare at Cullen. She reminded me of an overacting vaudeville performer from another era, mugging and grimacing in exaggerated style. The only thing she didn't do to show her displeasure was use hand gestures.

"Well," he said, "I guess I should check her in, but let's get together."

I found myself nodding. "Yes. I'd like that."

"Psshaww," said his mom. Really.

"Still have my card?" Cullen asked.

"I do." And I did. *Of course I did, though after meeting Udi, I might have tossed it like so much garbage.* I didn't, however, tell him that I had been thinking of calling. I remembered really enjoying the time we'd spent with each other, despite the fact I'd been slightly embarrassed that he'd used the opportunity of my purring Aphroditty to start a conversation. I'd actually thought about him quite a bit before I'd met Udi (B.U.), but after I met Udi (A.U.), I was consumed with Udi, even if things with Cullen might have ultimately worked out better. Of course, at this point I *know* things would have worked out better. Cullen was still alive, after all.

Here fate had thrown us together again—in a cancer hospital, no less. I hoped it wasn't a bad omen; certainly it was no worse than Babeland.

He turned and, over his shoulder, mouthed, "Call me."

"Very good-looking," Kiki whispered in my ear as we watched him roll his mom toward reception. "And he loves his mom. That's nice to see."

She was giving me a very non-Kiki expression. In fact, Kiki seemed to be breaking through at least some of whatever had been bothering her. She seemed more content, somehow. And that day she was looking and acting less like the grown-up married Kiki and more like the Kiki I'd known fifteen years ago. She was wearing her hair kinky and wild—the way she'd worn it before she'd met Saul—and her clothes were less conservative. *Deliciously Disturbed* had worked some kinda magic on her after all. I just couldn't tell what it was yet.

"You realize that he's the one I met in the vibrator store," I told her, no longer too concerned she might give me a lecture on safe sex.

She nodded then turned to face me when Cullen and

his mother rounded a corner, out of sight. "I think I can forgive him that."

CHAPTER 24

"Good to see you again," Cullen said when we met up one afternoon several days later for coffee.

"Yes," I agreed. "Though seeing you at the hospital was a little jarring, particularly after meeting the way we did."

"Mmm, I see what you mean—sex and cancer don't naturally go together. Then again, why shouldn't cancer patients have sex?" he asked. "My mother has a vibrator—not the fancy one you have, but I'm sure it gets the job done."

Good for her. Everyone should stay sexually active, I thought. We'd all be happier.

"I was hoping you would call me," he went on. "I thought we had a nice connection that day in the Andalucia." Cullen, now in a dark blue version of the light blue shirt he'd been wearing at the hospital, lifted his cup to his lips.

"We did," I said, trying not to smile too provocatively.

We *had* had a connection, but so much had happened since then, not the least of which was the death of a lover with whom I'd shared an even deeper connection.

Also: Vicki's lump had come back negative; Kiki had told Saul she wanted a trial separation and for him to respect her decision to go to church now and then; Jelicka had put together several more wild scenarios as to how Udi had met his end; Sarah had miscarried (which was sad but probably a good thing, since she didn't know who the father was); Paige was being stalked by a tennis dad whom she admitted leading on; Rachel was full-on into her new series of paintings entitled "Nude Men Without Faces"; and Lauren, even though she hadn't lost any weight, had started to consistently wear mini-skirts and high-heeled boots in marked contrast from her previous customary attire of baggy, though trendy, sweats made in countries that didn't treat their workers well. The book, and all that it had awakened in us, was still having positive effects.

All that and I'd forgotten just how easy the rapport had been with Cullen.

"It was a *nice* surprise getting your call," he said, taking another sip of his chai latte. "You look pretty today."

"You're not so bad yourself," I found myself saying. *Lame.*

I did look pretty good. On this particular day I wore fashionable jeans and a jacket borrowed from my navy blue power suit with a lacey, form-fitting blouse peeking out. Necklaces of different lengths completed the look. Though I was dressed for success of any kind, I was not yet over Udi, so *flirting* for success really wasn't on my mind. Still, I saw no harm in looking good while picking Cullen's brain about Jelicka's scenario regarding Udi's early demise.

We were in Peet's Coffee on Sunset Boulevard, across from Book Soup. I'd nixed meeting him at the Andalucia out of fear we might end up in the same booth, necking and groping each other as we had that day after Babeland—not that I wouldn't have considered that under different circumstances. I just didn't want Cullen thinking we'd pick right up where we left off.

Luckily, I had the excuse that I needed to go to Book Soup to get the book for the next Muff gathering at Paige's— *We Need To Talk About Kevin,* a depressing-sounding novel told from the perspective of the mother of a bad seed who grows up to be one of those school shooters like Dylan Kleibold and his gun-crazy friend who shot up Columbine High School and forever tainted the flower the school was named after. I was also sort of hoping Book Soup Steve might make an appearance.

"How's your mom?" I asked, stirring the whipped cream into my mocha.

"Well, other than having cancer, she's fine. She's still very much my mom, you know? That hasn't changed."

"But she's hanging in there?"

"Oh, yeah. Plays with the vibrator, eats a lot, listens in on my phone calls, tells me what to do—you know, same old Mom." He smiled. "She's not that bad, really."

"How did you end up taking care of her?"

Cullen put down his cup. "She showed up one day and hasn't left. Now she says she's going to die soon so there's no point in spending the money on air fare to get anywhere and she might as well die here."

I wondered if Cullen's mom's surprise arrival in Los Angeles had anything to do with his girlfriend leaving. I didn't ask, but I couldn't imagine it was much fun sharing a duplex in West Hollywood with the mother of your grown boyfriend. I'd also gotten a glimpse of her character that day in the cancer ward—a hundred miles of rough terrain.

"I'm not sure what I should say."

He shrugged. "Nothing *to* say. She's my mother and there's really no one else to take care of her."

"Well, it's great of you to do it. Not everyone would."

"Onto more interesting things. How did it go with your Babeland purchases?"

I felt my cheeks flush. I could actually feel the color—more accurately blood— rush to my face. "Good. How about yours?"

"Fine. One night Mom fell asleep on the couch watching *Terms of Endearment*. I got the thing out . . . both things I guess, and gave 'em a try. The Fleshlight was—well, you know, it feels all right, but it's still just a metal-encased collection of silicone and I was aware of that the entire time. Difficult to clean if you want to know the truth."

"I would think."

What had been easy before now felt awkward. I still found him attractive, but the magic had morphed and we were now decidedly mortal beings—no longer each others' temporary sexual fantasy. We also sort of knew too much about each other——TMI, as they say. At any rate, I knew a lot about him *and* his mother. But a lot of what I knew wasn't sexy, and I had the melancholic thought that the magic between us had gone.

"What are you working on now? How's the new book coming?" I asked, taking another consoling sip of cafe mocha.

He gave me his lovely smile again. "Quite well, I think. Thanks for asking."

"So it's going to work—this new erotic detective genre you wanted to invent?"

He shrugged. "I have no idea. There's nothing like it on the shelves, but that could be because people have tried it and tanked."

I put my coffee down. "I read in the *New York Times Book Review* that erotica of all kinds is supposed to be very big right now. My book club loved the one we read."

"Well, that's positive." He wiped his mouth with a napkin and with it his mood seemed to go a few shades darker. "If I can't make it work, I'll probably pack Mom up and go back to Portland."

"Why would you give up so easily? It takes some people years to write their first novel." I sensed my opportunity had arrived to segue into my most pressing question. "You know," I said, letting it hang there a second, "it's actually your new erotic detective genre that I wanted to talk to you about."

"And I thought you called because you wanted me."

He was giving me that suggestive expression again and I felt myself make an effort to get turned on. *But I couldn't have sex with Cullen so soon after Udi had expired* in flagrante. *Could I?*

Gathering myself, I stared into my mocha, though I doubt he was fooled. Luckily I'm told I'm quite skilled at hiding my emotions when I mediate.

"You've done research, right?" I asked, once I'd recovered my cool. "Criminal databases, FBI protocols, security checks, global positioning systems?"

"Yes. Hours' worth, days' worth—possibly months' worth. Why?"

His mind was now off Mom, and he was genuinely intrigued with where I might be going with this.

"So, I have this story and I'd like to pitch it to you. You know—see if you think it's plausible."

"Do you want me to sign a release, just in case it's a great idea and I end up writing a bestseller?"

"I'm a lawyer, remember? Forget the fact that ideas aren't protectable."

"That's sexy," he said, mocking me. He was returning to the playful guy I'd met at the Java Joint. "Ok, I'll shut up. Go."

"It starts with a woman who's reading a very sexy book . . ."

I told him the whole thing, using this other "woman" as the central character. I told him about her reading a book that got her libido going, meeting the guy at a party, the great sex they had, the guy's potential Mossad connections, the untimely death—

and the possibility that the death was not from natural causes. I told him about the woman's "friend" and a group of thugs who, though they said they were from an airline, had really been sent to get the body, and how the woman had become suspicious and now had to find out the truth because the cover-up could involve a threat to national security. Through the entire story he nodded and cocked his head with interest.

"What do you think?" I asked when I'd concluded.

He tapped his tapered fingers on the table.

"I like it," he said after a few seconds. "I could buy all that happening. And it's fun and silly—like *Sex and The City* meets *The Women's Murder Club*."

"I hope I told it well," I went on. "It just sort of came to me, you know? Maybe it was the sexy book we read and then, of course, I met you and the idea of detective fiction was running around my brain. I couldn't actually *write* it. But you know, *you* could." The sun was streaming in through Peet's windows, but it wasn't the sun, so much as the telling of the story, that was making me perspire. I blotted my brow as demurely as I could with a napkin.

His eyes narrowed and he studied me. It was the first time I felt that the sexual element of our interaction was not a factor. He was weighing what I'd said along with how I'd said it. Though I sort of missed the sexual undercurrent, it was nice that he was taking me seriously.

"I could . . . ," he mused, still assessing me, which made me want to fidget. "Why'd you pitch me that story if you weren't going to write or produce it yourself? This is Hollywood."

I shrugged. "And that means . . . what?"

"It means you don't just give a good story away. Didn't you tell me you have a friend who's a talent agent? Yes, you did tell me that. She was supposed to meet you at Babeland to help you shop for a vibrator."

"Shhhh. Not so loud."

"Sorry."

I really like it when a guy can apologize and make me believe him. "Accepted. Anyway, ideas are a dime a thousand. It's all about the execution."

"Of course . . . but I still feel like you're leaving something out." He sat back scrutinizing me.

"What do you mean?"

"I mean you're leaving something out."

"I'm not. It's just a story that sort of landed on my lap. I thought you might need one. New writer, new genre and all."

"Very generous." He wasn't buying it. "You called me and drove in from—where was it? Agoura? To meet up and tell me this story?"

"Not just that. It's . . ."

It wasn't just that, of course. I liked Cullen and he was an attractive guy. But the main reason I was meeting with him was I wanted to run Jelicka's idea by him. He was objective, or someone whom I *thought* was objective. And I needed an unbiased, undramatic opinion to help me decide what to do. After all, it might be dangerous.

"I'd consider writing it, but there's just one thing—" He stopped and took my hand. "This woman in the story—she's you, right? I mean, you're the one who read the sexy book. In fact, I think you told me about it."

I didn't want to look at him. He'd seen right through me. I had to treat him like a party in a mediation. "I did read a sexy book. That's true."

"Your hands are shaking."

I looked down and noticed my hands *were* shaking. I clasped them together on the table in front of me to steady them. Then he put his own hands on top of mine. They provided cool comfort and strength.

"For all I know," he went on almost wistfully, "when I met you, you were already reading that racy book. If that friend's philandering husband hadn't come into the wine bar, you and I might have gotten together, but instead—and I'm not saying anything about what happened was wrong—but *instead,* you went to this *other* friend's dinner party and met a sexy Israeli spy and the rest, including the spy, is history."

Cullen was no pile o'rocks. That's why I'd liked him in the first place. And he was funny. But it was clear I wasn't going to get anything past him.

"You're right," I said, staring into his welcoming eyes. "*I'm* the woman. But timing's everything, right? I don't know why Nate walked in that evening, but he did."

Cullen sat back, pensive, taking his hands from mine.

"What was his name? This Mossad guy?"

"Udi."

Cullen nodded.

"He had another name, but we're not sure what it was."

He looked up at me as if considering his options. "So as things turned out, you didn't need to get that Rabbit after all."

"Well, I didn't *need* it. I mean, when I met Udi ..." *How to get out of this?* I took a breath to regroup. "It's a nice thing to have."

He nodded again. He seemed to be wrestling with some changed view of me. I thought he even appeared a little hurt.

"I'll probably get it out again soon," I said, finishing the thought, "just to try to take my mind off things."

He scrunched up his face in concentration then dove to the floor for his messenger bag. My last comment hadn't even registered. Guess I'd been wrong about hurting him.

"OK," he said, pulling out a yellow legal pad. "Tell me the whole story again from the beginning, with as much detail as you can remember. Just leave out the graphic sex descriptions of you and the other guy, if you don't mind."

So I told him everything again, just as he'd requested, from the very beginning, trying not to leave anything out. From reading *Deliciously Disturbed* to Berggren's dinner party, to what she'd told me about Nissim and Udi meeting in the army, through Nissim and his associates taking Udi's body away and Jelicka's subsequent wild speculations—all of it with as much detail as I could recall, though I'd probably left something out. I told him everything except, of course, the intimate sexual details, per his instructions.

And as fast as I could talk, Cullen was taking it all down, every word of it, with great solemnity, legitimizing and elevating what I'd considered Jelicka's delusional musings into the realm of possibility.

CHAPTER 25

"Just because Cullen thinks your scenario is plausible doesn't mean that's what really happened," I told Jelicka the following morning. "The fact is, we may never know why Udi died or why Nissim and his thug associates came to take him away."

I'd agreed to meet her at the Century City Mall before my mediation session for a little shoe shopping at Bloomingdale's, followed by lunch and non-alcoholic margaritas at *Pink Taco*—a restaurant named after a woman's labia. I was slightly put off about eating there, for obvious reasons, but Jelicka said it was fun, so I agreed— at least they hadn't called it *Beef Curtain*.

"Yay, and say unto him, I speaketh the truth," said Jelicka, mocking me *and* the Bible as she opened a shoebox, picked up one of the Louboutin metallic flats inside, then dropped it back in dismissively.

"It still could be very *un*true," I went on, slipping my foot into the fourth pair of boring black work pumps I'd tried on so far—these with a low cut opening that revealed my toe cleavage. "There is no evidence that Udi died of anything other than natural causes."

I didn't want to totally twist her knickers because the whole thing with Udi had taken her mind off Roscoe and she was relishing her role as *crime solver extraordinaire*, but I still didn't think it was good for her continued existence to be entertaining the idea of exposing a murder plot involving the Mossad.

"You're not thinking, Maddie. It appears nefarious and *it is*. You're still too upset to fully grasp what I'm saying." She assessed the shoes. "I like those on you. They make your ankles look sexy."

"Stop saying I'm too upset to know what I'm talking about. I really liked Udi, but it *wasn't* love."

"How do you know it wasn't love?" Jelicka had an almost ingenuous expression on her face—like she'd lost her definition of love and needed a new one. I could relate. Love had become mysterious and inexplicable.

"It was lust," I said. "He didn't live here and he would never move here, so I knew going in that there were limitations. I really couldn't fall in love with him."

"Sorry, but that's bullshit," Jelicka said with conviction. "You fall in love with who you fall in love with. It doesn't matter where they live. You can feed yourself any line of crap you want, but falling in love is out of your hands, girl."

She was right, of course, though we still hadn't come up with a definition of love we could agree on.

"OK, then, how about this? I was protecting myself from falling in love because Udi was unavailable and younger than I." I sounded like a shrink. I probably could have used a good shrink.

"That's still crap," she said. "But at least it's honest. Now, when this is all over, I'll help you find a more appropriate love interest."

I opened another shoebox—a pair of black pumps exactly like every other pair of black pumps. "I can't shop for shoes right now. Let's eat."

"How's it going with Roscoe and the divorce?" I asked once we were seated in our booth at Pink Taco. The restaurant was as pink as Babeland had been, which was appropriate, considering its namesake.

"Horrible, but there are no more tears left—I've cried enough. It's time to move past all that and own my anger, you know? I hired a shark lawyer a few days ago, so I feel pretty good, actually. Of course, the Xanax isn't hurting."

"Here's to moving on," I said, laughing and lifting my non-alcoholic margarita in toast.

There we were, both of us enduring major upheavals in our lives, toasting ourselves on a weekday afternoon—granted with virgin drinks. Other women might be kicked to the gutter and stay there after getting dumped or having a lover die on top of them, but neither Jelicka nor I would be kept down for long, with or without pharmacological assistance.

Our glasses clinked and Jelicka took her first sip.

"I need the tequila," she said. "Where's our waiter?" She stood up and waved at the first cute guy she saw in an apron.

"So what's the next step?" she asked.

"What do you mean?"

"With our investigation."

"We don't *have* an investi— I don't know what the next step is," I said. "I don't think there should even *be* a next step. It's too dangerous."

"Once we get the government involved, you'll see this isn't some idle hunch."

"We are not doing that!" I caught myself behaving in a manner unbecoming a mediator and brought my voice under control. "You mean the U.S. government?"

"Of course. They'll want to know. We're doing a service for our country."

"No," I said as firmly as I could. "There's no evidence."

"OK, then we'll *get* some evidence. We just need to probe a little further. That's how we're going to *find* this evidence you say we need. *Then* we'll call the government. What did Berggren say?"

"About what?"

"About Udi and his friend and everything? Did she tell you anything juicy?"

"Well, I didn't want her to suspect I was digging, you know, so I just sort of asked some general questions. But she's having a dinner party on Saturday night and I'm going. I'm hoping to find out more." I most definitely was not going to mention the word *assassin* at this point.

She sat back, thinking, her eyes squinting as if she were looking very far away.

"What?" I asked with a certain modicum of dread.

"Did she invite the friend?"

"Nissim? I don't know. Why?"

"Because if we could find out where he lives and we could get him out of his house and over to, say, Berggren's house, then we could go through his stuff—see what we find. Get some *evidence*."

I'd already thought of that, despite my better judgment. In fact, it was my plan to get Nissim's address just in case the recent events came back to haunt me, but I didn't see the wisdom in telling Jelicka any of this. "If Nissim is a spy," I said, "don't you think he'd have his house rigged with all kinds of cameras and things? There could even be an explosive device or something triggered to go off when somebody opens the door."

"Maybe we'll wear disguises."

"A lot of good disguises are going to do if we get blown up. You're acting like you're in some movie that we already know ends happily," I told her. "We don't have an ending, and if it turns out there really was a crime committed, then you— me or *we*—might end up very dead, just like Udi. And please can we leave the other Muffs out of this?"

"Fine. But you're really overreacting. All we need is a little proof."

"Like what, a written confession that Nissim

poisoned Udi?"

"I'll know it when I see it. Remember, I've been to Israel and I can read a little Hebrew."

"That was twenty years ago, not that it's even relevant. If someone *does* go, it shouldn't be one of us. Maybe Cullen would do it."

"Hey, great idea. Ask him. He's a writer so he'd just make up a good excuse."

I frowned at her then glanced at my watch and realized I was going to be late. "I have to get to my mediation."

"Divorce?"

"Neighbor dispute in the Marina."

"Somebody not pick up his dog's poo?"

"Something like that," I said.

"Well, good luck, but don't let it distract you. You have to get Nissim and his fiancée invited to Berggren's dinner party."

Something was telling me—other than, of course, Jelicka telling me—that I should trust her instincts. Despite the fact that the Jelicka I knew, wife of Roscoe and member of the Muffia, was the only one I'd ever known, people always have another side. It could well be that the Jelicka I knew was being subsumed into another Jelicka I hadn't known existed. Perhaps the one I knew was the cover and the real Jelicka was starting to emerge, wearing more than a new pair of shoes.

CHAPTER 26

"Hello. Welcome. As you know, mediation is the process of resolving disputes where a third-party neutral assists the parties involved in a dispute to come to a satisfactory resolution. My job is to listen to all of your issues and concerns. But unlike a judge who imposes a decision on you, *I* try to help you find a solution to your dispute that both of you can live with. I want to commend you both for your willingness to try mediation today, and I want to assure you I will do all I can to remain unbiased and guide you toward a resolution that is win-win."

I was addressing a very serious looking man and woman sitting on the sofa in front of me in my friend's underused real estate office in Marina Del Rey, a community comprised of expensive real estate on and off the water north of the airport. Looking down at them from my perch on a wooden chair opposite the sofa wouldn't be my first choice of an ideal seating arrangement—I prefer everyone to be at a round table so we all at least *seem* on equal footing. But these two people, like some of my friends, seemed almost phobic about driving to the Valley; hence our meeting in this office at the Marina.

"You found me through the Southern California Mediation Association website. Is that correct?"

"Yes," said the man grimly. "That's correct." The

woman just looked like she didn't want to be there.

The man, about fifty, wore glasses and appeared to be roughly halfway through hair transplant surgery. The woman struck me as a cool professional type with a steely determination—for what I couldn't tell. And as a trained mediator, I could feel the power imbalance between them immediately.

"I want to assure you both that I don't know nor have I ever heard of either of you prior to receiving your email, and I believe I can be completely unbiased as we go through this process. I'll be taking notes, but they're just for me and will remain, like the mediation itself, completely confidential. None of us should talk about what happens in this room outside of this room."

Both still wore stern expressions but neither offered any reaction to what I'd said so far, so I plowed ahead with my opening statement.

"The way this will work is one of you will talk and then the other will have a chance to respond, adding whatever you think is important. If you forget to say something, don't worry. You'll have another chance to talk, and then another, until everyone has said all he or she wants to on any subject he or she thinks is important to the issues we'll be mediating today." I paused then added firmly, "One ground rule though, and this is critical: We do *not* interrupt each other."

There was still no reaction, unless both man and woman, sitting on opposite ends of the floral sofa, looking at their cell phones is a reaction. I gave them my best flight-attendant smile and prepared for take off. "And now, I'd like us to put away all handheld electronic devices."

Reluctantly, it seemed, they put their phones away, particularly the woman who dashed off one last text message before tossing her Blackberry into the black Longchamps briefcase on the floor in front of her.

I shifted my attention to the man since his body language told me he was the one with the grievance.

"Would you like to start?"

"Well," he began, shifting his weight on the sofa. "I'm Stan."

"Hello, Stan."

"Hello. Susan and I are neighbors. We live in the same condo complex in the Marina." He still couldn't or wouldn't look at her.

"OK." I had questions, of course, but it was better for now that I sit patiently and listen to what he wanted to tell me instead of asking him what I wanted to know.

"For the last three months, Susan has been making a lot of noise—"

At this Susan rolled her eyes, but Stan didn't see it.

"Anyway, she's loud and I find that to be a problem."

"Have you talked to her about it?" I asked after a pause.

"Well, I've told her I have trouble sleeping from time to time."

"I see. Stan, let me ask you—have you told her that there's too much noise coming from the apartment?"

"No. I thought by telling her what I told you I told her she would, you know, get it."

At that point, I smacked right up against one of my own personal biases—that men are lousy communicators—and had to make an effort to hide it. I took a breath and visualized a sweet, non-confrontational woman—the kind I'd never be. "Have you ever spoken to her directly about the noise you've been hearing and perhaps holding it down?"

"It's awkward, you know? The condo development—it's not the greatest construction, if you know what I mean. But she doesn't need to be so loud."

"I see. OK, so, let me see if I can reframe . . ."

Reframing is one of the important tasks of any mediator—by skillfully rephrasing what the parties are saying in slightly different words, they know they've been heard and understood. There's also the hope that one party might come to understand the other party's point of view and give a little.

"What I hear Stan saying is that he is unable to sleep because of the noise coming from your condo, Susan. He's hinted that the noise bothers him, but so far he hasn't really confronted you. Would you say that's accurate, Stan?"

Susan shrugged while Stan nodded, running his hand over his head and the forty or so visible hair plugs. So far this seemed pretty straightforward—neighbors living in close proximity in apartments and condominiums often had noise issues. All I needed to do was get Susan to agree to quiet down or limit the noise to certain hours and to get Stan to accept that he's going to hear things he might not want to living in a poorly constructed condo complex.

"All right, Susan, what would you like to say?"

"I don't think I make a lot of noise," she said. "No one else complains."

"You wouldn't know," Stan said, flustered. "You are—you are out of touch, with that iPod plugged into your ears all the—"

"Stan, remember the rule. You'll have another opportunity to talk when Susan is finished."

"No one else has complained to me, anyway," she went on. "Besides, I believe people enjoy hearing others having a good time. Stan is making too big a deal of it."

I took a deep breath, smiled and tried to validate both of them, another function of a skilled mediator. "Susan," I began, "Stan may be making a big deal about this, but we're talking about *feelings* here—no one's right, no one's wrong. I mean, if you agreed, you wouldn't need me to find a solution to what amounts to a difference of opinion, right? None of us can judge the worthiness of anyone else's emotions. What we need to do is find a way *through* the feelings."

I didn't know if they were feeling validated but it would have been hard to sound more patronizing.

Smoothing her pencil skirt, Susan crossed her legs. "Of course, Madelyn. I think the whole problem comes down to the fact that I have a boyfriend who makes me scream like a banshee every time we have sex and Stan just can't deal with it. He's started doing this ridiculous hair transplant surgery, but it's all since I broke up with him about six months ago when I started dating Juan Carlos."

How do I reframe that? "Stan? Do you have anything you'd like to add?"

Stan shook his head vehemently, chagrined.

"OK. Well. Let me try to reframe what's been said to this point. Susan doesn't believe she makes a lot of noise but she believes that even if she were making a *little* noise, it's the kind of happy noise people like to hear. Then there's the issue of the poor construction of the condominium complex, which you seem to agree on—and, by the way, I want to commend you both on this point. It's very good that we have this to agree on. Very good. Consequently, it is indeed possible that sounds might appear louder than they actually are."

Suddenly, as I sought a way to maintain some professionalism to the proceeding, Stan sprang to life — red faced, hair plugs on end.

"When she comes, or, more accurately, when she *pretends* she's coming—because it's all faked—"

"It is *not* faked! I faked it with *you!*"

"She sounds like an orangutan. It is *not* a happy sound. Frankly it's scary to everybody. Parents don't want their kids to hear screeching like that, and that's regardless of the construction. Besides she's just doing it to get back at me because I wouldn't pay for her boob job."

"All right, now. Stan, let me—" I started to say, using my non-threatening voice again to no avail.

"I told him to just move out of the building if it's so

upsetting to him that I have a new boyfriend. I don't know what else I can do."

"I'm not going to—" Stan blathered, indignant.

"Would it help, do you think, Stan, if Susan could restrict the hours she has sex with Juan Carlos to the hours that you are not at home?"

"And I'm not loud," Susan said. "That's ridiculous. Other people would have complained."

"They have."

"Name them."

"OK," I said, hoping to diffuse the escalating anger. "Let's see if we can—"

"Oh, and by the way," Susan said, cutting me off, "this has nothing to do with my boob job. I paid for that myself." She was sitting up taller and thrusting her new voluminous breasts forward for both Stan's and my benefit. Thirty-six C, I guessed.

"I'm a writer," exclaimed Stan. "I work at home. And I seriously doubt his name is Juan Carlos. He looks like an Irv or Abner. He probably paid for those big tits."

Susan was starting to get red in the face. She was so worked up she was having trouble forming words. Before anyone could say anything else, I stood up and raised my hands along with my voice. "OK, let's see if we can move forward here. If Susan has loud orgasms, and I emphasize the 'if,' do you, Stan, feel that your right to complete quiet—given that you both live in a poorly constructed condo complex where many noises travel—is more important than Susan's right to enjoy sex with her partner in an uninhibited fashion?"

"I think I should be able to have sex whenever I want to," Susan said, choking out the words.

"Susan, I realize this is difficult, but I asked Stan."

"You're a whore," Stan spat.

"I'm not a whore. You're a withholding asshole."

Clearly, I'd lost control of the mediation. "Alright, let's see if we—"

That's as far as I got before Susan attacked me. "Stop rephrasing or framing or whatever it is you're doing." Then she went after Stan. "You didn't give me enough sex, Stan. What am I supposed to do? Masturbate every night?"

"How could I give you enough sex when you got home at eleven o'clock and I go to bed at nine-thirty?" Stan was screaming now, standing tall at his full five feet nine inches.

"Well, who the hell goes to bed so fucking early?" Susan was standing now, too, towering over him in her heels with her fake breasts thrust out. She looked like she could eat him for breakfast. "And if you're asleep, then tell me how you hear us screwing and making all the noise you say we make. Huh? Huh, little man?"

Sometimes in a mediation I become immobilized— amazed that the parties to a conflict once co-existed in a more peaceable state. I then find myself wondering how they got to such a low point. These two people had supposedly loved each other, and it seemed that much of the current conflict was about old hurts. Perhaps what Stan and Susan needed was a gifted psychologist. Their problems went deeper than I was trained to deal with.

"I went to bed early every night because I was trying to finish writing the book so I'd get an advance to buy you your fucking boob job!" Stan yelled. "It doesn't mean I couldn't hear you, you ungrateful baboon."

"Stan! Susan!" I moved between them, almost yelling, hoping to shock them into silence. It worked. Before they could start yelling again, I picked up my handbag and placed their deposit check on the couch between them.

"Thank you for attempting the process of mediating your dispute. Under the circumstances, I think you're both very brave. But I can't help you. I'm afraid I can't see coming to a resolution of this dispute that you both can live with and frankly, I think the issues presented here today are beyond the scope of mediation. Good luck."

As I walked out, gesturing to the receptionist that we were finished with the room, I was shocked to discover that, despite the tension that had arisen and the unresolvable nature of the dispute, all the talk about Juan Carlos and Susan's screaming had made me horny as hell.

CHAPTER 27

Returning to the house that afternoon, I was stressed and self-flagellating. I had never just flat-out given up on a mediation and I felt like a failure, even if Stan and Susan *were* crazy and needed to undergo therapy before they could begin to think about mediating. On top of that, my negative attitude was compounded when I got a call as I began my drive home along the Coast Highway, telling me I didn't get the job with the sports mediation panel. The vice president of the mediation group—a small, Poindexter of a man who'd never been an athlete of any kind, I was quite sure—gave me some lame excuse about how I was unfamiliar with modern Olympic gymnastic and decathlon practices, and that they'd decided to go "another way." Total bullshit, of course—the typical non-excuse-excuse which tells the interviewee nothing about why they *really* didn't get the offer. Any way I looked at it though, it was back to networking and the job boards before child support ran out.

I had another hour until it was time to fetch Lila from school and I needed to unwind. Dropping my briefcase on the kitchen counter, I considered pouring a glass of wine then nixed it, acknowledging the early hour. I scratched Stipple under the chin and headed up the stairs to my bedroom. I considered making a larger dent in *We Need to Talk About Kevin* but, no matter how well written the book was, a story about a high-school shooter wasn't the kind of escape I was looking for.

Slipping out of my simple brown pumps, I tossed my navy suit jacket onto the chaise and unbuttoned my pleated dress pants, letting them drop to the floor before lifting them onto the chair along with my other discarded clothes. Then, in shirt and undies, I crossed the white carpet to my bedside and dropped to my knees, drawing out the flowered case that lives under the bed and holds both the Rabbit and Aphroditty. I didn't even need to touch myself to know that my pussy was already warm and wet from the tantalizing thought of what was to come.

Opening the small brass latches, I lifted the lid, then the piece of red lace I'd draped over my toys. Staring into the box, it took a few seconds to realize the truth of what I was looking at—the Rabbit wasn't there.

So where was it? The last time I used it was . . . I couldn't remember. Before Udi was dead, that was for sure. It *had* been in the bedside table, but where was it now? I *knew* I put it back.

I looked under the bed again hoping I'd missed it. There was a dust bunny or two, but no Rabbit. I pushed the empty box back under the bed and stood up.

Opening the drawers of the bedside table, I saw that there was, again, no Rabbit. I went to the other side of the bed and checked those drawers as well. I really had to get rid of some of this stuff. Audio cassettes? The last time I'd had an audio cassette player, I was sixteen. And what's this? Leftover invitations to Lila's tenth birthday party? I stopped cold, taking a sharp breath.

Lila! Would she . . .? Oh my God, I really didn't want to think about it. No, she wouldn't. I must have done something with it myself. I'd been stressed lately and I just couldn't remember.

Inside the spacious master bathroom, I pulled open

the cabinet doors and began rummaging under the sink. There was an old set of curlers, facial cleanser that was at least four years old and other miscellaneous curiosities—but no Rabbit. The drawers were similarly cluttered with things I didn't use.

The dresser in my bedroom contained things I actually still used, but rummaging through my lingerie, scarves and T-shirts still did not yield my purple vibrating Rabbit.

Standing up tall, I glanced around the room one more time. Then spun on my heel and headed out the door.

Entering Lila's very girlie room of pinks and pastels, I had no idea what I would do if I found the Rabbit there, but I knew I would at least need to have a more explicit talk with her—possibly put her on the patch. Starting with her bedside table, I opened the second drawer and there, under a couple of naked Barbie dolls, was my purple Rabbit. That was almost too easy. There certainly didn't appear to be much effort expended putting it somewhere I wouldn't find it.

Staring at that length of purple for what must have been a full minute, all kinds of thoughts ran through my mind. The biggest question I had was for myself: How could Lila's sexuality have reached the level of wanting or needing a vibrator without my knowing? I felt like a failure as a mother.

Pulling my grown-up toy from the midst of my child's dolls, I pressed the *on* switch and the Rabbit hummed to life. Though this could have meant Lila had replaced the batteries, I chose to believe she hadn't used it. Either that or the Energizer bunny really did keep going and going. At this point, I realized the rabbit imagery had gotten out of control, threatening to turn into some kinky version of an A.A. Milne story.

Turning for the door, vibrator in hand, I stopped before I'd gone more than a couple of steps. *What was I doing?* The moment for self-pleasuring myself had passed. I couldn't get the visual of my innocent fourteen-year-old daughter playing with the vibrator out of my mind.

I returned the Rabbit to the drawer, figuring it would give me more options to bring up the subject later—"Oh look, Lila, what's this under High School Musical Barbie?" or "*There's* my vibrator!" Well, the appropriate thing to say would come to me, or so I hoped as I headed back to my room.

CHAPTER 28

Who do you talk to when you find your vibrator in your teenage daughter's bedside table? I was just picking up the phone to dial Paige, the mother of a daughter herself, even if Carlotta *was* only six, when Cullen called. I was so fraught that before he could get out the reason for his call, I blurted my news about Lila taking the Rabbit. I guess I figured he didn't know her and might be able to give some interesting, unbiased feedback.

"Rock on," he said. "That's taking charge of your sexuality from the get-go."

"She's fourteen, Cullen."

"So what? People in other countries go to war at fourteen. Might as well have sex first."

"I don't know if I like those choices."

"Kids grow up faster these days. I wouldn't worry about it, Madelyn. Just wash the thing."

"That's good advice. Thanks."

"Anything new on the Udi front?"

"I'm a little too worked up about Lila at the moment to think about Udi."

"OK, I'll call back."

"You're rather provocative, you know that? What makes me think I can discuss my daughter's sex life with you? Some guy I met at Babeland."

"Ouch. Come on, I told you why I was in there. I'm

not like that."

"Like what?"

"Like the kind of guy who frequents sex shops for the latest stimuli—plastic or human."

"Still—" I let my angst hang there.

"She was probably just curious. Nothing wrong with that," he said with a spirit of conciliation, which I ignored. "You should be glad she feels comfortable enough to explore her body in the safety of her own home."

"Wait until you have a daughter. I doubt you'll be so cavalier."

"I'm not trying to be cavalier, but you're right. I'd probably flip out. In fact, to tell the truth, I don't think I could handle having kids. I like them and everything but, seriously, I wouldn't know what to do with 'em. Especially when they're in that diaper stage and can't talk. It might be all right once they get to adolescence . . ."

"When you give them sex toys before they go off to war."

He'd heard me but continued talking.

"I guess I'd have to see how it went, you know, and if I had the right person to parent with."

"Nobody knows how they're going to be as a parent until it happens. That's what's bizarre. Something takes over and you don't recognize yourself. I didn't, anyway. But looking back, I wouldn't have wanted to miss all the early stuff—even the diapers."

"Step-father—that's a job I could be good at. None of that blood-connection confusion that keeps you from looking at a situation objectively." Something about the way he said it seemed almost like an offer, but I didn't pursue it.

"I do have one bit of Udi news," I said, changing the subject. "There's something I didn't tell you at Peet's. You know how I said that Berggren told me that ZsaZsi told *her* that Udi and Nissim served in the

Israeli army together and that's where they met?"

"I think so, but . . ."

"Well," I continued. "Berggren also told me that ZsaZsi told her—in the strictest of confidence, you understand, which is why I didn't want to say anything—that when he was in the army, Nissim's job was as an assassin for the Israeli government."

"So?" He sounded unimpressed, but maybe he was just waiting for the punch line.

"What do you mean *so?*" *How could he not be impressed?*

"The guy's in the army, you figure he kills people."

What a guy thing to say. "What I was thinking is that because Udi and Nissim knew each other in the army—and yes, this is a bit of a leap—maybe Udi was an assassin, too. Of course, I haven't said anything about this to Berggren because she might say something to Nissim or ZsaZsi, which could end up getting ugly if Nissim thought I knew something I shouldn't. So please don't say anything."

Luckily, he didn't know any of the players so his telling someone wasn't likely.

There was a pause during which I could almost hear his brain working. "So you think Udi could have been a killer? A real spook? That *would* change things."

"It's possible. He was really strong the way he could—"

Was I really going to tell Cullen about how Udi could throw me around the bedroom like so many decorative pillows?

"Put it this way," I said, "you could tell he was physically trained."

"And you're not talking about ballet," he said without a trace of sarcasm.

"No. He was like a perfect physical specimen; almost machine-like. And he had this vigilance about him. His eyes were always"—here I felt the need to edit a bit—"active, which makes me think of Daniel Craig for some reason."

"Do you think that maybe that's what some of the excitement was about for you? What woman doesn't like the idea of being with James Bond? And that's *any* of the Bonds I'm talking about, though if I were a woman, I'd go for Daniel Craig, too. Actually, as a man I could go for Daniel Craig. He goes both ways, I've heard. But alas, I prefer women."

"Don't be ridiculous, Cullen. I didn't know anything about any of this until a few days ago. Udi and I just hit it off. I didn't know that he was a spy—assuming he was a spy. I just thought he worked as a sky marshal and had excellent physical discipline."

"*Yeah right*—sky marshal. There's a ruse if I ever heard one."

"You're saying you buy that he was a spy but *not* a sky marshal? Why wouldn't I believe him?" I protested. "I admit I fell for the accent and maybe I didn't care what he did. I don't know—. The point is, I didn't know anything about him and I still don't know, but we have it on reasonably good authority that Nissim was once an assassin."

"And once an assassin, always an assassin. Is that what you're saying?"

"It seems like something that would be hard to get over, don't you think?"

"Makes retirement kind of tough. An old assassin is usually a dead assassin."

Something was bothering me. "But they were good friends. Why would Nissim want to kill Udi? Wouldn't he need a motive?"

Cullen didn't respond right away.

"Wouldn't he?" I repeated.

"Usually, yes, you'd need a motive. But some of these guys were or still are Mossad, right? I mean, that's what you said. Maybe they don't use the same motivation system we do. If I'm going to write the story, this is a point I need to think about."

"You need a motive, Cullen, or your reader isn't going to be satisfied. We need to know why Nissim would kill Udi."

"We don't need to know the *real* reason. We can make one up."

"Yes, for the story, I suppose we can make one up," I said, getting a little irritated with him. "But we also need to know the real motive."

"Do you really? If Nissim did kill Udi, maybe you don't want to pursue this. I mean, think about it. Those guys you described—the Subzero and the one with the red hair and shifty eyes—they could do a real number on you. And you can forget about your friends in the Mafia ever finding a body."

"Nice thought. It's the Muffia, by the way. And, anyway, he didn't have shifty eyes. I know for a fact I never said he had shifty eyes."

"In my version of the story he has shifty eyes. And it works. The shifty eyes works."

I took a deep breath. I was getting confused at this point about what was real and what wasn't—what was truth versus what was being fictionalized by Cullen and Jelicka

"You know, you're right. I *don't* really want to pursue it. I never did," I said. "It's Jelicka. She believes the Israeli government needs to know about subversive activity being committed in the United States by some of its errant operatives. She says I need to trust her because she's Jewish, has been to Israel and has a good idea about how the Mossad operates. Her reasoning is not completely wacked and she's convinced she's right. I guess she's also sort of convinced me."

"I like that," he said excitedly. "Let me write it down."

"This isn't funny, Cullen. Jelicka wants to go over to Nissim's house during Berggren's dinner party on Saturday night to see if she can find some evidence to take to the authorities."

"I agree with you there—that *doesn't* sound very smart."

"No, it doesn't. But she won't listen to reason."

"She shouldn't go alone. I should go with her."

"Nobody should go!"

They were both crazy. "Look, you're both making too much of this. But it's my own fault. I keep letting you get me all carried away. Udi just died—hard as that is to admit."

"Well, I'll keep Saturday night free, just in case something interesting crops up." He paused then he let out a sigh. "You sound really wound up."

"I *am* really wound up."

"Sorry. I hope I didn't make it worse."

"Nah. It's . . . you didn't. It's been a fruitless kind of day."

"What did you end up doing with the vibrator?"

"Left it in Lila's bedside table so I could pretend to discover it when I tuck her in tonight."

"Go get it."

I knew where he was going with this and I wasn't sure I wanted to play along. "I decided to leave it there so we could have a little heart-to-heart sex talk with visual aid."

"You can put it back."

His tone, more than his words, had me getting off the chair where I'd tossed my discarded clothes and where I was, up until that point, putting them back on, and head for Lila's bedside table.

"Wash it off," he told me, once I was back in my room.

"Cullen, if you're asking me to—"

"Go on," he cooed.

"I don't have much time. I have to pick her up in—"

"Wash it off, Madelyn." His voice had dropped a register or two and I got a wave of that same feeling

I'd had kissing him in the tapas bar. Still, I didn't move. "Don't you need to write? It's still so early in the day."

"Warm water." *So insistent.* "I'll wait."

Once again, I did his bidding. Of course, I must have *wanted* to, I just needed that little bit of encouragement. And I *did* have a little time before I had to leave. Gently, but quickly, I washed the Rabbit, toweling it dry as if it were a newly circumcised penis. Then I returned to the chair and picked up the phone. "OK, done."

"Now lie back on your bed. Tell me about your bedroom."

"Well," I said gazing around my room, which I'd made my refuge after the divorce. "It's pretty; maybe a little too girly, you know?" I stretched out on my king-sized bed, still lumpy after a poor bed-making job. "But definitely a woman's room."

"Are you on your bed?" He had a mellifluous voice that soothed me and wound me up at the same time.

"I'm lying down and very comfortable."

"*Mmmmmm* . . . Tell me what the colors are like in your room?"

"Shades of grey and blue which are soothing, and then some cream mixed into the curtains and duvet. The floors are maple and the fixtures are sort of a dark reddish color. It's kind of cool and warm at the same time."

"Sounds nice. How about you? Are *you* warm?"

"I *am* warm." I was getting very warm and I knew I was already wet.

"Pull your panties down."

There was no more resistance. This was exactly what I needed to be doing. A wave of desire pulsed through me and I felt my vagina involuntarily tighten in anticipation of what was to come. Positioning the receiver on the pillow next to me, I could hear him talk while not having to hold onto the phone, leaving my hands free to fully maximize my toy of joy. I lifted my buttocks, slipping my panties clear of my ass.

"Are they off?"

"Mmm-hmmm."

"You're surprising me, Madelyn. This is getting interesting."

"How am I surprising?"

"When we met I thought I detected some fire there inside you, but the last couple of times we've seen each other you've been sort of distant."

"We were in a cancer ward."

"Peet's Coffee?"

No excuse there. "Maybe life intervened."

"I'm going to intervene now. Turn it on—just the vibrator first."

I remember wondering for a fleeting instant if the thing would have enough juice to go the distance. But it purred to life and kept on purring.

"Now," he said, " I know you're wet."

"Mmmm . . ."

"I want you to rest it on your thigh and just let it purr there for a few seconds."

I did as he bid me. Closing my eyes, the second it touched my soft, sensitive thigh, I was vibrating all over, especially high between my legs, still four inches away.

"Mmmm, I like the way it feels," I murmured.

"Very slowly now, bring it up your thigh. Easy— take your time. I can hear you breathing. That's it. Feels good, doesn't it?"

"Yessss." It did feel good. And the anticipation of feeling even better was making me quiver.

"Now bring it up higher—slowly—slowly. You know the spot, that tingling piece of flesh. On you it must be so beautiful."

I *did* know but I was trying to let myself go. Part of me was still feeling a little odd letting him talk to me this way. Though in retrospect, given the way we'd met, it seemed the best, the only way for him to talk to me, really. "Mmmm, yes . . . right . . . there," I breathed out.

"Don't stop. You're almost there... I can feel the sensations going through your body. Yeah, it feels good."

"*Oh*—" It was working.

"You're so hot, Madelyn. So hot. Now turn on the rotation. Keep the vibration level where it is."

Breathlessly I whispered, "Ahhhllright . . ."

I really needed to take my mind off things—a situation I'd been finding myself in with greater frequency—so I surrendered to him, even if it was over the phone. I gave up the last bit of me that I'd been holding back, not that it had been much. It was just sort of weird to not be doing this in person, particularly with someone who I hadn't had actual sex with.

But, as previously noted, I'd reached a point in my life that if a reasonably suitable guy looked at me right, something could happen. I really didn't hold out much hope anymore for *the* right guy, who also believed I was *the* right girl, to show up, meet each others' critical criteria and give each other the happy ever after. I just wanted a happy hour here or there.

"Listen to you. You're a real screamer, aren't you? I can hear you all the way over here in West Hollywood."

"Yeah? You . . . don't . . . know . . . that," I managed to say, moving the bunny further up my purring pussy. "Ahhh!" Sometimes I amazed myself.

"That's it. I can picture you—all moist and ready. Almost like the real thing, huh?"

"Mmmm, no, but . . . oh, it's good. Don't stop."

"Do you want me to come over? Or do you just want to come?"

"There's no time, I'm . . ."

"You're close aren't you?"

"Keep going, don't stop."

"I can be over there pretty fast. It's not rush hour."

"Mmmm, not fast. *Really* good. *Oh!*"

"Do you want me to come?"

"I like you talking to me."

"I like to talk to you. I like talking to you like this. And I loved meeting you, kissing you in the tapas bar, I was so turned on. I wanted to take you right there."

"Mmm, yeah. Those booths were sexy."

"And then that guy you knew came in and spoiled the mood."

"*Shhhh.* Don't *you* spoil the mood."

"No, we don't want to do that. You feel good, baby? Is that bunny rabbit taking care of you?"

Cullen didn't sound stupid saying baby either.

The Rabbit was moving in and out, then I let it rest inside, the little bunny ears pressed up against my clit and I could feel the orgasm churning deep inside me, threatening to blow. "Oh, yeah."

"You're so hot, baby. Don't stop. You sure you don't want me to come over?"

There was no stopping now. I'd reached the point of no return. "Oh, yeah!"

"You want me to come over?"

"I want you to . . . I want to . . . Oh, God."

"What do you want? You want me to come over there and take you and make you scream?"

"Oh, my—I'm—I want to—"

I can't think straight during sex. For me, that's most of the appeal.

His voice urged me on, so sexy, adding to my pleasure. But I couldn't tell if he was getting any himself.

"You want to what?" he asked, drawing it out of me. "Tell me what you want."

"I want to— I want— Oh, I'm going to . . . *come*—"

I screamed out a couple more times and felt my body twitch involuntarily for those many lovely seconds when all is release and nothing matters. Then all is warmth and glow.

"Wow."

"Yeah, wow," Cullen said. "You did that all by yourself, you know."

"I had a little help."

"That was all you, Madelyn. You're wild. Are you sure this is your first vibrator? You seem pretty good with it."

"Yes, I'm sure. Was I really loud?"

After the case I'd tried to mediate that afternoon, I had to wonder if any of my neighbors had heard me.

"Eight on a ten scale. I wish I were there with you," he said sweetly.

"Mmmm. Maybe next time," I said, not ready to let go of the glow just yet. "That was great, Cullen. Thank you. I feel much better."

"It was my pleasure."

"Was it?"

"I'm not twenty anymore. It's no fun if it's all about me."

"You and I have an interesting relationship." We did, I thought. I'd never had another one like it.

"That's an understatement." He laughed.

I glanced at my watch. "Shit, I've gotta go."

"Hey, what about me?" he demanded.

I did feel bad that there'd been no reciprocity, but hadn't I'd told him up front that I had to pick up Lila? *Why was he guilting me?* "I'm just playing with you." He *was*, too.

"I *would* like to return the favor sometime," I offered, half hoping he wouldn't hear me.

"No pressure." It seemed as though now, the passion spent, there was an awkward silence where neither of us seemed willing or brave enough to venture the suggestion that we physically get together.

"I'll call you later," I said finally. "After I talk to

Berggren's assistant and try to get Nissim's address which, and I repeat, is against my better judgment."

"Great."

Still slightly embarrassed, I thought of a whole new subject to take our minds off the unsaid. "How's your mother doing?" Even though the woman had been hostile to me, it did seem polite to ask.

"Pretty well, thanks," Cullen said. "A lot better. Her doctor told her the cancer was in remission, which kind of shocked her, I think. So she just left yesterday for a cruise up the Nile with a college friend and fellow cancer survivor from Smith."

"That's great." There was another healthy pause so I continued, "I mean it *is* great, isn't it?"

There came a silence during which I considered whether or not he would have preferred her to actually die. Finally he said, "Yes, I mean, of course it's great. But it *was* a pretty sudden turnaround—for me, I mean. And then she announced she wanted to see the Pyramids before she died. She was going to buy me a ticket to go along, but I really need to stay here and get my life in order."

To my relief, he was talking about his mother in a different tone of voice than the one he'd been using bringing me to orgasm, which is, of course, as it should be when a man talks about his mother.

"It *is* one of those places we're all supposed to see before we die," I said in support. "I don't know about you, but I haven't seen much on that list—The Grand Canyon. New Orleans."

"Not on the list," he said.

"Should be, shouldn't it? Even after Katrina."

"The weird thing is," he went on, "I can't remember my mother ever telling me she wanted to see the Pyramids. She tells me everything. You'd think that would be something she'd mention."

I wasn't sure how to respond because I felt an instinctual awareness that there was something slightly off about Cullen's relationship with his mother. His tone of voice sounded more like that of a jilted lover than a son.

"Well," I said, "thanks again. You made my day."

After we hung up I lay there for a few more seconds, thinking about the extremes of cancer and self-stimulation. Maybe they weren't opposites. As I've said, the older I get and the more experiences I have, the less I'm sure about anything. Or maybe it's that I know more, but it's about less of what really matters.

If anyone had told me back in my thirties that I would one day be so easy to arouse, I wouldn't have believed it was possible—by *any* guy, with or without mother issues. And if anyone had told me I'd become the kind of woman who could be satisfied with the little gifts life handed to me, I wouldn't have believed that either. Generally, I find these days that I'm filled with gratitude for what I *do* have and I've stopped moaning about what I don't. But there was no more time for philosophy. Lila had a volleyball tournament.

CHAPTER 29

"Thor?" I said into the phone upon hearing a man pick up at Berggren's house.

"This is Nestor." *No wonder he didn't sound like Thor.*

"Hi, Nestor," I said. "I don't think we've met. This is Madelyn Scott-Crane calling. I'm a friend of Berggren's."

"Oh hello, Madelyn," said Nestor, dripping with the superior attitude of the insecure.

"I need to get some contact information from Berggren, if that's possible." I was secretly hoping Berggren hadn't yet returned from New York and that he'd not been instructed to keep people's contact info private. All he needed to do was type Nissim or ZsaZsi into the big database and I'd have what I needed.

"That won't be possible," Nestor said. "Berggren is very protective of her list, as you must know."

"Yes, but this isn't a celebrity actor's information I'm after, if that's what you're worried about," I said. "This is just the guy who's engaged to Berggren's producing partner. I think he's in real estate. You must know ZsaZsi—"

"Of course. But I'm afraid I've been instructed not to give out any information of any kind, except the dates of upcoming Spoken Word events."

"I see," I said. "Nestor, are you new?" His silence told me I'd assessed the situation correctly. "Is Thor in?" I continued, thinking that by asking for a more senior member of the staff I could guilt Nestor into giving me what I wanted.

"No. He had to—"

"Who's that on the telephone, Nestor?" a voice demanded. I identified the timbre and vocal characteristics as those of the mighty Norseman, the blonde and beautiful Thor.

Nestor hesitated. "It's a friend of Berggren's."

"Well . . . who?"

Someone covered the mouthpiece and all I heard for several seconds were garbled sounds. Then, "'Allo, Madelyn," Thor said. "How's it going, *yah?*"

"Thor," I said, trying to sound as cheery as I could without sounding sappy. "I'm fine. How are you? Nice to hear your voice."

"I'm good, thanks, yah. What can I help you with? Berggren won't be back until late tonight."

"Well, I'm trying to find out the address of ZsaZsi's fiancé. I can't remember his name," I lied.

"Of course. You mean Nissim, yah?"

"Yes, that's it. Nissim."

"So sorry, Madelyn. I can't do that. Besides we don't have it."

"Shoot," I said, already armed and ready for the next line of attack. "You see, I wanted to send them an engagement gift."

"Oh gee," said Thor, sounding stumped. "An engagement gift. Yah, that's different, I think. Hold on."

He put me on hold. I don't know what he thought I was going to do with the address anyway. It wasn't exactly saleable to the guys who hand out maps of Hollywood so tourists can drive around to celebrities' homes.

Thor came back on the line. "Here is ZsaZsi's post office box: four-zero-five-six, Beverly Hills nine-o-two-one-o."

A post office box is useless. "Don't you think it's kind of impersonal sending an engagement gift to a PO box?" I asked as mournfully as I could.

"Yah, but so sorry, Madelyn, that's all we have here," Thor said. "Maybe Berggren can get you the street address, but at the moment she is somewhere over Nebraska, maybe."

His sing-songy accent was lulling me to torpor when I heard him blurt out, "I know what you can do!"

I waited for him to tell me what had sparked his *ah-ha* moment.

"Why don't you bring the gift on Saturday?" he asked. "They will be here for the dinner party, yah."

"Really? What a good idea," I said. It wasn't a good idea, really, but it was at least a workable idea: I'd arrive at Berggren's early, find out the actual address and then call Cullen and Jelicka. Based on the zip code of Nissim and ZsaZsi's PO box they could live anywhere. But I seemed to remember they lived in the Hollywood hills. And knowing what traffic was like between the hills and Mar Vista, after they left their place for Berggren's, there'd be plenty of time for Cullen and Jelicka to snoop around while we were all partying. I thanked Thor for his brilliant suggestion and hung up.

CHAPTER 30

"So—" I began, coming into the upstairs hall bathroom as Lila began rinsing the green soapy avocado cleanser from her face. The bathroom, which had been done in shades of orange and peach, was in dire need of redecorating. *What had I been thinking when I chose those colors?* It must have been right before the divorce when I wasn't really thinking straight. "What's going on at school?"

We'd had our dinner—frozen Mandarin Orange Chicken from Trader Joe's—during which time I'd kept the discussion topics to ballet, her recent disappointing "C" in math and what we might do for summer vacation. Of course, I just wanted to come out and ask her how my vibrator got into her bedside table, but I had to wait for the right opportunity.

"What do you mean, what's going on at school? It's school, Mom." She had her long blonde hair tied in a loose knot on top of her head and it wobbled there, threatening to come undone whenever she moved.

"Yes, I know it's school, but what's going on with your friends? What's going on in PE? That kind of thing."

"Nothing," she said. "More girls have obvious pubic hair, maybe. Is that what you want to know?"

This wasn't my idea of easing into it. I handed her a décor-appropriate orange towel and she began drying her face. "Any problems with your teachers? How's Mr. Rodriguez these days?"

Mr. Rodriguez, Lila's social studies teacher, had a reputation for belittling everyone in ninth grade for being uninformed about history. It was true they were uninformed, but he was probably overly optimistic thinking he could improve Americans' awareness of world history by criticizing the country's hormonally challenged teens. The truth was, the average American didn't care about history.

"He doesn't bother us anymore. We reported him."

"Ah." I *had* encouraged her to be assertive, but I didn't like the sound of this. "How did you do that?"

"Linda, Savannah, Kim and me—"

"Linda, Savannah, Kim and *I*—"

While hanging the towel back on the ceramic towel bar, her fourteen-year-old face revealed feelings of boredom, intolerance and disgust, which consisted of rolling her eyes, puffing up her cheeks then dropping her jaw as she let out an unnecessarily dramatic sigh.

"Linda, Savannah, Kim and *I* walked into Principal Jenner's office and said Mr. Rodriguez was acting inappropriately toward us."

Now I really didn't like the sound of this. "Was that true?" I asked with trepidation.

"Yes. I mean, I guess it's all in how you define *inappropriate*, right? He has no reason to tell us we're bad students because we don't know all the details of whatever war we happen to be talking about. That's inappropriate."

"But the word inappropriate suggests something different," I said. "It's not a word one uses lightly— especially when you're talking about a male teacher and a group of young female students."

"I know," she retorted. "That's exactly why we used it. Principal Jenner probably wouldn't have told him to shape up if we said he was being mean because we couldn't remember which century World War II was in or something, so we did what we had to do to protect ourselves."

"But he also has a reputation that *he* has to protect. And he has a family. What will his wife think? Lila, you don't want to be one of those women who makes accusations when they're not true."

"Why not?"

This couldn't be *my* daughter talking. *My* daughter had more integrity.

"Because they're not true, that's why," I stuttered. It was difficult to believe that, despite her youth, Lila couldn't grasp the seriousness of her offense. "And because . . . because you don't hurt people like that—especially when it's a lie. It was the wrong thing to do."

She shrugged. "But for the right reasons."

"No, it wasn't. You *should* know when World War II was."

"Well, whatever... he's a lot nicer now—to everyone. So it worked." She made a move to exit the bathroom, but I blocked the door.

"Ends don't always justify the means, young lady, and I'm going to call Linda's mother tomorrow to discuss this."

"No," she whined. "Don't."

"Don't you say 'don't' to me. I am the parent here and you are the child."

Then I lost my patience with her. Maybe I'd lost patience with myself as well. Lila was her own person—I had to remember that— but she was still my daughter and living under my roof, which gave me permission to complain about her bad behavior. It never would have crossed my mind to be so manipulative. I also liked to think none of the women I knew could behave in such a way. That said, I realize there are plenty of women, probably many whom I knew—even women in the Muffia—who would do this kind of thing and worse to get what they wanted. It just wasn't the kind of behavior I wanted to encourage in my daughter. Well, I'd made my point and I'd continue to work on her, but at that moment, there were other issues I needed to deal with.

"We'll see. I'm very angry with you right now and I want to sleep on it. But I'm still going to be angry in the morning."

"I know when World War II was, in case you want to know."

Then she gave me the kind of smile that told me she was already far more skilled than I'd ever been, or ever *would* be at manipulation. I didn't have time. I was tired and I wanted to get to the point—why was my vibrator in her drawer? Still, I tried to segue into it.

"Is there a boy you're interested in?"

She sucked her teeth and sat down on the toilet lid. "No, Mom. Just like there wasn't a boy I was interested in last week or the week before. What are you fishing for?"

"I'm just curious about whether there's a boy in your life."

"No. There's no boy," she huffed. "I should never have told you about Amy Villetta giving a blow job to that tenth grader at Claremont. Then you wouldn't be hounding me like this."

"I'm not hounding you." Glimpses of similar conversations I'd had with my own mother came flooding back, though none had been about blow jobs. Neither would I believe Mother ever owned a vibrator. Nor, if she had, that I would have borrowed it.

"Things aren't like they were when I was fourteen," I went on, "I realize that. Kids are exposed to more, earlier in their lives, and they grow up a lot faster. That's really what I wanted to talk to you about."

"Mom, we've already talked about this."

"Listen, you—*I'm your mother.*"

She gave me her best glower. "*Really?*" Sarcasm dripped. No one's better at it than the teenage girl.

"Yes, *really*. Like it or not," I went on. "And I'm going to *continue* to talk to you about sex as much as I want to because it's important and I don't want you, you know, making a mistake and getting in trouble."

Again she rolled her blue eyes as she pulled the knot out of her hair, letting it fall over her shoulders. Her freshly washed face glowed with youthful beauty. Any mother would be terrified of such a girl being taken advantage of, though I realize her personality had already shown itself as one not to be toyed with.

I was trying to be cool. Not fourteen cool. I was aiming for around twenty: young enough to be listened to, but old enough to have some authority. As far as she was concerned, at forty-two I was practically dead. I wanted her to trust me and listen, but I had to establish some kind of a parental line at the same time.

"You're at the age when boys will try to get in your pants—plain and simple. When you get to be my age the situation gets reversed."

"Huh?"

"Never mind about that. But boys *will* try to get in your pants, if they haven't already. It's normal. And with your looks, I'd say you can count on it."

"I'm not really interested in boys yet, Mom. I've told you that. I'm still into sports."

"OK. Well, let's just have this little discussion before you need to, then. You must be curious about sex—birds and bees, that kind of thing." I thought I was doing a pretty good job of keeping up a casual yet upbeat demeanor.

"Can we talk about it tomorrow? I'm kinda tired and I want to go to sleep." Lila yawned and got to her feet.

Realizing I was still standing in the doorway, I moved aside to allow her to pass then followed her into her bedroom, where I conveniently needed to be for Act II of the sex discussion: The dildo in the drawer scene.

She pulled the covers back and began to climb into her princess bed—painted pastel yellow and white, with the pink duvet decorated with yellow flowers—while I, meanwhile, opened the drawer of the bedside table and pulled out the Rabbit.

"There it is. I've been looking for this," I said, trying to sound surprised, not angry. "What's this doing in your bedside table?"

Flipping around she saw what was in my hand and the rosy color drained from her face as she gasped.

"Lila? How did this get in here?" I asked again, still maintaining my upbeat, non-accusatory tone.

"I—"

"You . . . what?"

"Remember when Kim came over and spent the night and you went out?"

I did remember. It had been the week before when I'd left them alone while I went out with the scheduling coordinator for a mediation group. "Yes."

"Well," she went on, "we were in your room... trying on your shoes and stuff..."

"You're not supposed to be doing that."

"I know. Sorry."

"Why do you say you're sorry when you're not at all sorry?" I said, then stopped myself from going further. "Forget it. Go on."

"OK, so she was sitting on the floor and she saw this box under your bed and she asked me what it was so, I, like, looked under the bed and I didn't know what it was, so... so then we pulled it out and opened it."

"And—"

"And then we found that."

I scanned her face. She *appeared* to be telling the truth. "OK," I said. "So how did it get into your room? Why didn't you just leave it in the box?"

"Well, because we knew what it was and we wanted to see how it worked. So we brought it in here and just turned it on and off...you know? Watching it."

Sounds semi-believable.

She had propped herself up on a couple of pillows encased in linens featuring intertwined cats and dogs and wasn't looking at me. I was sure there was something she was leaving out. "You just turned it on and off."

"Yeah. And we laughed."

"You laughed."

"It was funny."

I glanced at the purple vibrator with the little rabbit face and little rabbit ears and fake pearls around the middle. "Yeah. I guess it is."

I sat down on the bed and placed my hand on one of her legs, both of which were tucked under the duvet. "Did you try it?" I asked.

Her face contorted into one of total disgust. "*Ewww,* nooo. . . ," she squealed.

"It's OK if you did," I said calmly. "You're a little young, but it's not weird or anything."

"*Are-you-kidding-me?* That thing is huge! And it's *gross.* Totally, totally gross. Look at it. *Oh-my-god, oh-my-god.*"

Still holding the Rabbit, I tried to assess it with a fourteen-year-old's eyes. It was odd-looking, particularly for a girl growing up an only child of a single mother who didn't have many opportunities to see a real penis, but it didn't look *that* huge. At that point Stipple jumped up onto the bed and licked the Rabbit.

"Stipple, that's nasty," said Lila, laughing as I shooed the cat away. "No, Mom. I definitely did *not* try it. And neither did Kim. We turned it on and off and watched it wiggle and stuff, but I mean, really? No. That thing is just plain scary-gross. I don't think I'm ever going to have sex. How can you stick it inside you?"

How was I to give an honest answer to this question? I'm not one to sugar coat the truth for anyone. "Well, honey, it's like you said in the car the other day—grown-ups have sex. I guess when they don't have sex, this is sort of a safe substitute."

"Why do you, like, even want a substitute?" She was staring at me open-mouthed, clearly appalled.

"We don't need to talk about this anymore," I said, patting her leg. "I just thought that since it was in your drawer maybe there was something you might want to tell me."

"Nothing. *Really*, Mom. I'm serious."

"Because even if there's nothing you want to tell me right now, there may be something you want to tell me soon and I want you to feel you can talk to me."

"I know. I do. I'm just sleepy now."

"You're just at that age when . . ."

She shook her head vehemently. "There's nothing to tell. I'm serious. I'll tell you when there is, Mom. Promise. And I'm sorry I took that thing. I really am. I just forgot to put it back."

"OK," I said. *What more was there to say at that point?* She and I had a good relationship, I thought, for mom and adolescent, hormone-riddled daughter. I wanted to believe her. But even if she were telling the truth, there would always be secrets and always be issues— like the incident with the Social Studies teacher, Mr. Rodriguez. I leaned down to kiss her goodnight.

"Sleep tight," I said standing up, Rabbit in hand.

I was about to turn off the poodle lamp on the bedside table when she asked, "Hey, what happened to that guy you were talking to on the phone? Wasn't he going to come for a visit or something?"

She'd finally asked me about Udi and for some reason I felt a sharp pain in my chest.

"Yes."

"So . . . did he?"

"Yes. He did."

"And—?"

"And we had a nice time together."

"Well, that's good, I guess," she said, making an effort. "Is he still here? You know, in California?"

"No. No, he's not." We were getting dangerously close to my having to decide if I should continue with the truth.

"Is he coming back? You seemed to really like him. Where's he from again?"

"He's from Israel and, um, no honey—I'm pretty sure he won't be coming back." I felt my throat tighten, surprising myself that I'd get choked up at this point. I sat back down on the bed.

"Why not?" She yawned, trying to hide it.

"Well—" I looked into her eyes, drooping but filled with concern, and I couldn't think of a lie that wouldn't come back to haunt me in one way or another; nor could I tell her the whole truth. So I deflected.

OK, so maybe I was being a little overprotective. But the day was right around the corner when I would no longer be able to shield her from life's cruel realities. This was one I didn't have to share. She was going to be fifteen in two months and that was plenty soon enough to warn her about the possibility of a guy dying on her during sex. Come to think of it, I'll most likely delay that indefinitely.

She yawned again. "So why isn't he coming back?"

"Family commitments and government regulations and that kind of thing," I told her.

"Ohhh." Her eyes were just slits by this point, her head deep into the pillow.

"Yeah, so that's kind of sad, but maybe it's for the best. He wasn't geographically desirable anyway."

"Oh," she yawned and turned on her side.

No, poor Udi certainly wasn't *geographically desirable any more.*

I could tell by the sound of her breathing that Lila had fallen asleep, stuffed poodle under her arm and Stipple, purring blissfully, at the foot of her bed.

CHAPTER 31

"Why are you so interested in whether Nissim is still an assassin?" Berggren asked the day of her dinner party, as together we secured the large round table top and dressed it with a black tablecloth and white napkins.

"I'm not *so* interested. I'm just asking." *Clearly I wasn't doing a great job of covering my curiosity.*

"Well, I can tell you, ZsaZsi simply would not marry a working killer. Trust me on that. He's completely committed to real estate."

"But if he *were* still a Mossad assassin, like you said he once was, that wouldn't exactly be something one goes around advertising, now would it?" I tried to keep the tone conversational so as not to alert her to my ulterior motive. "Nor is it something one easily gives up. You think the Jackal or any other hired killer walks away from that kind of work and lives? Too many skeletons."

She shrugged. "Ask him."

Finished with *that* topic, she walked to the laminated sideboard, picked up a black and white wire sculpture featuring those terminally happy and sad Commedia Del Arte characters, and placed it in the center of the table. She stood back to admire it and I thought I saw her face go from happy to sad to happy in the course of a second and a half.

Turning to me she said, "I'm waiting for a call from Toni Collette's agent. Can you man the phones while I'm in the shower?"

"They're going to call on a Saturday?"

"These people are insane. They never stop working. Just tell him I'm talking to Jude Law on the other line and that I'll have to call him back." Then she turned toward her bedroom.

"Hey, wait!" Jude Law was one movie star I'd really like to talk to—actually, more than talk to. "Have you really spoken to Jude Law?"

She smiled lasciviously, starting to undress. "I've seen him naked."

"Really? Berggren, your life is just too shockingly rich. He's gorgeous!"

"You should see his body. He's a god." She raised her eyebrows as she cocked her head, suggesting that she had a slough of stories she could share if so inclined. Not many of my friends got to see nude male movie stars, but given her work with celebrities, Berggren was one who could.

Then she turned on her heel once more, saying, "It was in a play but so what?"

"Berggren!" I said, disappointed. I was annoyed because she'd destroyed my vicarious thrill as fast as she'd created it.

"I take my excitement wherever I can get it, Doll. His body was worth the Broadway ticket price, I'll tell you that. He walked down this long stairway really, really slowly so everyone could get a real… *good…* look." We sighed in unison then she winked and disappeared behind the door to her suite, leaving me to sigh alone.

I'd gone to Berggren's early on the pretext of helping her get ready. I would have helped her anyway, but the real reason was that I needed to find Nissim's and/or ZsaZsi's physical address so I could alert Cullen. I'd decided that not telling Jelicka was the way to go, but she'd remembered that Berggren was having her party that night and had been bothering me to get the address. I planned on avoiding her calls for as long as I could, then telling her I couldn't find it.

I'd brought Lila along because I couldn't get a babysitter and Lila's dad was busy with a Republican fundraiser—his politics being one of the many issues in our marriage that I'd found to be an obstacle to maintaining intimacy. Fortunately, Lila and Berggren's identical twins, Sadie and Mavis—often reduced to Say and May,were all friends and only a year apart, Sadie and Mavis being the younger.

When Berggren went off to shower, the three girls were playing Canadian doubles badminton on the ten-foot by ten-foot patch of grass that Berggren referred to as the back forty inches. Through the sliding glass doors that ran along one side of the living room, I watched the shuttlecock hurtling back and forth while appreciating the view— that *poquito* Mar Vista of the ocean. Berggren had instructed the girls to take the net down and put it away, but clearly that hadn't happened yet. I moved toward the glass doors to remind them, but before I got there, Berggren's voice boomed out from her remodeled bathroom window, "Say-May—that net needs to come down!"

"OK, Mom. We heard you the first ten times," one of them yelled back.

"I shouldn't have to *tell* you ten times." Berggren said *this* sentence as if she often had to say it. I could relate. If there's one thing about mothering that I don't like, it's feeling like a nag. Why is it necessary to say, "Please remove your dirty sneakers from the counter" more than once?

"All right, I'll take it down—*geez*!" Sadie stomped around the yard. She was as dramatic as her mother, while Mavis, a math geek, said, "Told you," to her sister.

By this point, I was outside and facing a partially-naked Berggren through the open bathroom window. "Take a shower," I said. "I'll deal with it."

"They never listen."

The window slammed shut and I turned to the girls and said, as firmly as I could while still smiling, "Ladies, this is the first and only time I'm going to say this. Pack it up and put it away and I'll be back in ten minutes."

Thus came my opportunity to find Nissim and ZsaZsi's address. I walked back into the house casually but with purpose and, once inside, I dashed into Berggren's office and woke up her computer. Staring at me was Berggren's open contact database and probably more than I wanted to know about Toni Collette and her agent.

Moving toward the door, I listened for approaching steps—nothing. Where was the mighty Thor? Where was newbie Nestor? I didn't have time to wonder. I could faintly make out the sounds of the shower and teenage voices. Returning to the computer I typed "ZsaZsi" and, faster than you can say "badminton net down," up popped ZsaZsi Sullivan and Nissim Ben Gurvitz. It *was* in the hills—2561 Lookout Lane, Hollywood, along with more phone numbers than one couple should have.

Then there was a noise—*a door?* I quickly noted the information on an envelope rescued from the recycling bin and stuffed it in my tiny front pants pocket. Coming out of the office as casually as I could, I almost collided with Mavis, who looked past me into the empty office.

"Hi," I said. "All set?"

Mavis shrugged. "It's put away if that's what you're asking."

Lila and Sadie stepped up beside her. "I told you Berggren was a little weird," said Lila.

"She's not weird. She asked the girls to do

something and was upset when it didn't happen. You know how *I* get when I have to repeat myself."

"You're a nag."

"That's right. I'm a nag and I don't like being a nag and Berggren doesn't either."

"She's still weird," Mavis said. "She's weird *and* crazy. Probably borderline neurotic."

If Sadie had said it, I would wonder if she really knew what she was saying but Mavis, I suspected, knew what it meant.

"She's just being Mom," said Sadie practically.

"I think it's just that your mom is having a dinner party and she wanted the yard clear of obstacles so people could be out there. Which reminds me, the guests will be getting here very soon. What are you three going to do? Can I set you up with a movie in the den?"

Lila looked at me, then at Sadie and Mavis, then back at me. "Say and May have some friends and one of them has an older sister and they're all going to the Westside Pavilion. Can I go?" Lila pleaded.

"What are you going to do there?" I asked, like any concerned parent would.

"Just walk around and stuff."

It was the *stuff* that worried me. The Westside Pavilion is one of those huge lifestyle shopping malls, one of several in greater LA filled with mostly expensive stores, where teens like to congregate to look at each other and at each others' clothes, bags, iPods and G4 mobile devices. Such expeditions often resulted in these same teens returning home with an urgent need to go shopping.

I didn't like the idea of Lila hanging out with so little constructive purpose other than to possibly stimulate sales in a down economy, but I was of the mind that if I prohibited something, the backlash could well be worse. When I was growing up, the closest mall was forty-five minutes away and there was no way my parents would drop me off to hang out with my friends. But times had definitely changed, and after the vibrator-in-the-drawer incident, I wasn't sure which way to lean.

"Hailey's sister is seventeen and she's really smart in school," offered Sadie. "She'll watch out for us."

"She's sort of smart," agreed Mavis.

I nodded, doing my best to remain open-minded yet non-committal as I considered whether a young woman's smarts could ever put a stop to any of the more horrible events I could envision. "And Hailey's sister's name is—"

"Georgia. We've gone with them before," said Sadie. "Nothing's ever happened."

It was coming back to me. Berggren had told me a few days ago that the girls might have a chance to go out. I guess I hadn't paid enough attention.

"Well, that's certainly a plus," I said.

"Our mom is totally cool with it," said Sadie. "Go ask her."

"So now your mom is cool? A minute ago she was weird and neurotic."

They stared back at me. I think they missed the sarcasm but I couldn't be sure. Plus they wanted something from me.

"She's only neurotic when she has dinner parties," said Mavis.

Which we've established was often. "All right," I said, acquiescing.

"Yeah! Thank you. Woo-hoo!" They squealed, grabbing each other's forearms and jumping up and down in unison. One would have thought they'd made it to Hollywood week on *American Idol,* the way they were carrying on.

"But please be careful and make sure you bring your cell phones. Also—and this I'm also saying only once—*all* of you must be back by ten."

They nodded vigorously.

I hoped I wasn't making a mistake, but I was always fighting my overprotective streak and, at some point, I was going to have to let it go. After all, it was only the mall. They might have wanted to go to a club on Sunset Boulevard. *Shit, why did that have to enter my mind? Now I'd worry even more.*

"And stay together," I blurted. "Close . . . together."

"We will. We'll stay *really* close together. Don't worry," Lila said, giving me a hug. "Thanks, Mom." She was still just a wisp of girl but in that hug, I felt her love and gratitude, which gave me some assurance that she appreciated the permission, maybe even trust, I'd given her, and she wouldn't abuse it.

"Hey," said Sadie. "Let's go put on some makeup."

"Oh, yeah, we are!" Lila agreed, in the way kids do that sounds grammatically incorrect.

Mavis pursed her lips. She wasn't one for makeup.

The doorbell rang and they sprinted toward the bedrooms, leaving me to answer it. I glanced at my watch. It was too early for the dinner party crowd.

"Don't worry, I'll get it," I said to anyone within earshot. Walking the length of the hallway to the front door, I opened it to Sadie and Mavis's friend and her older sister—both preternaturally tall blondes. I was pleased to see that neither appeared to be the type who might drag my daughter into the gutter.

"You must be Hailey and Georgia."

"Yes," said the older one. "You're Lila's mom?"

"I'm Hailey," said the younger one. "Hiyyee—"

Sadie, Mavis and Lila strolled into the foyer—each wearing a different top than they'd had on minutes before, Sadie carrying a large, clear plastic bag of makeup.

"That's a lot of face paint," I said, trying to sound unconcerned. They didn't *need* makeup and I didn't want them drawing any more attention to themselves than they already would.

"We don't have time to figure out what to bring so

we have to bring everything."

"See you later, Mom," said Lila, crossing the threshold.

"Ten o'clock," I said. "Georgia, you're in charge."

"Don't worry, Ms. Crane."

Then they were gone, ghosts in the dusk. Car doors opened then closed, with four distinct *wurrumph* sounds. An engine purred to life, grew louder then faded into the evening.

I was picking up the phone to call Cullen to give him Nissim's address when Berggren yelled as if she'd been stood up by her entire cast. "Maddie, I need help!"

"Coming," I yelled, putting the phone down and running to her aid. I found her, fresh out of the shower, hair dripping with a towel clutched to her breast, completely distraught. "What is it? What's wrong?"

"Where are the girls?"

I started to panic thinking I'd been duped by three late tweeners. "They left with Sadie's friend and her sister."

Berggren's face relaxed. "Oh, yeah. I forgot about that."

"That's OK, isn't it?"

"Stop worrying. You're such a worrier. But they could have at least said good-bye."

"You were in the shower."

"Right. OK. Well, can you do me a big favor? We're having salmon on cedar plank but I forgot to make the relish. We have to have that relish!"

"I can do that," I offered, once again amazed at Berggren's sense of drama. "I assume there's a special recipe?" This wouldn't be a problem. I'd make the call from the kitchen once I heard Berggren's blow dryer start up.

"*Very* special recipe," Berggren corrected. "Solomon's Salmon Solutions in the kitchen with the other cookbooks."

"Solomon's Salmon Solutions—I'm on it." Heading for the kitchen, I speculated that Solomon's Salmon Solutions was a horrible name for a cookbook and might better have been the name for a line of smelly skincare products or medicinal extracts derived from the Omega3 fatty-acid-heavy fish. Locating the cookbooks on a special shelf above the wine fridge, I pulled down Solomon's Salmon Solutions. Turning to the condiment section, I found there were seven recipes for relish.

"Berggren—!" I called. "There are seven recipes for relish. Which one do you want?"

I counted out the seconds, "One one-thousand, two one-thousand, three one-thou—"

"The one with lime and cucumber," she called back.

I looked down at the recipes again, flipping the pages quickly. Three of the recipes called for lime and cucumber. I wasn't going to be responsible for picking the wrong one.

"Berggren—! Three have lime and cucumber."

She appeared, hair combed out but still dripping, clad in a peach towel. "Lemme see. She fingered the pages and pointed. "That one." Then she disappeared again mumbling, "I don't know if it really matters."

So much for the very special recipe. Berggren cared a lot about most things but relish wasn't one of them. Lauren, who's all about the sauce and condiments, would have been appalled.

Glancing down at the recipe, I saw that in addition to the lime and cucumber, there was a very long list of ingredients. This wasn't going to be quick and Berggren still hadn't turned on the blow dryer.

I needed to call Cullen. I should have called already. He was probably waiting by the phone, desperate to get started. People would be arriving in less than half an hour and once they arrived, it might be too late to give him the time he needed to get to Nissim's house, make his way inside, look around and leave undetected. Presumably he was already in the Hollywood hills awaiting my call but I couldn't be sure. And now I realized that that was a stupid plan because cell service is spotty in the hills.

"Berggren, I need to make a call!" I yelled.

"Can you just chop the cucumber first? I'm almost done. I can whip up the rest of it while you make your call."

"Sure," I found myself saying before I realized the recipe called for the cucumber to be diced in half-centimeter squares. It could take an hour to peel the cucumbers and chop them into enough tiny pieces so that each of the guests could smother his salmon in it. And I already knew Berggren's food processor was broken.

I began peeling then chopping and I chopped and chopped and was almost done when the doorbell rang. *Shit.*

"Coming!" Berggren waltzed in wearing a fitted black dress, her eyes painted dark and glamorous and her hair slicked back into a chignon—no blow dryer required. "Can you get the door, Doll, and maybe you can wait a bit longer, until more people get here before you make your call."

"Sure," I found myself saying again. Part of me didn't want anyone I knew going to Nissim's house, so I welcomed the excuse to delay, even though delaying could potentially ruin the plan.

Going back to the living/dining area, I pulled open the door to reveal three chic people, a man and two women, none of whom I knew, all in their forties, standing on the stoop, each holding a bottle of wine.

"Hi," they said as a collective.

"Hi," I said back, ushering them into the room, taking their wine and helping them off with their various jackets and wraps.

Berggren flitted in from the kitchen and gave the

woman with the low-cut blouse and beautiful breasts a hug. "Daphne!" she exclaimed. Then she hugged "Esther" and "Samuel" in turn. "Thanks for coming. This is one of my oldest, bestest friends, Madelyn."

"Hi," everyone said again, adding things like, "nice to meet you," "pleasure," "traffic was terrible," "pretty outfit," and other similar pleasantries of the kind exchanged upon meeting someone for the first time.

I actually didn't want to get too deep into an interesting conversation because I still needed to sneak off and make the call, but as if reading my mind, Berggren said, "Maddie, could you get everybody a glass of wine? I'm still working on the *magic.*"

"Sure," I said again. "This way, everyone."

Heading back to Berggren's large gourmet kitchen, I poured wine for the recent arrivals and a small glass for myself. I needed a little help in handling the mounting stress I was feeling at not being able to call Cullen.

As soon as I'd had a few good swallows and had started to breathe easier, I noticed Berggren was chopping and stirring—already deep in conversation with Daphne, while Esther and Samuel were similarly engaged in the breakfast nook under the steady gaze of one of Warhol's Marilyns. This was my opportunity to sneak away unnoticed. Then the doorbell rang again.

"I'll get it," I said, once again heading for the front door. As I pulled it open, I found I didn't know this attractive couple either.

"Hi, hi, hi," we all said. *There is a certain predictability to these things.*

"Berggren and a few other guests are in the kitchen having wine," I said gesturing in the general direction of wafting aromas and conversation. "Go ahead and join them and I'll be in in a few minutes."

The couple had no sooner thanked me and sauntered off, than I was out of the front hall and into the bathroom, dialing Cullen's number. "Twenty-five sixty-one Lookout Lane," I said in a loud whisper when he picked up.

"I was getting worried. What took you?"

"This is the first time I could sneak away to call."

"It's seven-thirty already. Are Nissim and his girlfriend there yet?"

"No. But people are starting to arrive so they should be here pretty soon. Where are you?"

"About half an hour out, I think, but you know Hollywood traffic on Saturday night."

I did know. "Yeah."

My phone did its little double xylophone ding thing, which tells me there's a new text message. I took the phone away from my ear and saw the text was from Jelicka.

"So, I guess that's it then," I said to Cullen. "Anything else?"

"Nope. Can't think of anything," he replied cheerfully. "Tally-ho."

"Good luck and be careful and *please* make sure no one's in the house before you go in." *One would have thought that went without saying.*

"I thought I'd wait until they come back from the party and ring the bell, actually."

"You're not serious," I said.

"I'll just say I was lost or had the wrong house. But I could have a look at them and maybe decide whether you and your friend Jelicka are out of your minds."

"Right." I drew out my sarcasm, wishing I'd never agreed to tell him.

"I'll keep you posted." He rang off.

Jelicka's text should have been expected: *I'm at Hollywood Costume—need to get something to wear. Possibly going as stripper or homeless woman.*

What? I had to call her. But she didn't pick up. I called twice. Any minute someone would knock on the door. "You don't need to get something to wear," I said to her voice mail.

She was treating this whole spy/counterspy thing like a movie in which she was not only the featured player, but also costume designer. She was going to what I considered to be unnecessary lengths—truly unnecessary since I had no intention of giving her the address. Then again, perhaps this costume enterprise would keep her busy and she'd lose track of time. "Get the homeless woman outfit," I said, amending my message, "or the stripper. I mean, either could be good. And why not try on others?"

I hung up feeling pleased that Jelicka didn't know Nissim's address, nor had she asked.

"Please, Jelicka—" I begged out loud, *Don't call me.*

Crack-crack-crack! "Maddie, are you in there?" It was Berggren knocking on the bathroom door and talking in a hushed voice.

"Almost done," I responded.

"Hurry up. Someone out here I want you to meet." It sounded like her lips were literally on the crack in the door. "He's really hot."

"OK," I said. "Out in a sex—I mean sec."

My cell phone rang. Cullen again.

"Did you say twenty-six fifty-one Lookout Lane?"

I looked down at the address still in my hand. "Twenty-*five sixty*-one."

"I knew that," he said. "I just wanted to hear your voice one more time in case they've booby-trapped the house and I'm blown to smithereens."

"Cullen, you know, on second thought, I don't think this is a good idea."

"Ten-four. Too late."

"Then don't stay too long."

"Aye-aye, Cap'n."

"And don't forget to wear gloves."

"Yah-*voll.*"

"And if you move things, they're going to know. So put them back."

"Will do."

"Please, will you take this seriously?" He was making me laugh.

"Don't worry your purty head about me, li'l girl. You have fun at your party." Then he was gone. Maybe gridlock would keep him from getting there.

I stuck the address in my purse along with my cell phone and opened the bathroom door. Across the living room, up against the sliding glass doors, I spotted Berggren talking to a handsome guy with prematurely gray hair. He *was* kind of hot.

"Madelyn," Berggren called, beckoning me over with outstretched arm. The man standing next to her, calm and very cool, was about six-two and almost too perfect- looking. His hair was thick with multiple color shades ranging from light gray to black and his teeth were sparkling white and even. He was wearing a starched white shirt, no tie, and an expensive-looking sports jacket. Guys who look and dress like him don't usually go for me. I'm a little too eclectic. I find guys like this one want a woman who's the female version of them only more submissive. I can only play that role about one-tenth of the time. But perhaps, despite his perfect exterior, his inner life was interestingly imperfect—like mine.

"Rex, this is my dear, dear friend Madelyn," said Berggren. "We've been friends for twenty-two years."

"Hello," I said, extending my hand the way I always do when meeting someone new, hoping to convey an interesting blend of intelligence, warmth and self-possession. I knew I looked pretty good that night. I was wearing an updated halter-top and unusually trendy pants (for me) that flattered my curves and de-emphasized the bulges. I'd curled my usually straight, boring hair into cascading curls, which framed my face, and the overall effect took five years off my age—or so I thought.

"Very pleased to meet you," said Rex with his own

blend of intelligence, warmth and self-possession.

And he had an accent. Uh-oh, this could be dangerous. I'd learned I had a weakness for accents.

"Rex is from the British production company," said Berggren. "He's here helping us line up some strong actors for one of my new movies."

"Fantastic."

"Maddie is a mediator, lawyer and she has a daughter a year older than Say and May. They'll all be back in a couple of hours. So," she went on, "talk amongst yourselves. Dinner is just moments away."

Berggren moved off, in her element, chatting with people as she went, making all of her fourteen or so guests feel at ease. Looking around, I noticed that neither ZsaZsi nor Nissim was present and I made a mental note to call Cullen if they hadn't arrived in another fifteen minutes.

"So what does a mediator *do* in America exactly?" Rex asked, drawing my attention back to him.

"Well," I began, "a mediator is an unbiased third party who helps people solve disputes. Isn't that what they do in England?"

"We don't have disputes in England." He said this with utmost seriousness, smug as a character in "Downton Abbey."

"What a lovely, idyllic existence it must be for all of you there." He flashed a smile and I got the very clear impression that he was accustomed to having it work on the female of the species.

"I love London but it rains too bloody much."

"Hmmm . . . I like the rain," I countered. "I'm from the east coast—of America, that is. Here, it's too bloody sunny all the time, if you ask me."

"Well, who asked you?"

Now it was my turn to smile. Rex seemed playful and sexy, even funny. In my experience this was surprising for a guy with his looks. He also had an air of legitimacy about him and was more age-appropriate than most of the men I found myself attracted to. We probably could have had a very good time together, though I wondered for a few seconds why Berggren wasn't interested in him for herself. But I was distracted and not really into whatever game Rex and I could have been playing.

"Would you excuse me a moment?" I asked. "I'm sorry. I'd like to continue this conversation about rain and the dearth of arguments in your country—I'm not just saying that. But I have something I have to do."

"Far be it from me to keep a lady from doing what needs to be done," he said with a slight bow. *What play was he doing? One I was pretty sure I didn't want to be in.*

Before I'd gone very far, Berggren called, "Dinner everybody," and I saw her, along with the diaphanous Daphne, depositing platters of food in the center of the table. There was still no sign of Nissim or ZsaZsi.

"I thought Nissim and ZsaZsi were coming," I said to Berggren cheerily, catching up with her in the kitchen to carry more food to the table.

"He sent a text saying they couldn't make it. ZsaZsi doesn't feel well or something." Then she leaned in and whispered, "Since when do assassins take care of their women like *that*? Hmmm?" She glanced over to the living room where Rex was holding court with a couple of the other guests. "He likes you."

Regardless of Rex's level of interest or what an assassin with a sick fiancée might or might not do, I had to stop Cullen from going to the house. Placing two bright orange bowls filled with fish relish on the table, I picked up my bag and headed back to the bathroom.

"Abort, abort," I said into the phone.

But it was only voice mail. Why wasn't he picking up? I hit *end* and redialed. Surely he wouldn't have left the phone in his car. He probably just turned it off so as not to give himself away if it rang. Then again, maybe he was in one of those spotty cell service areas.

"A-b-o-r-t m-i-s-s-i-o-n," I typed a text. Surely this will get through, I thought, as I sent the text into the ether, then stared at the screen willing it to respond. "Acknowledge," I texted as an afterthought.

Jelicka still hadn't made contact. Perhaps she'd really gotten into a shopping frenzy at Hollywood Costume. In any event, I wasn't going to call her.

Sounds of the dinner party filtered through the bathroom door. I heard plates and silverware doing their dinner dance. I'd better get back there, but I needed to keep my phone close by. My pants were too tight to stick the phone into, so in order not to miss a call, I'd just keep the phone on vibrate and hold it on my lap.

Returning to the table, I found that Rex was seated next to me and I was happy to resume our flirtatious conversation, despite being distracted by international espionage. We talked about how expensive London was, how globalization really hadn't improved the lives of most people, Shakespeare, the decline of the English language and American versus British childrearing practices, among other things.

What I really wanted to do was get up and leave the dinner party—to drive to Lookout Lane and do... I had no idea what I'd do. Instead I made the effort to keep up with Rex and his sparkling wit, continuing to hope Cullen would call or text. I couldn't take off yet anyway. Lila wasn't back from the mall. Then I had a panic attack. Could Jelicka have talked to Cullen? Could she have found out the address some other way?

Rex must have thought I was a ditz. But then perhaps that made him feel comfortable. He'd probably met his share of ditzes, given his line of work and exposure to actresses —a section of the female population whom, in the course of our witty repartee, he said he'd sworn off.

He was polite, though, and never made me feel as

dumb as toast. The sad thing was he could have been a good match for me. Our meeting suffered from bad timing—the opposite of how it had been for Udi and me. On any other evening, Rex was the kind of guy I would have made an effort to get to know better, even though I could tell he'd be no vacation in a relationship. This guy would require me to stay on my toes—confuse La Rochefoucauld with Verlaine? No mercy.

I still hadn't heard from Cullen or Jelicka by the time we'd cleared away the dinner plates and the front door opened to reveal Lila, Sadie, Mavis, Hailey and Georgia, who had changed into a different outfit than she'd had on when they left. Instead of preppy, she now looked like a demure version of Lady Gaga, if such a thing were possible. So much for keeping a low profile.

"You're back," exclaimed Berggren. "How was it?"

"Well, it was, you know, the *mall*," said Georgia, elongating the word for a full three seconds. "But it was OK."

Behind Georgia's back, Sadie, Mavis and Lila gave us thumbs-up signs indicating that for them the mall was still pretty cool.

Glancing at Rex, I found him to be visibly salivating over the young beauties. *I knew there had to be something wrong with him.* I didn't need a guy with a Lolita complex—that was for sure — even if I suffered from the female strain of the condition. I consoled myself with the thought that I was at least aware of my hypocrisy.

Just then my thighs vibrated—not that wascally-wabbit kind of vibration, or even the Aphroditty, but the kind that happens when the mobile-wedged-between-your-legs-so-you-won't-miss-it goes off.

I practically jumped out of my seat, excusing myself as graciously as possible while peering down at the screen to see that it was Jelicka. "Where are you?" I demanded in my loudest whisper when I'd stepped a sufficient distance from the table.

"I'm at the costume shop."

"What?"

"You didn't call and the sales guy here was so good-looking and nice, not to mention knowledgeable. So we got to talking—don't worry, he doesn't know anything about the operation. Basically, I've been here the whole time."

"I've been so worried." *Nice of her to let me know.* "Hey, did I give you Cullen's number by any chance?"

"You said you didn't want us talking because you thought it would be weird that I knew all this stuff about him, which seemed stupid since we're supposed to break into a house together."

"Right." In retrospect that did seem stupid. So, if Jelicka and Cullen hadn't talked and he hadn't responded to my text, he could still be up there—dead even. *Oh, God!* Not to mention that I now had indigestion because all through dinner I had visions of my friends getting strangled by an assassin—ex or not.

"Why?" Jelicka asked, disrupting my fear mongering.

"It's just I haven't heard from him and I was worried he might have gone ahead with the plan without you."

"Don't worry—he's probably just not answering his phone."

I truly hoped that's all it was but, still, his not calling was really unsettling.

"Anyway, we're going out for dinner to that tapas place you went with Cullen, since you liked it."

"Who—? I was there *once* and I didn't eat anything"

"OK, whatever," Jelicka said. "Dan says it's pretty good, too."

"Dan—?"

"The *sales guy*. And guess what? He can't be older

than thirty." She squealed with delight and more than a little anticipation.

"Just remember, Jel, you're a little fragile right now. Take your time."

"Righty-o there, sister. But I won't break. And I doubt he'll die *in flagrante*, if we get that far. That just can't happen to two Muffs in the same year."

"Certainly unlikely." I sighed with a trace of self-pity that the Muff that it did happen to was me.

A beat or two went by and then she continued, in a more serious tone, "So something must have happened, right? I mean with Nissim and the fiancée? That's why you didn't call."

"They never showed up at the party."

"Then it all worked out for the best. Ta-da! Dan and I were meant to be."

"That's a bit of a leap, don't you think?" Not to mention selfish.

"It's just dinner, Maddie. Anyway, let's talk tomorrow about our next *opportunity*. Dan's letting me keep both outfits on an extended basis, so I can be ready at any time."

"Good to know," I said, with a trace of resignation.

"Soooo—" Jelicka floated the word ever so seductively, giving no doubt of her meaning, "Do you think it's too soon to sleep with him?"

"Too soon after meeting him, or too soon after Roscoe?" After all, these were entirely different questions.

"Either—or both, I guess. The real question is 'why *not* now?'"

Granted, Jelicka needed some male attention. After the whole thing with Roscoe's leaving her for the older woman, her self-esteem really took a hit. No matter how much she talked about seducing the pool guy, she'd never actually done it. Not long after the Muffs had talked about *Deliciously Disturbed and Distracted*, I'd realized that Jelicka lived in her head. And that was part of the reason she wanted to prove Udi'd met an untimely end. She just needed her life to become more exciting and visceral.

"No. It's not too soon," I said, thinking about all my own missed opportunities. "Particularly at our age. You never know how many chances we're going to get."

CHAPTER 32

The following morning, I still couldn't get Cullen on his mobile and he hadn't called in. What the fuck had happened to him? Before I could figure out who to call or whether I might assemble my own posse to find him—or, God forbid, recover the body—my computer dinged to life with Muff news and the beginning of the next pre-meeting email assault.

> <u>vonhooter@gmail.com</u>: Woo-hoo! Jelicka scored with an adorable costume designer named Dan! And Vick's cancer-free. Even more to celebrate since I finally nixed the tennis stalker (by restraining order)!! Hope you're into talking about *Kevin*. Am planning an Italian feast—lasagne—veggie and non—and an appetizer. Looking for you talented ladies to fill the gaps. Salad? Bread? Wine? And it's coming up on Lauren's bday (she's not on this list) Sarah, can you do a cake? Love, Paige
> BTW in case you forgot— Thursday at 7pm

I was glad to find out that Jelicka had seized the day, or night, as it were. And it was nice for a change that for our next gathering, Paige felt secure enough in her cooking to delegate the cake. I offered a variation on what I usually do:

> MSC@MSCMediate.com: I'm   bringing
> champagne   so   we   can   toast   everyone's
> successes.

Not that I had any thing of my own to celebrate. And though there were clearly things to be happy about, Jelicka, undaunted by the fact Cullen had gone missing, still wanted to get into Nissim's house. So any full-on celebration might have been premature. But there was no reason to burst everyone else's bubble just because a couple of Muff lives might be in danger.

> Sapizz11@connect.net: Lemon cake?... or white chocolate coconut? And here's a shocker--I read the book. For some reason I identified. Yikes. BTW—Nate and I are getting along better than ever and he's stopped drinking.

Sarah had reason to rejoice, except for the fact she identified with the narrator of *Kevin* whose son turns out to be a school shooter.

> kookykiki@hotmail.com: I'll make a salad. Sorry, can't get into book. Troy would never do anything like that little creep. ~K

It was a foregone conclusion that at least one of us wouldn't like the book. It's just the Muff way. This time it was Kiki who, as it happened, also had trouble with *Deliciously Disturbed.* Her lack of interest in our most recent reads was probably due to whatever was going on in her life that she had not, as yet, shared with us. At this point, however, I felt we had waited long enough to find out, so I vowed that at our upcoming gathering I *would* get it out of her. I felt she owed us that.

One afternoon, several days after Kiki and I went to see Vicki through her second lumpectomy, I had attempted to broach the topic and may have even scratched the surface. Kiki's never been one to expose those corners and crevices of her life she considers private, but she did confide in me that day, probably because I was the one who'd gotten her involved with the Muffia to begin with and she knew I could keep a secret.

Tears began to form in the corners of her lovely honey-brown eyes as she told me she'd recently miscarried for the second time in two years. She said she couldn't believe how deeply sad it had made her— that she really wanted another child and now she didn't know if it was possible. And because she'd been having such a hard time increasing her family's size, it had hit her particularly hard when Sarah seemed to treat the whole idea of childrearing and fidelity as cavalierly as people flip through television channels.

"It's so callous," she said, drying her eyes.

"She probably wouldn't have acted like that if she'd known what you were going through," I offered. "You can be certain she didn't mean it as a personal affront."

"Maybe not." Kiki sighed and a pensive look came over her face. "Maybe I've been blaming Sarah and Saul and everybody else for my misery when it's me," she whimpered. "I just didn't or couldn't accept that my body was not doing what I wanted it to. I think deciding to become a nurse has something to do with my wanting another child. I want to take care of something else."

"That part is great."

She looked at me, confused.

"I mean that after you take care of Saul and Troy, you still have something to give. Most people aren't so generous."

She nodded then smiled, and we hugged our goodbyes. Later that day, though I didn't say anything to the Muffs, it was as if Vicki and the others sensed Kiki needed our support, not our ire.

> victoriamendoza@mac.com: I've missed a great many meetings over the last four years, for which I'm sorry (living thousands of miles away is not on Paige's excused list). But I have read every book and I am much more interested in being introduced to the books that moved you all than I am in the hyped tedium of the safe choice. Funnily enough, the thing I most value about our book group is being collectively coerced to read books I otherwise never would have read. I've gotten almost as much out of the ones I didn't like as the ones I did. I would never, EVER find the time to read anything like *Kevin* otherwise. I think it'll be fascinating talking about it. At the very least, it's made me love writers all the more who are bold, shameless, playful, and energetic. And a woman wrote it. Yes, it's a bleak worldview but there are kids like Kevin out there and we should read it on that basis alone. Anyway – this is the stuff that's interesting. The irritation is interesting. And the odd love found at the end. Plus, this was a book that was already read and liked by one of us – and that's a good enough reason for the rest of us to give it a shot.

I loved Vicki for saying what I hadn't. But I worried there might be something more she *hadn't* said. It's just that when a friend or relative has had the big "C," part of you never stops worrying. If anything happened to her I…

Meanwhile, the email assault continued.

> LBSweet@aol.com: I've got the bread covered and I'll bring a couple bottles of Chelsea Handler Vodka (amazingly she gave us six cases). Also invented a yummy herbalized vodka sauce. Hard to describe but great on everything!

> cunningquinn@Talentpool.com: Hi all. Still in Japan at the slowest Internet café in Kyoto. I could write you all individual letters, get on a boat and deliver them by hand and it would be faster. It took

about 13 hours to wade through the e-muff mail of the past few days and it's like "10 Days That Shook the World". Congrats all. My news is: Kubota tractors replaced Vince V with Viggo Mortensen who looks more natural on a tractor (and in every other position). Will think of you all on BC night. Wish I could be there. I predict disturbing discussion. Way more disturbing than *Deliciously Disturbed* which was really only just delicious. What's going on with the spy stuff, M? Get the goods? And what happened at Berggren's latest dinner party?

While I was wading through all these exchanges and more, Rex called to ask me out. He said he was in LA for another five days before returning to London and wanted to see me. But after Berggren's stressful dinner party, during which I'd behaved in a scatterbrained, unappealing fashion—no matter how good I'd looked in those uncomfortably tight jeans— and during which I had occasion to observe his lust for young flesh, including my daughter's, I found myself with only excuses for every rendezvous opportunity he proposed. I suppose I could have moved some planned event, like reading the manual for my new food processor, but I guess I just plain didn't want to. I'm one of those who believe people do what they want to do, not what they *say* they want to do.

Perhaps if he'd proposed meeting in Hollywood, I'd have been more open to seeing him, but he wanted to make sure he came to Agoura and got to see Lila as part of the deal. Seeing him ogle my daughter at Berggren's hadn't turned me on and it wasn't likely to get me going the second time.

In other words, in thinking about Rex, I didn't think sex. I didn't think anything. B.U. (Before Udi) I might have been able to put aside the reservations I had about Rex and just follow where it led. But A.U., having all the feelings I'd had with Udi, I realized putting up with Rex just wasn't worth it. Plus, at the end of the day, he was a creep.

In assessing my feelings about Rex, my mind drifted—more like back-flipped—to Cullen. He and I had certainly avoided the traditional, possibly even staid, beginnings most relationships suffer from and the typical march to the missionary position. Instead we'd met at Babeland, the über-adult toy store, and moved directly into vibrator-assisted phone sex, which had been amazing. But then he'd failed to notify me that he was just fine that night of Berggren's party. He had not been captured, tortured and trapped in an airless tomb, as I'd imagined. And his lack of awareness that I might be worried made me quite sure I didn't want to date him either.

It was Udi I was still dreaming about, which my rational mind knew was completely ridiculous, but which my irrational mind was helpless to stop. In hindsight, I must have loved him.

What Udi and I had had, if we'd had anything at all in the short time we knew each other, was *crazy love*— wild, passionate, animal attraction. It was romantic, it was exciting, but it wasn't a mature relationship the way my friends both in and out of the Muffia defined one. Nevertheless, that's what I wanted. Does this situation beg the question: Why does it seem to be impossible to live a truly romantic life and, at the same time, a fully conscious one?

The idea of therapy crossed my mind, but I'd read my share of self-help books and had come to the conclusion that everyone has issues—everyone. By the time one hits forty, most people have baggage— previous relationships, children, health issues; no one escapes unscathed. The question then becomes: Whose set of issues do you want to deal with and who do you feel you can trust with your own issues who won't pretend he doesn't have any, too?

So, what was the reason Cullen gave for not

calling? Not texting? Not letting me know the night of Berggren's dinner party that he was fine and thereby sparing me the worry and torment over what had happened to him? Well, it's pretty anti-climactic, really. And maybe I should have guessed. There'd certainly been plenty of hints about what might have occurred but, no, he let me imagine him getting his fingernails torn off and worse the entire night. I mean, how many keystrokes would it have taken? When he finally called, it did put an end to my imagining him being water-boarded and instead made me want to torture him myself.

"Sorry I didn't call but something came up," he said.

"Yeah?" *Could he be any more cryptic? Something came up?* "It better be good," I said. "I visualized you getting your toes nailed to the floor." The truth was, I was too angry with him to bother figuring out a less direct approach.

He made a weak attempt to laugh. "I'm really embarrassed," he continued. "See, my mom called and they're twelve hours ahead or something."

I wasn't sure what the time difference and his mom calling had to do with anything, but I went along. "Is she all right?"

"Oh, yeah. Fine… but it was the only time we could talk, you know, before I leave."

I didn't remember him telling me he was going anywhere. My silence apparently spoke volumes.

"I thought I told you. I'm going to the Middle East."

"I didn't know you were going to the Middle East."

"*Well*, you know *wwwww* . . . " he said, drawing it out and trying his best to sound reluctant about an exciting trip to Egypt and Turkey. "That's my mom— a real character." Cullen and his mom were becoming a pattern.

His mom apparently couldn't let him go—that's in the metaphorical cutting-the-umbilical kind of letting go. Or he couldn't let *her* go. In any event, I was suddenly feeling very uncomfortable about the phone sex we'd had.

"I'll be meeting her in Istanbul. She said it might be her last trip and she wanted me to be there."

Her last trip. What a drama mama.

"Well, have fun." It did sound like fun—East meets West, Topkapi Palace, Kayseri carpets… I wasn't going to lie, even though I suspected Mom pulled this kind of thing frequently. Probably any time another woman pulled focus from her.

"She said Egypt was so incredible, she insisted I come over and see it for myself. The ticket came FedEx this morning and I leave tomorrow."

"Wow. Sudden."

"But when I get back, I'd like to see you again."

He had absolutely no awareness that a potential love interest—me—might think his relationship with his mother was more like that of a middle-schooler than a fully grown man and that his recent behavior had been obtuse at best.

"I don't know, Cullen. I think we should let it go."

"What's the matter, Madelyn?"

"I guess the only way to say it is I feel odd."

"Odd how?"

"Odd with *you.* Odd that I feel like I'm competing with your mother. Odd that you wouldn't think to call last night—"

"You aborted the mission!" he protested.

"Odd that you didn't think I'd be worried about you, even though I aborted the mission, and call. And I don't feel like it's my job to tell you that these things might make a girl feel odd. Sorry, but that's it."

"It was the phone job, wasn't it? If I'd known I—"

"It's not the phone sex. I mean, all right, the phone sex makes me feel a little odd now, but it's not only the phone sex."

"What do you mean it's not only the phone sex?"

He wasn't a bad person, but it was as if he hadn't heard me, hadn't taken in how I felt at all. "Nothing," I said, not wanting to prolong the futility. "I'm glad you called to tell me you're all right."

"I'll call you when I get back?"

"Sure," I said. And even though the subtext was probably lost on him, what I was really saying was, *"Don't bother."*

CHAPTER 33

"Fourteen-fourteen Mockingbird Lane," Jelicka said with a faux-eerie tone that worked in counterpoint to the sunshine as I negotiated the Prius through the narrow streets of the Hollywood hills. Cars were parked in any available spot with no regard to other vehicles that might need to get by, while fallen plastic bins for garbage, recycling and lawn debris created an obstacle course on this windy day.

I groaned. "You have quality sex for the first time in however many years and you're making jokes about something inherently *not* funny."

"I thought it was funny."

"Besides," I said, "the *Munster* family lived at thirteen-thirteen."

"Really? I watched that show like it was homework."

Jelicka seemed oblivious to the magnitude of what we were planning to do, which was to break into Nissim and ZsaZsi's house. She'd been dogging me about it ever since the previous aborted attempt during Berggren's dinner party a few days earlier. This time, I'd reluctantly agreed to join her—more out of worry for her than anything else.

"I don't feel good about this," I said.

"What do you mean? Do you think they're home?"

"No, they don't work at home. ZsaZsi told me when I met her that she sometimes makes calls before she leaves in the morning, but she's always out of the house by noon, and it's—" I looked at my watch. "It's two.

"So we're good," Jelicka said.

"No. We're not *good*. I need to know you're going to start being serious."

"I *am* being serious."

"You're not focused."

"I *am*. Focused just looks different on me."

I pulled over behind a van to allow a mattress delivery truck to pass and looked at her intently. "What we're planning on doing here is dangerous—not funny."

"But it might be *fun*," she said. "Don't you think?"

"Not really, no. Exciting and dangerous, possibly. Not fun."

Pulling the car from behind the van, we continued traveling up and up some more. My little hybrid might be good on gas, but it sure is gutless on steep hills.

"Maybe I just feel good, you know?" she said. "Because of the sex. And the sex *was* good. But that's not why I'm in a good mood. I'm in a good mood because we are possibly doing the world a service."

"I'm happy for you, Jel, really. You needed to get laid. Just don't confuse the post-coital glow with being invincible. Having great sex does not equal the cloak of invisibility—or whatever." I didn't want to be a total downer but come *on*—doing the world a service?

"From your tension level, Madelyn, I'd say the good sex you enjoyed not so long ago has worn off and you need another dose yourself."

"Thanks for pointing that out." I *was* wound up, but even if I'd just come from a satisfying romp with a very alive Udi, I'd still be worried about searching the house of an ex-assassin, even one I knew.

"What can I say?" Jelicka said cheerily. "Regardless of whether or not there's a deadly plot afoot, I will not let it get me down." Then she started *doo-doo-doo-ing The Munsters* theme song and I had visions of Herman,

Grandpa and Eddie hopping on for the ride, when she stopped mid-*doo*. "Did you know Al Lewis's cousin was married to my mother-in-law at one time?"

What was she talking about? Then an *oh-my-God* recollection from years ago reared its ugly head: Hadn't Jelicka once been diagnosed with a mild bipolar disorder? *Yes!* She was having a manic episode. This was getting worse by the minute.

"No, I didn't," I said. "I think we should turn around. This is suicide. You don't have a child. But if I die, Lila won't have a mother. Let some person whose job it is figure out if Nissim is plotting something terrible."

"We could have asked your friend Cullen, the masturbator's friend, to join us."

"No, we couldn't. And please don't call him the masturbator's friend. It was just that one time and—"

"That you *know* of."

"Fine, that I know of." It didn't much matter if Cullen was a repeat phone-sex offender.

"If he was good at talking you off he's done it before."

"What does that mean? That I'm tough to talk off? Whatever—he's unavailable. He went to the Middle East with his mother," I said, trying to put an end to the topic.

"Another guy from the Middle East? What's with you and the Middle East?"

"Cullen's not *from* the Middle East. He's just visiting Egypt and Turkey."

"Turkey. . . now there's a bizarre place. Remember that book we read? Or *tried* to?"

I'd been the Muff who hosted an evening for a book by Orhan Pamuk that was set in a remote part of Turkey and told the heartbreaking story of young teenage girls being driven to suicide, among other things. I'd loved it but most of the other Cliterati hadn't read it. After that we decided we should only read books under two hundred and fifty pages.

"It was called *Snow*. But that took place in Kars—way east. Cullen and his mom are going to Istanbul and then up the Turquoise coast to see all the ruins."

"Who needs him anyway?" she offered. Then something caught her eye and her head did a one-eighty. "That was it—twenty-five sixty-one. Some house."

The house was cute, in a mixed up kind of way—probably built in the 1970s and "updated," which in LA often means architectural confusion of some kind. Large anodized pieces of aluminum protruded at "artistic" angles from the roof and the tiny graveled front garden was suggestive of a miniaturized metal Stonehenge. The front walkway was lined with a row of glass cubes sitting atop a lime-green stucco wall, which asymmetrically matched the glass cubes in two of the windows. The house itself had been painted slate grey and might have been mysterious at night. But during the day it just looked drab. The overall affect was less-than-pleasing to the eye.

"Let's park down the street a little, then we can walk back up to the house undetected."

She had a point and I had to apply some of my mediation training about peoples' different communication and reasoning patterns, which I've been known to forget when my own emotions get involved. One of the behaviors we're taught to observe is that when something's important to a person, he often gets locked into thinking there's a right and a wrong way to handle it—childrearing, war, home invasion: it becomes a *my way or the highway* kind of thing, even if on a conscious level someone is willing to admit that intelligent minds can differ. We're also trained to look at why people become entrenched in their own belief systems—whether they've acquired those systems as a result of their parents, school, life experience, fear (actually I've come to believe that fear drives most human behavior)—so as to acknowledge it and hopefully move beyond it. But when you're in a relationship, the theory can get muddied with the reality and you're just confronted with the vast differences between people. When I'm mediating *other* peoples' disputes, I can be empathic about each of the parties' entrenched positions and try to help them move off them, while having no vested interest in the outcome. I am, however, not nearly as successful in applying these theories to myself.

"You probably think I'm having one of my bi-polar episodes, but I want you to know I haven't had one of those in years. Honest. I'm religious about the meds."

I stared hard into her eyes. We'd come this far, I thought. *What could it hurt to walk around the house and look in the windows?*

Once the Prius was wedged between a Peugeot and a Porsche, we got out and walked back up the hill a few hundred yards. It was another gorgeous southern California day that makes most people feel glad to be alive, but which can also make some residents fear their luck won't last and that an earthquake is imminent.

When we reached the house, Jelicka motioned me around the side. "They always put keys under flower pots."

"Shhhh—" I shhhhed. "Who does?"

"People!"

"Not everybody," I whispered. "I don't."

"I do!" she whispered louder, about to pick up one of several bright green flowerpots that perfectly matched the walls.

"Wait! Gloves." I pulled two pair of leather gloves from my bag and handed her a pair.

"What about under mats or on ledges?" I asked. "People put keys there, too."

"On TV maybe," she said.

"In real life," I protested in an even louder whisper,

though it seemed silly to argue about where to search for the key to a house we shouldn't have been looking for a key to in the first place.

"So look already," she said, picking up a pot then placing it down in a different spot.

"Always put stuff back exactly where you found it." How could she not know this basic rule of snooping?

"I thought I did," said Jelicka, mystified, as I nudged the pot a few inches further from her.

This was exactly what I was worried about—okay, one of the things.

Feeling above the door, I found nothing except dirt and soot, and there was no mat to even look under.

Meanwhile Jelicka looked under the last of the flowerpots. "No key," she announced.

"So much for that theory," I said, moving all the pots back to where they'd come from. "Better we just peek in the windows anyway."

"Don't worry. I have this." She whipped out what looked like a miniature screwdriver set.

Glowering at her, I said, "Please tell me that's not a lock-pick kit."

"I could tell you that, but it would be a lie."

I stopped. There'd been a sound and neither of us had made it. "Shhh," I warned, touching my ear.

"What is this, charades? We're trying to get into the house," Jelicka said, opening her kit.

"Shhh. I heard something."

Jelicka listened for five seconds before she walked over to the door with me close behind.

"How do you know how to pick a lock?" I asked.

"How hard can it be? I see them use these things on TV everyday."

"That's what I thought you'd say."

"Don't start with me again. I'm taking this seriously."

She knelt down and began futzing with the lock, trying various long pieces of metal. The locks looked as old as the house—the original house—not what you'd think a Mossad agent in the twenty-first century would use to keep people out.

"I'd say these locks suggest there's nothing nefarious going on, Jelicka. Which means it might be a good time to leave."

"Possibly."

"Do you come by all this knowledge from writing screenplays or just from watching crime shows?"

"Both. And before that there was *Harriet the Spy, Nancy Drew* and the original *Bionic Woman.* I wanted to be a spy but I didn't like the training, so I kind of trained myself in a way that still permitted me to shop and have weekly manicures. I should have taken lock-picking though. And I could be a better swimmer. I *am* good with a Glock, however."

"Don't tell me you brought a gun. We're already breaking and entering. We don't need to add armed robbery."

"You won't say that if we find something."

"Where is it?" I asked gravely.

"Purse," said Jelicka, inserting another long pick into the lock and poking around.

I slowly lifted what looked like a real gun from her Alexander McQueen handbag then carefully placed it back with a shudder.

"This is harder than it...ouch." Jelicka dropped the pick and gripped her right index finger—the finger*nail* to be specific—which was hanging by an acrylic thread. "Goddamn it, I just had these covers put on."

"Maybe they're not designed to stand up to the rigors of lock-picking," I said.

We'd made no headway in the roughly ten minutes she'd been working on the lock and I was ready to call an end to the escapade when, from behind us, came a voice:

"Hullo, there. Can I help you with somethin'?"

Jelicka dropped her nail tip and we both wheeled

around to face a grizzled man who had to be seventy, if a day. He wore tie-dyed pirate pants, a black beater and the expression of someone who enjoyed a daily bong hit.

"Good afternoon," I said, casually taking off my gloves and extending my hand to shake his. Fortunately, I'd prepared for a nosy neighbor and had my story ready. "Gail Russell, Century Twenty-one. How are you?"

"Ain't that that big real estate racket? Whatch doin' back here?"

"We were just trying to determine the best place for the lock box, Mr.—" Jelicka had by this point stood up next to me, smiling broadly. She and I were both dressed in upscale street clothes and, other than the fact our behavior might be perceived as questionable, we seemed like normal women.

He stared at us with red eyes. "You can call me Joe. What'n the hell's a lock box?"

"It's one of these," I said pulling the device from my own non-designer handbag. "Surely you've seen these, Joe. They allow realtors to enter a home and show it to clients without bothering the seller's agent or the occupants."

"Don't they usually put 'em on the front doors?" he demanded.

"Not necessarily," said Jelicka. "That can ruin the curb appeal."

"Well, all right. But these are nice folks. Nice young couple. Surprised they're selling. I thought they liked it here."

"Oh, they do," I said. "They like it very much. But you know, they're getting married, planning a family. Living in the hills just isn't practical."

He cleared his throat and I thought he might say something else, but that stoner's glaze came over his face and he walked off as suddenly as he'd appeared.

"We might consider leaving now," I whispered.

"That would be silly. Especially since . . . We're in." Jelicka placed her hand on the knob and beamed when it turned.

She'd done it. The pick that had broken her nail had also tripped the lock. I high-fived her. Despite all my earlier trepidation, I now found myself getting into it. Even if Joe called somebody, we'd be in and out before they could arrive.

Opening the door, we poked our heads in and peered around. We hadn't seen an alarm panel while walking around the house and no sound was emitted, but that didn't mean there wasn't an alarm going off at a local police dispatch. However, if Jelicka was right about Nissim and he *was* Mossad—a one-in-a-hundred-thousand chance, I thought—he might not want an alarm going off that would bring U.S. law enforcement to his lair.

Stepping inside, we closed the door. Still no noise emanated from the interior. The faint whirring of city life somewhere outside, along with the hum of a distant appliance, was all that my ears could detect. We found ourselves in a simply appointed, mid-century styled living room where, at least by appearance, nothing seemed suspicious.

"See that painting?" Jelicka asked in a hushed voice.

I followed her gaze to the dining area and spotted a few paintings hanging on the walls, none of which, I thought, would be considered a desirable acquisition by the board of the Museum of Modern Art. One painting in particular looked as though Jackson Pollock's progeny might have produced it while suffering from both Parkinson's and Alzheimer's. "The abstract?"

"What do you want to bet there's a safe behind it?"

"Jel, no one does that anymore. That's cheesy and obvious."

"What's past is prologue, right? It's *such* a dated place to put a safe that it's the logical place to put one."

"Whatever."

I went over to the painting—an acrylic in hues of that same lime-green color as the house's exterior, along with black, grey and the occasional splash of neon blue, hanging without a frame—and lifted it. I expected to find absolutely nothing. Curiously, there was no safe but there was a hole, a six-by-six-inch cave carved out of the wall.

"See." Jelicka was thrilled. "What did I tell you?" She walked closer to peer inside.

"What I see is a hole in the wall," I said. "They probably just put the painting here to cover it. Besides, there's nothing inside."

"Let's keep looking."

I returned the painting to its place and followed her through the dining room to the kitchen. "Are we going to check all the cabinets?" I asked, opening the spice cabinet—empty, except for the spices.

She closed the dishwasher, peered into the microwave—nothing. Then at the same time we saw it . . . the freezer.

"You," she whispered.

"No, you."

She didn't move. "OK, together," I said.

Together we walked to the freezer—one of those pull-out kind and very large. Each of us took one side of the drawer and looked at each other, silently counting. "One, two, three . . . *go!*"

We pulled hard and the heavy drawer snapped against its tracks, disturbing the automatic icemaker and causing a loud rattling of ice.

"Shhhshshhh!"

Unsure of what might be in the freezer—food? severed heads?—together we ventured a peek inside. It looked like a normal freezer to me though there were a suspicious number of packages of frozen *edamame.*

Very slowly, Jelicka stuck the hand with the damaged nail into the drawer and started pushing the frozen food around. If there were any body parts, they were cleverly disguised as chicken tenders.

"Let's check the other rooms," whispered Jelicka.

We were walking down the hallway, carpeted with sisal, when I heard a door open somewhere.

"Madelyn?" The voice calling my name was familiar but it wasn't a welcome familiarity.

Jelicka, who was in front of me, whirled around.

"Nissim," I mouthed silently.

"What's he doing here?" she whispered frantically, as if she finally realized that what we were doing entailed such risks as the legal owner returning to his home.

I had no idea what he was doing home at two o'clock in the afternoon on a Tuesday, but there was no time to discuss it. I pushed her further down the hallway.

Jelicka began reaching inside her handbag and I snatched it from her.

"No gun," I said as softly and firmly as I could.

"But—"

"No. No gun!"

Nissim spoke again, this time sort of sing-songy. "Ma-de-lyn—I think you're in here. I saw your car outside."

Why hadn't we taken Jelicka's car!

The windows wouldn't open enough for us to fit through, so true to crime cliché, she and I dived into the closet with me clutching both our handbags, and we held our breaths.

"My neighbor called to tell me there were a couple of women in my back yard and I was just down on Vine having lunch, so I decided to come up and see what was going on."

"Give me the gun," Jelicka whispered, grabbing at the handbags, which I tried to keep out of her reach without knocking clothes from hangers or overturning shoes.

"OK, Maddie, you can come out now." Nissim sounded almost playful. I wouldn't have felt particularly playful toward an interloper in my house.

"Stop. Jelicka, shhhh!" I said, pushing her hands away.

"I know why you're here, Madelyn. Berggren told me you were asking questions. And to tell you the truth, if our situations were reversed, I'd be curious, too."

Why was he saying all this? To soften me up somehow? He didn't sound upset or even alarmed, but then again, he was a professional, and he was moving steadily toward us. *I had no game plan. There was nowhere to hide.*

"You and your friend were right, by the way. I used to be Mossad."

Jelicka reached out and clutched my arm. I felt for her other hand just to make sure she hadn't snagged the gun somehow. No Mossad agent would take kindly to having a Glock pointed at him.

"But it was a long time ago," he went on. "I've been exclusively into real estate for about six years now. That is the truth."

His voice was getting louder. Soon he would open the closet door and the jig—as they say— would be up.

"I'm still friends with those guys, though. I worked with them a long time. So sometimes they ask me to help them out. This was one of those times."

He was very close now. I tried to see Jelicka's expression in the dark, which was impossible, but from the death grip she had on my arm, I knew she was terrified.

The closet door opened, throwing light onto us and revealing Nissim's smiling face. "Ladies . . ." He didn't seem to think we were a threat.

"Nissim—" I said. "Hello."

"Boker tov," said Jelicka.

Nissim turned his attention to Jelicka. "Other than the fact it's the afternoon, good morning to you, too."

Jelicka's Hebrew, like most things about her, was inconsistent.

"Let me introduce my friend. Nissim, Jelicka. Jelicka this is Nissim," I said as cheerfully as if I were at the Southern California Mediation Association annual dinner instead of in a guy's closet with one too many overcoats.

"Shalom," said Nissim.

"Shalom," responded Jelicka.

Nissim was being very gracious and understanding, I thought. Hardly the kind of behavior one would expect from a man finding uninvited persons in his house.

"Please . . ." He gestured for us to step out of the closet.

"Nice to see you again," I said in my friendliest voice as I followed him out of the room, Jelicka close behind me.

He turned to face us, once he'd reached the dining area. "You broke into my house," he said.

Clearly he was correct, so there was no point in denying it. Instead, I switched to my empathic mediator voice. "Yes. We did. I'm *so* sorry, Nissim." I spoke as if I'd only just learned that his father had passed.

"I should call the police."

"From previous experience I know you don't like to call the police."

He smiled, clearly recalling that day at my house when he and his friends came for Udi's body. "It depends," he said. "I've been known to make exceptions."

Jelicka had been pretty quiet up to this point, but she was starting to recover her nerve. "We had to get in to find out what really happened. I know a little something about Israel and the Mossad."

"And this would mean what?" asked Nissim, his body language difficult to read, even for me, an astute reader of body language.

"She's been to Israel and has friends there," I said.

"Madelyn told me how you showed up at her house that day but it didn't sound on the up-and-up. In fact, it stinks like an overflowing Van Nuys garbage can in August."

Nissim gestured to the dining table and we obediently sat down.

"Look at the situation from our point of view," he said. "An Israeli citizen dies in your country while having sexual intercourse. If he were to go to a U.S. morgue, what would be gained?"

"How about 'we follow the rules' is what would be gained?" Jelicka said with a smile.

I gave her a kick under the table to get her to call off the attack-dog antics.

"Perhaps," Nissim said, "but this Israeli citizen who died is not insured in your country. His last will and testament—in a safe-deposit box in Tel Aviv—says nothing about being buried in the U.S. His family is in Israel. His Israeli employer, the safest airline in the world, can get him home quickly and for free. What would you have done?"

"Well, what was that about implanted chips?" Jelicka asked in her "softer" voice. "That sounded really suspicious to me."

"As I told Madelyn, El Al implants microchips in all its employees."

"But why would they do that?"

"Why not? Training people is expensive. They're protecting their investment."

Jelicka scowled.

"People do put chips in a lot of things these days," I said. "Dogs, horses. Why not people?"

"It's very cost-effective as well," Nissim went on. "Israel produces most of the microchips for human implantation, so they're very cheap. People in Israel are putting chips in their children so they won't wander away from the playground."

If this were true, I could consider putting one in Lila, just in case she forgot her phone.

"When Udi's movement stopped that day, these friends of mine knew it immediately. They called to ask if I knew what Udi was doing in Agoura Hills and I told them I thought he was having sex with you, or perhaps he was sleeping. Then later they called back and said he was still not moving, so something was wrong and would I come with them. And that's what we did. The rest you know. That's it."

"But those guys with you... especially the one who was built like a Sub-zero," I protested. "He looked like a hired thug from the WWF."

"You mean like him?" Jelicka asked, pointing behind me.

I turned to see the refrigerator-like man who'd been at my house that day. "Yeah, like him." Alarm bells went off inside me, but I tried to keep it together. I brought my hand up in a small effort at a wave, like we'd originally met under more auspicious circumstances. He smiled in return.

"Who *is* that big guy?" Jelicka whispered, a little too provocatively.

I shot her a look and said, "Listen, Nissim. I'm sorry we broke in. It wasn't right. I know I didn't know Udi very well, but I kind of felt I owed it to him to, you know, turn over all the stones."

Nissim nodded—a concession—then he said, "He was crazy about you. When they got him back to Israel, the airline did an autopsy and it turned out he had large amounts of a drug in his system that he shouldn't have been taking."

I was stunned. "A drug? He didn't act like he was taking drugs. He barely took a drink."

"Maybe you just weren't aware of the symptoms.

And anyway, this drug is legal."

Jelicka gasped.

"He was taking Viagra," said Nissim the same second I realized myself what the drug must have been.

"I thought of that, but he was so young! Did he need it?"

"That stuff is deadly," Jelicka said. "My husband—well, ex-husband— went off it because of a heart condition. That's the choice—sex or a heart attack."

Nissim tilted his head to the side and exhaled slowly. "There you have it, exactly. Udi had a small problem with his heart, but because he wanted to be with Madelyn so badly, and to please her, he took the risk. As it turned out, this was not a good idea."

"So, *I* killed him." *This was horrible.*

"No, not you. Love killed him."

Nissim seemed almost wistful for a second or two before ruining the mood. "Believe me, there are far worse ways to die. I should know."

He was looking at me now. I did believe him, but I didn't want to know.

"Was he a Mossad agent, too?" Jelicka asked.

"Udi? No," Nissim guffawed. "No. Udi just liked people to think he was Mossad but Udi was what he said he was—a sky marshal for El Al."

Almost like it had just happened, I felt the fresh hurt of Udi dying on top of me. "Occam's razor," I said.

"Him again," Jelicka sighed. "What's with the razor? Why don't they just say Occam's principle?" She paused. "What is it again?"

"It's the idea that the simplest, most obvious explanation for something is usually the right one. I knew he'd died of natural causes, but I guess some part of me wanted it to be something more."

"Well, my version of events *could* have happened," said Jelicka. "It was possible."

"Yes, it was possible, but I'm sorry to tell you it is

not what occurred," Nissim said.

"You could have told me more, as things were going on," I told Nissim. "You didn't even tell me his real name when you had the chance. You let me continue to believe his name was Udi Hamoudi. What was I supposed to think?"

"Would you have listened?" asked Nissim. "I could have told you Udi was really a double agent conducting affairs with women in several different countries and wanted for murder in at least five of them. This probably would only have added to the excitement. Which is not to say you weren't genuinely attracted to each other, I think you were. I also think that you were excited by the idea of Udi more than by Udi himself."

Part of me resented what he said but I had to admit at least a little of it was true. Udi had been mysterious and different from anyone I'd ever met. I hadn't wanted to know more for fear of destroying the fantasy.

"Do you want to know his real name?"

I thought about the question for a few seconds. "No," I said. "What would be the point?"

If he was gone, that was it. He'd always be Udi to me.

"So what are you going to do to us?" asked Jelicka.

"Nothing," Nissim said. "Let's just say we had a misunderstanding. I'll overlook the fact you broke into my house. Was it difficult, by the way?"

"Ten minutes," said Jelicka. "But a pro could have done it much faster."

"I'll change the locks."

Nissim stood and we did the same. Jelicka picked up her bag, the gun and lock-pick kit out of sight inside, and slowly we moved toward the door. Refrigerator Man stepped aside to let us pass. I think he might have winked at me.

"It must have been very good sex—you and Udi,"

said Nissim.

"Yes, it was," I said, looking down at my shoes. How much had Udi told him, I wondered.

"Sounded *very* good to me," added Jelicka, smiling. She was probably thinking about her own recent romp.

"Try not to feel bad, Madelyn. If he had a choice, I think Udi would have chosen this way."

Jelicka and I walked to the car, and I was struck once more by how quickly life can change, for good or ill, and that it was best just to roll with whatever comes. Most of all, it was important not to have regrets. As far as Udi was concerned, I didn't have any. Of course I wished he weren't dead, but his death wasn't really my fault. If he hadn't died with me, it probably would have happened with some other woman, some time in the not-too-distant future.

One thing I could say for sure was that I would have regretted not meeting Udi and not spending those blissful hours with him. If it hadn't been for the Muffia, my book club made up of slightly flawed women, and our reading *Deliciously Disturbed and Distracted,* he and I might never have gotten together. So no, I had no regrets about anything that had happened.

Even Jelicka's hyping an ordinary death into a matter of national security had its upside. She and I had gotten to know each other better, she'd found a boyfriend and Nissim and I had cleared the air — proving that even insane things happen for a reason.

I pressed the power button on the Prius and my ears picked up that comforting no- sound sound of a charged battery. "So, how far are you into *We Need to Talk About Kevin,*" I asked.

She grimaced. "Just started it. I'm with Kiki —it's a downer."

"Not completely. You've been spared having a school shooter for a son. That's got to be uplifting."

"Oh my God—I just thought of something," she said, that look of suspicion coming over her face. "Do you think the author is writing in code about some future incident?"

"What are you talking about?"

"I'm talking about the possibility that there's a school shooting that's going to occur, and that the *where, when* and *how* are contained in the pages of *Kevin*."

I put the car back in park and faced her, ready to nip the next would-be adventure in the bud. "You've really got way too much time on your hands. You need a job. Maybe you should go home and sear something."

"I'm kidding," she said, giving my shoulder a gentle shove. "Let's get out of here."

CHAPTER 34

Paige lives in an area the Los Angeles realtors like to tout as "Beverly Hills Adjacent." This wanna-be neighbor of BH covers miles of pavement, mini-malls, apartments, condos and small, overpriced homes bearing little relationship to the 90210 zip code made popular by the 1980s television show.

The evening after Jelicka and I made our narrow escape from Nissim's, the Muffia met at Paige's charming, if over-priced, three-bedroom house, a little too close to the freeway, to feed our souls and talk about *We Need to Talk About Kevin*, among other things.

"So different from *Disturbed*, but I actually found it a lot more disturbing," I heard Sarah say.

"You read it?" Jelicka asked, genuinely surprised.

Sarah nodded. "I'm making an effort to be a better person—you know, read the books, not fall into destructive relationships."

"That's two books you've read now," I said in support.

"She's seeing a therapist," Lauren mouthed so Sarah couldn't see, then she drew her palm across her forehead in a show of relief before leaning in to give Sarah a hug.

"We needed a change of pace, don't you think?" Rachel said—Rachel who reads and loves almost everything and never has trouble adjusting to whatever genre gets picked.

"From love-making all the time to worrying about whether or not your kid is a psychopathic mass murderer? Yeah, that'll do it," Vicki said, camera panning the Muffs while we consumed Paige's Middle Eastern feast.

Again with the Middle East! It just so happened that even though *Kevin* was another book set in New Jersey, the narrator of the story, Eva Khatchadourian, is Armenian—granted, not quite the Middle East—but she's a great cook. Paige's fare rose to the occasion, but Lauren still felt compelled to show up with a sauce made from an alcoholic celebrity's vodka. I begged off because it didn't really work with the shwarma Paige had prepared.

"To be honest…I missed all the sex in *Deliciously Disturbed*," said Jelicka. "But Eva sure made me want to see the world with her 'Wing and a Prayer' travel guides."

"Those did sound fun," everyone agreed and I flashed on Cullen at the Blue Mosque, rolling his mom around the whirling dervishes.

"The way the book was written, it's hard to believe Eva and her husband ever had sex," Sarah said. She had a good point.

"Well, they must have—at least twice," I suggested.

"Oh, that poor little girl when she lost her eye. I wanted to *kill* Kevin," Lauren almost shrieked.

"I wish you had," said Kiki. "It would have saved us having to read any more."

"Shriver sure was successful in getting us riled," Paige confirmed.

Kiki shrugged. "You mean in getting some of us not to like her book? Yeah, I guess." I saw Kiki smile at Vicki. Something had transpired there and I could see it had been something good. Maybe I wouldn't force her to come clean tonight after all but just let it evolve.

"Successful in getting people worked up a little," I offered. "She was drawing attention to something more…what? … more sociologically significant, even if it is upsetting. You can't just stick your head in the sand."

Vicki pointed her at camera at Kiki who pursed her lips.

"They don't do that, you know?"

"What?"

"Ostriches. They don't stick their heads in the sand. I don't know how that got started. And what kind of a name is Lionel for a woman anyway? Is she gay?"

"Does it matter? In the notes at the back of the book, she says she didn't like her given name so she changed it and she has a husband, not that *that* means anything anymore," I pointed out.

I remember taking in the group that night, and thinking of all the things that had happened recently. I felt sentimental and sappy and content. I couldn't help thinking about my mother's book groups, both of which she's been in for years. She has one that consists of a bunch of academics that ONLY discuss the books, and another that is full of friends who seem to discuss everything EXCEPT the books.

I have always felt lucky, and never more than on that night, that I was a member of a book club in which we can do both—and more.

"It was definitely a different kind of read," I went on. "Really clever how the author told the story in letters. But if I had a kid like Kevin, I definitely wouldn't have waited around hoping my husband would eventually see what I saw—though, of course, by then he was dead."

"No," said Paige, her bob once again blown out perfectly. "I agree. He'd be off to military school in a heartbeat. Maternal love or not."

"You say that, but you'd have a harder time than you think," Sarah said.

"Fortunately Enrique doesn't have the temperament," said Vicki. Then added with some concern, "I don't think."

"It would be hard," Paige went on. "But it's a question of protecting flesh and blood on an unstoppable path of self-destruction versus protecting a bunch of innocent strangers who get in his way. No," she said with the tough demeanor of the tennis champion she once was, "I know I could do it—it would be my duty to do it. But the point is, we should all feel pretty damned lucky none of us has a kid like Kevin."

"That's all I could think about with this book," said Lauren. "I mean, *God.* None of us has kids we're worried about like that. Do we?"

The question hung there awhile before Paige said, "My babies both loved breast feeding."

"That *was* the start of it all, wasn't it?" said Vicki, her camera focused on Paige. "Kevin didn't want to take his mother's breast."

Paige shook her head.

"Amanda was colicky and really couldn't drink breast milk, but then girls are different," Lauren said in an apparent attempt to convince herself.

"Has there ever been a female high school shooter?" someone asked.

"Wait—you're suggesting most mass murderers either never got, or rejected, their mother's breast milk?" asked Jelicka. "I'd buy that."

"Interesting idea. But if true, it could mean mandatory breastfeeding—women forced to become cows," Vicki said. "More legislating on how to be a mother."

"There's already that pressure," I said. "I actually mediated a case between a husband and wife who had differing ideas on how long to breastfeed their baby. She said six months, he said two years."

"What happened?" said Vicki, focusing the lens on me.

"They compromised—a year and a quarter. The

term of art is they *split the baby*, though when an actual baby is involved, it's kind of a gruesome image."

"*America*," groaned Vicki. "I mean, in Spain no one goes around asking if you plan on breastfeeding like people do here, ready to seal your fate as an unfit mother if you give the wrong answer."

We all agreed, to a Muff, on the pressures of being perfect—perfect mothers, perfect hostesses, perfect wives (those of us still married), perfect in every way. It was a burden I'd been trying to rid myself of with mild success.

"Getting back to *Kevin*—" said Rachel, "I have to say I preferred it to the last book we read. Though I liked *Deliciously Disturbed* it was a little…let me put it this way: too much perfect sex is unnatural in my experience, so it didn't really turn me on in that sense."

"Poor thing," said Jelicka. "Not that surprising a comment coming from a woman whose new series of paintings is entitled 'Nude Men Without Heads,'" she added.

"'Nude Men Without *Faces*,'" Rachel corrected.

"Whatever—men with something missing. And I say that in the most loving way possible."

"Well," said Paige, "they do have something missing. I mean, don't they? They would never do anything as cool as our book club."

"They have poker night," Jelicka said. "I mean, Roscoe did. Or so he said, but he could have been schtupping the secretary. Ah, hell, what do I care? I'm being delightfully distracted by a thirty-year-old."

"Seriously, men don't generally have the kinds of deep commitments and support we have with each other," Paige went on.

In my experience, what Paige said is true: Men's friendships aren't generally as deep. And this group of women friends *is* deep, solid and longstanding. In honor of our commitment to each other, we routinely reaffirm our gratitude for whatever forces of nature and planetary movements brought us together. This was such a night.

"There's something we get from each other that only other women can provide," I said. "You all know I'm pretty self-sufficient, but you must know that that's in large part to knowing that all of you are nearby, ready to lend support if needed. Whether it's trauma over lovers, husbands, disease, death, children—"

"Breaking into houses owned by ex-Mossad agents," said Jelicka, injecting much-needed humor into the melodrama.

"Whatever—I know you're there for me. People come and go, but we will be Muff sisters 'til the end. Here's to you, and to the absent Quinn. I'm glad you're all in my life."

I held up my glass of Veuve Clicquot in toast, and the others brought their glasses to meet mine. "To the Muffia."

"To the Muffia," came the collective cheer.

CHAPTER 35

It's always been a little strange to me how so often we seek out companionship and then, equally as often, we destroy the connection we sought so hard to find— spinning off into our own separate orbits once again, either from neglect, fear, self-interest, or something else. But changed, one would hope, ever so slightly, as a result of the contact that's been lost.

I loved and will always cherish those brief glimmering moments of blissful union I'd had with Udi. But he and I never reached the point when we would have had to make that big decision—do we go on together or move off alone.

Through this whole experience, the old bonds were still there. I had Lila and my wonderful friends to help me get through whatever sequence of events might be headed my way. But when it came to my physical needs, I'd made no new contacts I cared to cultivate. That physical need to be touched, held and loved would have to be satisfied by smaller things—a warm greeting from a Muff, a shared hug with Lila, even Stipple, rubbing his body against my leg at dinner would provide for the foreseeable future.

That night, when I got home after talking about *Kevin*, I went into Lila's room and watched her sleep. *How lucky I am.* I have a wonderful daughter, fabulous friends and my health. So I don't have a guy. So what?

I won't settle, I told myself. If I'm going to make room in my life for a man, it has got to be better *with* him than it would be without him. Otherwise, I'm just filling the void, as it were. In the meantime, I'll just keep an eye out for the next Udi—a meteor of a man to strike me broadside and change my world for as long as it lasts.

I'm not saying people should live their lives as I'm living mine. Being alone is not the state of existence I envisioned for myself at any point in my life. But at this juncture, that's the way I find myself. Alone. But not lonely.

And so ends the first *Chronicle of The Muffia*. There will be more adventures to come for sure. In the meantime, I'll just keep trying to live life to the fullest while balancing the interests of a child and the need to stay financially solvent. But don't worry about me. I'll keep busy—hold on a second—where is it? Ah yes— under the bed where it's supposed to be.

Bzzzzzzz . . . weeee . . . urrrr . . . weee—urrrr, weee— urrrr, weee—urrrr . . .

Ahhhhhhh . . .

Mmmmm. Oh yeah, that feels *good.*

At the end of the day, it sure is nice to know a girl can take care of herself.

EPILOGUE

Lying in the drowsy afterglow of mechanically orchestrated orgasm, I was shaken awake when the phone rang. I glanced at the clock on the bedside table—it was three in the morning. Who would be calling now? It had to be an emergen—*Lila!* I panicked. Then I realized she was in her bedroom down the hall. I'd given her a kiss a few hours earlier.

Picking up the receiver, I heard that telltale long-distance sound—far away and underwater. *Cullen?* Why would he be calling? Please not Cullen. And from Turkey? I couldn't imagine him missing me, especially after our last conversation. "Maddie? Are you there?" It was Quinn's voice and I realized I hadn't said hello.

"Quinn?"

"Hey, yeah, it's me. Sorry to wake you up, but I didn't think this should wait." She paused for a beat. "Are you alone?"

I sighed. "Of course."

"OK, well, I'm at the airport in Tokyo on my way back to LA and something really weird just happened."

Her tone was very focused and extremely serious. I woke up fast. "What do you mean 'something weird'?"

"Well, I saw something and I had to tell you before I got on the plane. I mean we could, god forbid, crash or something and I might never get the chance to tell you and then you wouldn't know and then that might—"

"Quinn—Quinn, stop. The plane isn't going to go down. You'll be back tomorrow. But could you just tell me what you saw?"

"All right. This is going to sound bizarre and impossible, but I think Jelicka was right."

"About what? Quinn, what are you talking about?"

"Udi, or whatever his name is."

"Udi . . . What about Udi?"

"I just saw him. Here. At the airport."

"How could you see him? He's dead."

"I know. But I did. I saw him. You know those, like, bulletproof glass or maybe they're plastic partitions that separate passengers coming off planes from the ones going into the waiting areas?"

"Yeah. Sure."

"Well, as I was heading to the waiting area for my flight, I saw him coming down the hallway in the middle of a group of people on the other side of the partition. He must have gotten off a plane and was just getting to Tokyo."

"Everybody is supposed to have a twin somewhere." A warm sensation filled me at the thought of Udi being alive. *Could he be? No, it was impossible, of course, but then again, what if…?* I shut myself down; this line of thought would only lead to torment.

"I wouldn't put too much stock in it," I said.

"Maybe…" The way Quinn said it, I could tell there was more to her story than a quick sighting. "But I followed him. I went back through security, which you know is a gargantuan task these days, and I saw him at the pay phones in between Satusmaya Okutani and the Chibanippo Books shop. I walked over and picked up the phone next to his and pretended to make a call and I heard him speaking Hebrew. I mean, I think it was Hebrew. It sure wasn't Japanese."

"I'm still not convinced it was Udi. I mean, I saw him and he was dead. You saw him, too. We both saw him dead. Not to mention that Nissim, who is his friend, confirmed he was dead. Nissim and those other guys came to take his body back to Israel—his body, which was stiff with rigor mortis. How do you get *un*dead from that condition?"

"Look, I don't know what Nissam's motives may have been, but I'm telling you, Maddie, the only way this guy isn't Udi is if he has an identical twin and that's just too Hollywood. Even *I* wouldn't suggest that."

"If you only saw him lying down *after* he collapsed and died, do you seriously think you'd recognize him?"

"Absolutely. I studied him good. I mean I studied him *real* good and I bet if I could have gotten his pants off, I would have recognized his penis, too, along with the birthmark on his right thigh."

She really had gotten an eyeful. "Quinn—" I protested.

"Uh-oh, gotta go. They're calling for us to board. Luckily they say it in three languages before they shut the cabin doors. Sorry to wake you up and everything, but I thought you'd want to know."

Truthfully, I wasn't completely appreciative of Quinn's call. Mostly because I didn't think what she'd told me was possible. Udi was dead. I'd seen him. Besides, what would he have been doing in Japan? If it was
Udi . . .

The only way it could have been Udi is if he really was Mossad. How else would he have been able to pull it off? Nissim would have needed to be in on it. But why would he fake his own death? With *me*? And then, why walk around a major airport without disguising himself if he had?

As I lay there in my darkened room, lit only by the moon, I let myself consider all the delicious and disturbing possibilities.

IF YOU HAVE ENJOYED *THE MUFFIA*, YOU MIGHT ALSO LIKE
MORE MUFFIA,
OUT SOON. HERE'S A TASTE...

IF THERE'S ONE THING I'M SURE OF, it's that if *my* dear friend and fellow Muffia book club member had called *me* from half way around the world to tell me that my stupendous Israeli ex-lover—who, by the way, *died* while we were having unbelievable sex—was actually walking around Narita Airport very much *alive*, I would have jumped on the next plane to Tokyo.

If it had been me who'd been awakened with this news in the middle of the night, *I* would have been apoplectic and immediately gone online and booked a ticket. How dare Maddie react with her typically unique combination of disbelief and ennui? She should reserve all that composure for her freakin' mediations. What's wrong with people? And on top of that, now I was going to miss my plane! No good deed goes unpunished, right?

who knows not only what she wants, but who she wants, and how many times a day... I recommend it highly."
—*Becca Petersen, Amazon Verified Purchaser*

"A great read, couldn't put it down. *The Muffia* should be required reading for every book club in America. It's fun, sexy and smart. Hope this is the beginning of a series. Loved it."
—*Susan Hito Shapiro, artist, filmmaker and attorney*

"I didn't know what to expect when I bought my wife this book on the basis of the *Godfather* style font on the cover. The blurb on the back sounded sort of fun--a story about a bunch of wacky women in a book club (my wife's in a book club). I started reading it on my flight home and I have to say it held my attention (I'm usually reading Malcolm Gladwell or the Wall Street Journal). *The Muffia* is well written and that vibrator shopping chapter cracked me up. Now I'm wondering what else my wife's book club gets up to beyond reading books."
—*Jeffrey Malibu, An Amazon Verified Purchaser*

"The Muffia Book Club babes may talk like sailors when they meet, but they are sensible, condom-packing ladies. Soon enough, you're reading about vibrators and female sex aids, as discussed by a group of "cliterati" (the author's term, not the reviewer's), as if it were a gardening club comparing the virtues of daisies and sunflowers. The literary proposal is that of a "whodunit?" and both in flavor and presentation, *The Muffia* is urbane, erudite, and ironic."
—*Stephen Siciliano of Sidewalk Smokers Club, Highway Scribery, Vine Voice*

"Best serious love/thriller/comfort read ever! Wish I could go back in time and be those women! Their lives are serious and dark and fun!"
—*Linda Mohan, Amazon Verified Purchaser*

"I live in LA, where *The Muffia* takes place, and these women are spot on. They're so realistically drawn, that I could swear I even know a few of them personally! Very enjoyable."
—*Amazon Kindle Verified Purchaser*

"Ann Royal Nicholas writes in a breezy style making this the perfect beach or airplane read when you don't want anything too demanding or heavy. *The Muffia* is the first in a series and I can't wait to read what the smart and wacky Muff women will get up to next. I also really liked that the author and her book club are giving 10% of sales to women's causes. That's cool!"
—*Amazon Kindle Verified Purchaser*

ABOUT THE AUTHOR

Ann Royal Nicholas is an author (*Homegrown: The Terror Within*, published under the pseudonym Cialan Haasnic), *Royal Mack's Teeny Tiny Wine Guide*; a journalist (*LA Times, Vine Times Magazine*), an essayist ("Of Wine and Men," printed in Penguin's *In My Mother's Kitchen*) an award-winning filmmaker (*Univers'l*), screenwriter (*Big Bang Theory*), playwright (*Villa Thrilla, Petting Zoo Story*) and actor. She's a graduate of the UCLA Writers Program, former Managing Director of the Ojai Playwrights Conference, a mediator and single mom.

Find out more at:
annroyalnicholas.com/annanicholas.com